Dear Rafe
Mi querido Rafa

KLAIL CITY DEATH TRIP SERIES

Dear Rafe
Mi querido Rafa

Rolando Hinojosa

With an Introduction by
Manuel Martín-Rodríguez

Arte Público Press
Houston, Texas

This volume is made possible through the City of Houston through The Cultural Arts Council of Houston, Harris County.

Recovering the past, creating the future

Arte Público Press
University of Houston
452 Cullen Performance Hall
Houston, Texas 77204-2004

Cover design by James F. Brisson

Hinojosa, Rolando
    [Mi querido Rafa. English & Spanish]
    Dear Rafe = Mi querido Rafa by Rolando Hinojosa
    p.   cm.
    ISBN-10: 1-55885-456-8 (trade pbk. : alk. paper)
    ISBN-13: 978-1-55885-456-7 (trade pbk. : alk. paper)
    I. Title: Mi querido Rafa.   II. Title.
    PQ7079.2.H5M513   2005
    863'.64—dc22   2004055424
                                                      CIP

∞ The paper used in this publication meets the requirements of the American National Standard for Information Sciences—Permanence of Paper for Printed Library Materials, ANSI Z39.48-1984.

5 6 7 8 9 0 1 2 3 4   10 9 8 7 6 5 4 3 2 1

Contents

This work is dedicated to three friends:
Jaime Chahín
Arturo Madrid
Ricardo Romo

Introduction

Few literary works are as at home in the shifting sands of signification as those of Rolando Hinojosa. Ever since the 1973 publication of *Estampas del Valle y otras obras,* a title that already demonstrated the author's preference for inconclusive and open works, Hinojosa has added volume after volume to his *Klail City Death Trip Series,* weaving and unweaving narrative lines and incorporating new literary forms at each step. More than anything else, he has created one by one with every new text an ample gallery of characters—some intimate friends, others hated enemies—each of whom pulls us unavoidably toward that passionately historical portrait of the fictitious Texas in which almost all of the action unfolds.

The fourteen volumes that make up the series are perhaps the most ambitious experiment of contemporary Chicano literature yet. His project is nothing less than to combine Hispanic and Anglo traditions in order to construct a total novel, encyclopedic in scope, with the understanding that the effect on the reader will be the opposite of what is expected: the more material added to the series, the greater the degree of uncertainty about the world it narrates. This process is demonstrated in exemplary fashion by *Dear Rafe/Mi querido Rafa.*

The historical action of the series reaches back to the year 1765, and from that date it brings us back up through the final years of the twentieth century, encompassing some two centuries of intense economic, social, and cultural change in the south of Texas. As a reflection of these changes, we also find a dizzying array of intertexts in Hinojosa's work, which together take us through the domains of oral tradition and the various textual traditions from which Chicano literature derives its sources, as well as into the technified realm of pop-

---

*Translation of "Introduction" into English by Elizabeth Cummins Muñoz.

ular culture (including the world of music and recording, of television, etc.). At the same time, we are immediately aware that the diverse installments of the series do not presuppose a chronological progression through the universe of these characters. The series does not invite us to start "at the beginning" in order to bring us up to the narrative's present bit by bit, but it presents us instead with a slanted history, a dis-order in the process of constant reconstruction. To a certain degree, we can and should understand this strategy to be a broad commentary on Chicano history and historiography. Hinojosa's series seems to remind us at every moment that the lived experiences of Chicanos (and their ancestors) have been excluded from official histories, and therefore every new narrative with a historiographic impulse should originate in an awareness of this marginalization. In this way, it may become an ethnographic endeavor, an archival task, guided more by the rule of the accumulation (and articulation) of a variety of materials and voices, than by the synthesizing work of the historian.

With this end in mind, Hinojosa proceeds to decentralize his narrative to the extreme, adopting a series of techniques which should be mentioned here, if only briefly. One of his clearest stylistic techniques, for example, is an absolute renunciation of authorial control. In contrast to more traditional historians and novelists, Hinojosa opts for "putting the author to death," a strategy that appears in *Mi querido Rafa* and *Dear Rafe* in parodied form, by way of P. Galindo's constant reminders of his precarious health. In its place, the *Series* is articulated as the product of multiple narrators (Jehú Malacara, Rafa Buenrostro, and P. Galindo, among others) who, in turn, transmit the voices and memories of many other characters, either by oral means or through the reproduction of letters, diaries, and other documents. The result is a perspectivist narrative that continually contrasts different points of view and even levels of knowledge about *what happened*. Furthermore, the generational distribution of these different narrators, as well as that of the characters who inform them, creates a very effective sense of intrahistoric depth (and continuity). Whatever Rafa does not remember can be remembered by P. Galindo or by the elderly Esteban Echevarría. In this way, these memories, along with the supporting documents added by each narrator, come together to create a novelized history that the characters refer to as the chronicle of Belken County. Simply leafing through the pages of *Dear Rafe/Mi querido Rafa* the reader comes to understand the dynamics behind this polyphony of voices, narrators, generations, and texts (letters, in this case) that join together to construct the Hinojosian novel.

For this reason *Klail City Death Trip Series* demands not only an attentive and careful reading but also a constant re-reading. The fourteen volumes are so intimately connected that the reading of one text can (and, in fact, often does) modify the knowledge of the narrative world of Belken County that we, the readers, have up to that point. To be more specific, what we read in one installment of the series might complement, contradict, or modify in any conceivable form the episodes with which we were already familiar, and which, consequently, we must consider once more, this time in the light of the new information provided to us at every reading. For example, it is only by reading *Klail City y sus alrededores* (the second volume in the series, published in 1976) that we are able to understand the death of Alejandro Leguizamón, which had been narrated previously in *Estampas del Valle y otras obras*. Of course, as we are repeatedly warned by P. Galindo in *Dear Rafe/Mi querido Rafa*, the reader should take care not to believe all the stories that are told, and should certainly not give the same attention to all the stories' characters.

Within the ambitious narrative project created by the series as a whole, *Dear Rafe* and *Mi querido Rafa* play a special role: in these texts, we as readers come upon the threshold of the unknown, this change in direction by which Hinojosa catapults us into an artistic dimension heretofore unknown. Beginning with the thematic universe of the series, we find ourselves in a moment of transition between the more traditional culture presented in *Estampas del Valle* and *Klail City y sus alrededores* on the one hand, and the more recent and integrating culture of later books like *Rites and Witnesses* or *Partners in Crime* on the other. Furthermore, *Mi querido Rafa* stands out to an extraordinary degree because of the way in which it explores the bilingual world of the south of Texas with more skill

and detail than any of the other texts in the series, to the extent that
a good deal of the text remains inaccessible to monolingual readers.
Without a doubt, this is the novel in which Hinojosa's commitment
to allow the characters to express themselves in the language (or mix
of languages) most natural to them is developed to the extreme.

This is so evident that upon publishing both *Dear Rafe* and *Mi
querido Rafa* together for the first time we must avoid the temptation
to qualify this volume as a bilingual edition; how could it be if *Mi
querido Rafa* is already an absolutely bilingual book? In fact, the linguistic circumstances of the two pieces reproduced in this edition
demand that we examine the motivation behind the English versions
of his books that Hinojosa himself has continued to write since the
1983 publication of *The Valley*, in which he recreated the world of
Estampas del Valle y otras obras in English. After all, each of the
pieces that had originally been published in Spanish up to that date
had already appeared in English translation, usually with the trans-
lated text included in the same volume. The difference between
those "bilingual" editions (with the original text and the translation
appearing together) and the edition that the reader now has in hand,
is rooted not so much in questions of language, but in differences of
culture. Hinojosa's English versions do not simply take the text from
one language to another, but carry it across cultures.

In this sense, in addition to more than requiring a careful reading and re-reading, *Klail City Death Trip Series* invites us at times
(whenever Hinojosa decides to bestow one of these versions upon
us) to what I will venture to call a *transreading*, a phenomenon that
the readers of this edition, if they read the entire book, are on the
verge of experiencing. In *Dear Rafe,* as in all of Hinojosa's other
versions, the author alters, reorganizes, adds, or takes away according to his own re-creative needs; and he surely does it in order to
communicate with *another* public, one that does not read in the
work's original language and which, as a result, probably does not
share the cultural, literary, and even social baggage of the original
public. As a result, the changes do more than just reorganize, add up,
and take away narrative material. In fact, they amount to a transcul-
turation of the work, so that it may be accommodated to the needs of

the new readers. Take for example how the seventh letter from Jehú to his cousin Rafa does not include (in *Dear Rafe*) a half-paragraph about the *"raza papelera,"* which might have caused some sort of misunderstanding in the transculturated text. In other examples, the eighth letter adds a paragraph about the relatives on the other side of the river, a passage missing from *Mi querido Rafa*; and a small passage is added to the interview with Rufino Fischer Gutiérrez (chapter 35 of *Dear Rafe* and chapter 34 of *Mi querido Rafa*) in order to describe mesquite trees and their significance to readers who are unfamiliar with the Valley. The changes, of course, are far more numerous and varied and also include cultural and literary references that differ from those found in *Mi querido Rafa*. With these changes, Hinojosa demonstrates a clear awareness that Chicano literature's reading public is multicultural and multilingual, and that in order to connect with this public one must navigate its varied and various worlds and languages with ease.

Furthermore, and as proof that the Hinojosian versions are far more than simple translations, it is worth noting the intimate, organic integration by which each of these versions is drawn into the rest of the series. In order to stay close to the concrete case with which we are dealing in this publication, and to a specific example, the attentive reader will notice in *Dear Rafe* numerous references to Rafa Buenrostro's work as detective and police lieutenant in the homicide division, none of which appear in *Mi querido Rafa*. From the authorial point of view, the explanation is simple: between the writings of the two versions of the work that appear in this edition, Hinojosa had been working on *Partners in Crime*, published (like *Dear Rafe*) in 1985 and focused entirely on Rafa Buenrostro's new "life," which was completely unknown to the readers of *Mi querido Rafa*. From the point of view of the reader's reception, however, things become more complicated, because the newly added elements in *Dear Rafe* obviously make the text required reading for anyone seeking a profound understanding of the narrative world of Belken County, and not just for those readers who might approach the text for linguistic or cultural reasons.

The present edition should therefore be received as one more milestone in the history of Chicano publishing, as it offers us for the first time (in a single volume) the possibility to embark upon a transcultural reading of one of its most important novels. In this volume, readers will find an exemplary synthesis of the style that has made Rolando Hinojosa famous: the multiplicity of narrators, the mix of genres, the narrative openness of the work, the constant irony, the counter-play between popular voices and official discourse, and many other stylistic subtleties waiting to be discovered in the reader's personal experience.

As in a postmodern dance of death, the moribund P. Galindo convokes in this work the principal representatives of each social class in Belken County, Texas, one by one. Along with their respective declarations, Galindo also offers us (from second-hand sources) the letters sent from Jehú Malacara to his cousin Rafa Buenrostro during the latter's convalescence in the Veteran's Administration Hospital, William Barrett. While the immediate objective is to guess the whereabouts of the disappeared Jehú, by means of a complicated play of narrative mirrors; the reader is presented along the way with a profound reflection upon the economic, political, cultural, social, linguistic, and even sexual life of the Valley. It is worth repeating that these texts require a careful reading of every detail, but in the end the reader will not be disappointed.

Manuel Martín-Rodríguez
University of California, Merced

Bibliography on Rolando Hinojosa

_____. *Ask a Policeman.* Houston: Arte Público Press, 1998.
_____. *Los amigos de Becky.* Houston: Arte Público Press, 1991.
_____. *Becky and her Friends.* Houston: Arte Público Press, 1990.
_____. *Claros varones de Belken.* Tempe: Bilingual Review/Press, 1986.
_____. *El condado de Belken: Klail City.* Tempe: Bilingual Review/ Press, 1994.
_____. *Dear Rafe.* Houston: Arte Público Press, 1985.
_____. *Estampas del Valle.* Tempe: Bilingual Review/Press, 1994.
_____. *Estampas del Valle y otras obras.* Berkeley: Quinto Sol Press, 1973.
_____. *Estampas del Valle y otras obras.* Berkeley: Justa Publications, 1977.
_____. *Generaciones, notas y brechas.* San Francisco: Casa Editorial, 1978.
_____. *Generaciones y semblanzas.* Berkeley: Justa Publications, 1977.
_____. *Klail City.* Houston: Arte Público Press, 1987.
_____. *Klail City und Umgebung.* Frankfurt am Main: Suhrkamp, 1981.
_____. *Klail City y sus alrededores.* La Habana: Casa de las Américas, 1976.
_____. *Korea Liebes Lieder/Korean Love Songs.* Osnabrück, Germany: O.B.E.M.A., 1991.
_____. *Korean Love Songs.* Berkeley: Justa Publications, 1978.
_____. *Mi querido Rafa.* Houston: Arte Público Press, 1981.
_____. *Partners in Crime.* Houston: Arte Público Press, 1985.
_____. *Rites and Witnesses.* Houston: Arte Público Press, 1982.
_____. *This Migrant Earth.* Houston: Arte Público Press, 1987.
_____. *The Useless Servants.* Houston: Arte Público Press, 1993.
_____. *The Valley.* Ypsilanti: Bilingual Review/Press, 1983.

Secondary sources on Rolando Hinojosa

Akers, John C. "From Translation to Rewriting: Rolando Hinojosa's *The Valley.*" *The Americas Review* 21.1 (1993): 91–102.
Bruce-Novoa, Juan. "Who's Killing Whom in Belken County: Rolando Hinojosa's Narrative Production." *Monographic Review/Revista Monográfica* 3.1–2 (1987): 288–97.
Busby, Mark. "Faulknerian Elements in Rolando Hinojosa's *The Valley.*" *MELUS* 11.4 (Winter 1984): 103–09.
Gonzales-Berry, Erlinda. "*Estampas del Valle*: From Costumbrismo to Self-Reflecting Literature." *Bilingual Review/Revista Bilingüe* 7.1 (Jan–Apr. 1980): 28–38.
Illingworth-Rico, Alfonso. "Una aproximación sociolingüística a tres autores prototípico/canónicos de la literatura Chicana: Miguel Méndez, Rolando Hinojosa-Smith y Rudolfo Anaya." Diss. University of Arizona, 1994.
Lee, Joyce G. *Rolando Hinojosa and the American dream.* Denton: University of North Texas Press, 1997.
Martín-Rodríguez, Manuel M. *Rolando Hinojosa y su "cronicón" chicano: Una novela del lector.* Sevilla, España: Universidad de Sevilla, 1993.
Mejía, Jaime Armin. "Transformations in Rolando Hinojosa's 'Klail city death trip series'." Diss. Ohio State University, 1993.
Prieto Taboada, Antonio. "El caso de las pistas culturales en *Partners in Crime.*" *The Americas Review* 19.3–4 (1991): 117–32.
Randolph, Donald A. "La imprecisión estética en *Klail City y sus alrededores.*" *Revista Chicano-Riqueña* 9.4 (Otoño 1981): 52–65.

Rodríguez Presedo, María Begoña. "Rolando Hinojosa y su narrativa, The Klail City death trip series: hacia una reescritura de la historiografía social del Valle del Río Grande, Texas." Diss. Universidad de Deusto, España, 2000.

Saldívar, José David, ed. *The Rolando Hinojosa Reader: Essays Historical and Critical.* Houston: Arte Público Press, 1985.

Schäfer, Helmut. "Die Darstellung Der Chicanos Als Individuen Und Als Gruppe Im Erzahlwerk Rolando Hinojosa." Diss. Johannes Gutenberg Universität, Alemania, 1992.

Scholz, László. "Fragmentarismo en *Klail City y sus alrededores* de Rolando Hinojosa." *Missions in Conflict: Essays on U.S.-Mexican Relations and Chicano Culture.* Eds. Renate von Bardeleben, et al. Tübingen: Gunter Narr, 1986. 179–83.

Zilles, Klaus. *Rolando Hinojosa: A Reader's Guide.* Albuquerque: University of New Mexico Press, 2001.

Dear Rafe

I
A Reasonable Explanation of Things to Come*

What follows in Parts I and II consists of some firsthand facts and of diverse opinions, not all of which are soundly based or well-verified; there are also some asides and some commentary as well as other assorted data, dates, and events which (on the one hand) are well-known or which (on the other hand) are not and thus must be deduced.

The writer (The wri) is convinced that not all bases are sufficiently covered in Part I, and so, in Part II, he intends to add a shading of his own once in a while, but always on the side of truth, that necessary element.

Warning: The wri is not out to prove something beforehand and thus he expects to earn his reliability, his trustworthiness. The wri (considering his state of health) is also in no position to play fast and loose with the facts; he promises, furthermore, to go to the heart and core of the matter. He can hardly do anything else being, as he is, at game's end. He's been dealt the last card, and, alas, it's a singleton.

Background. The wri, interned as he was at the Wm. Barrett Veterans' Hospital, received a packet of letters addressed to and read originally by Rafe Buenrostro (Atty.-at-Law and currently a lieutenant of detectives in the District Attorney's office in Belken County). The letters had been written to him by his cousin, Jehu Malacara, at that time, the chief loan officer at the Klail City First National Bank.

The wri was convalescing at Wm. B. V.A. Hosp. as a result of a liverish condition. The liver (that treacherous organ) is unable to

---

Verbum sap.

1

defend itself against the smallest serving of 3.2 beer; both the liver and the wri, then, are in a bad way. Why? Ah, and you may well ask: drink, pure and simple. There is an accompanying shortness of breath: the wri has been a heavy smoker these last twenty years and thus one must add a lung deficiency as a corollary.

The icing on the cake came when Barney Craddock, Capt., M.D., came up with a further diagnosis: basal carcinoma. Not much, no, but just enough to spot the face here and there. In short, that's all the wri needed 1) to call it a day, 2) a night, 3) quits.

As for Rafe, who remained a patient there when the wri left, he was making his third tour of duty at the hospital; those scars above his left eye are due to injuries suffered during the Korean fracas and now, almost nine years after the fact, some high explosive fragments are cropping up and around the eyebrows, and, according to the oculists, these may bother his eyesight if not attended to. Nothing major, they say, but they should not be neglected at this time, etc., and one knows how doctors are.

An explanation: The wri doesn't have much time left; some eight months, perhaps nine, which may be enough for someone's gestation unless the kid's a seven-monther; 7-months have been known to appear in the best and in the worst of families. A matter of one's point of view, to be sure.

Time (a new topic) can eat through almost anything: friendships, loyalties, love, hearts, et alii. It marches, ambles, and races on, although at times it lays in wait, too. And, sometimes it merely goes away, like teenage acne. Obviously, time can do anything and the proof's usually in the mirror. Time, then, is something that the wri has little of; those eight months we talked about earlier. The wri acknowledges that this may be his last contribution to the Klail City entries; there's no need to cry or to wear sack cloth, brothers. Time is really nothing more than Hell all dressed up and with no place to go.

The wri has had more pleasant moments on the planet than the law may allow; no complaints, then. He does, however, recognize that he could have used his time in a more profitable manner, but he could be wrong about that, too. (The wri also acknowledges that he has been wrong in times past.)

What follows, and this is gospel, are the latest findings in re Jehu Malacara, the man/child born in Relámpago, Texas, and reared in Klail City, county seat of Belken County.

Final *caveat:* Belken County *mexicanos,* aside from their northern Mexican Spanish language, speak English, by and large; the Belken County Anglo Texans, aside from their predominant Midwestern American English, also speak Spanish, by and large. Proximity creates psychological bonds and proximity also breeds children, as we've been told. The truth, then, *über alles.*

At this writing, Rafe Buenrostro is either on his way home from the V.A. hospital or about to be released; it was a longer stay than either he or the doctors had reckoned. As for Jehu, there's no telling where he is, and hence this story.

Sufficit.

Part I
The Letters

1

Dear Rafe:

Here's wishing you a hale and hearty and hoping to hear that you're doing better, much better. According to Aaron, he claims you look as thin and pale as a whooping crane, and all I can say is "Fatten up, cousin," and you'll be up and out of that hosp. before you know it.

Not much to tell about the Valley right now, but things'll pick up when the primaries come around. The job at the Bank is a job at the Bank, and you'd be surprised (most prob. not) about how some people run their lives in Klail and in Belken County. Not a matter of a three-alarmer, no, but their accounts reveal that all is not well with some of the citizens in our tip of the L.S. State.

The trial for those killers you uncovered has been set for next Jan. 8. You're sure to be up and around by then; will you then be asked to testify?

Since you'll be in exile in Wm. Barrett for a while, I'll keep you up-to-date, as far as I can, on the doings here. For now, then, the primaries which are just around the corner.

Yesterday, and what follows is rumor, gossip, and hearsay, my boss, Noddy Perkins, called Ira Escobar into his office; it's soundproof, of course, and late that afternoon, Ira called on the interoffice phone: "Got to see you, Jehu." I initialed the tellers' accounts, popped my head in Noddy's office, and said good-night to him. On my way to the back lot, there's Ira again.

He could hardly stand it, whatever it was, and then, in a rush, he said that Noddy "and some very important persons, Jehu" had talked to him seriously and on a high level. It happens that our Fellow Texans want Ira to stand for County Commissioner Place Four. And, what did I think a-that?

My heart didn't miss a beat, needless to s., and poor Ira felt a bit deflated. Neither of us said a word for a second or more until I hit him for a light after having first accepted one of his cigarettes. (Ira's dumb, but not *that* dumb). He saw that, far from envy, it was plain disinterestedness on my part, but he still wasn't sure about my reaction or lack of it.

He looked at me again and asked if I didn't have any earthly I-de-ah what THAT meant: Noddy and the very imp. pers. wanted and had *asked* him to run, and that they were ready (and standing in line, I suppose) to help him all the way.

Wherever that may happen to lead, say I. But, who am I to go around breaking hearts and illusions? By now, you're prob. way ahead of me here since the only thing Ira was interested in was to let me know the Good News, and that was it.

Forward! Haaarch! The last thing he'd want from me would be some advice, and I'm not good at that either. There we were, two lonely people in a treeless parking lot, at 6 p.m., with 97 degrees F staring us in the face, and Ira saying: "Jay, Jay, don't you see? County Commissioner Place Four, the *fat* one, Jay." (Yes, he calls me *Jay).* About all I could think of was to wonder what Noddy, the Ranch, the Bank, etc. were up to this time; I mean, they already own most of the land 'in these here parts' and they have ALL THAT MONEY, SON; so it's prob. something else in that woodpile aside from the wood, right? I finally shook his hand, or the other way round, and then he went straight home to give his wife the second surprise of her life.

Ira and his wife are new to Klail, and I'm fairly certain you don't know her; her name's Rebecca Caldwell (we who know and love her, call her *Becky)* and she's from Jonesville-on-the-Rio. Her father's a Caldwell, but a Mexican for a' that. Her mother's a Navarrete, and enough said. I've seen her a couple of times at a Bank party and other Bank doings and what-not.

The phone! A call from one of the relatives in Relámpago; Auntie Enriqueta says she's coming along nicely; nothing serious. (Remember when we used to hit Relámpago fairly often? I wonder whatever-happened-to-those-baldheaded-tattooed-twins, Doro and Thea, right?). Anyway, getting back to Becky, she's a bit of a looker. We get along, and we do look each other in the eye when we've said 'hello' and such. Nice looking face to go with a well-rounded little *bod*. We'll see.

Now, it could be it's a false alarm, and it may be that the Central Powers are merely testing our boy here. You never know. If Noddy *were* testing the waters, and Ira's enthusiasm showed through, Noddy could read that as our boy's willingness to serve the public.

Old Man Vielma sends his best; ran into him at the Blue Bar. In re his daughter who now shares a house with your former sister-in-law, Delfina, our illuminated friends are up in arms about 'those two shameless women who live together.' Why go on? As you can see with that one good eye you've got left, we're still as nice and as sweet and understanding in Klail City as ever.

Well, cuz, take care, eat well, and I'm sure that before either one of us knows it, you'll be back hard at work at the Court House. (Thought I'd make your day: Sheriff Parkinson, he of the big feet, is taking much of the credit for solving those murders you and Culley and Sam cleared up. Big Foot's no fool; he says it was his *office* that solved them, and since he is the sheriff . . .)

Best,
Jehu

2

Dear Rafe:

First off: kindly do excuse the delay in answering your latest; it has to do with the work here, a rush on time, and then, before I know it, two weeks have come and gone, and I haven't dropped you line one. Second excuse: attended and participated in a sad funeral: Don Pedro Zamudio's, that old Oblate of Mary Immaculate, who graced the fair city of Flora long and well.

It happens that he had two older brothers (yes, *older*), and they came down from God only knows what aerie of His. Black hats, hooked-noses, and as bald as Father Pedro himself. Half the world and most of Belken County showed up, and I almost broke up thinking on that grand and glorious burial we gave Bruno Cano that bright Spring morning years ago. It's rained here and snowed elsewhere since that time, son. And now, sic transit.

On the way back to Klail, I stopped off at the old mexicano cemetery near Bascom. One of those things, I guess; I walked around reading the stones and markers, looking over the old and loved names. As you know, we're all one day nearer the grave.

Public Notice: The offer to Ira appears to be on the level. Noddy Perkins' sister (more on her in a minute) came by the Bank *eins-zwei-drei* times, and where there's smoke, there's a political barbecue, right?

Tidy-up time: you're wrong on the Escobar familial relationships, and I'll explain why in short order. Ira's an Escobar on his father's side (old Don Nemesio Escobar, who's related to the Prado families from Barrones, Tamaulipas. Got that?) But, Ira also happens

9

to be a Leguizamón, sad to say, and it comes from the maternal end of things: A Leguizamón-Leyva for a mother who's from Uncle Julian's generation. Of course, if you were to see Ira, you'd pick him out in a crowd, straight-off. It's the nose and jaw that gives the Leguizamóns away every time. And, as far as the Bank job's concerned, he got *that* because of his Leguizamón connections (this from Noddy, by the way). That aside, if I were Ira, I'd watch Noddy P. NP's not a lost babe, and our boy Ira is, in a word, blinded by the goal that glitters. To sum up, then, he looks as easy a prey as a jackass flats bunny, wide-eyed (and blind), ears pointed up (and deaf as a door), and ready for someone to pick him off with a .22 long. He seems to love it, though. It's God's truth that there's always someone who's willing to do anything in this world.

Ira himself told me that he'll pay the filing fee at the Court House this p.m. I've no proofs, of course, but I'm dead sure Noddy's got something up that sleeve of his. Yes, he do. I've been here three years now, and I've barely scratched three or four layers in that man's make-up. And he goes much deeper'n that, believe me.

As for you, I've got another surprise: you know Noddy's sister. Yes, you do. Ready? No less a body than Mrs. Kirkpatrick, our old Klail H.S. typing inst. Remember this?

A S D F G & don't look at the key

Q W E R T & keep your eyes on me!

Yep! Powerhouse Kirkpatrick is Noddy Perkins' sib. (The first time she saw me at the bank, must be going on three years now, she spotted me in my office & said, "Are you the Buenrostro boy?")

Well! I knew *she* knew who I was (it's their bank, dammit, and they know who they hire) but I went along, & we both wound up laughing and what-all. Getting up in years is Old Powerhouse, and "widowed all these twenty years, Jehu, but I've got all my teeth," she says. (And all that money Tinker Kirkpatrick left her, too, sez I). Her main interests these days revolve round the Klail City Woman's Club & the Music Club. If she rules there the way she did at Klail High, God help 'em.

By the by, Ira's not to run for Place Four, as he'd been told. (There's a note of sadness to that 'as he'd been told,' isn't there?)

This is what I think the play will be:

Ira's to run v. Morse Terry (Place Three) in the Democratic Primary. Do you recall MT? He was up at Austin with us; speaks Spanish (natch), and he's a friend of the mexicano. Sure he is. (Same old lyrics to Love's Old Sweet Song).

Here's the story, Your Honor: Looks like some toes were stepped on; or maybe a double cross or two, not sure, but *something* happened. Big, too. Soooo, Noddy's lining up some of our Fellow Texans against Morse Terry, and backing Ira Escobar.

Talk about your strange bedfellows. The rundown: Ira v. Terry with Bank backing, and our fair-haired boy's on his way to the victory circle. I can imagine Ira at night, alone, and softly, in the bathroom, facing the mirror, that Ira sees himself as a future Congressman in Washington; how's that for a dream? Still, stranger things have happened, mirabile visu et dictu.

There *is* one problem, however, and thus Powerhouse's comings and goings: Noddy wants Ira's wife's admission to the Woman's Club, and that's a tall order, Chief. More on this later as soon as the news develops.

Next week this here cousin a-yours is off to the Big House for a kickoff Bar-B-Q; Ira's announcement, most prob. One of the girls at the Bank says that a lot of people (she put the stress on *people)* have been invited out there; I'll keep you posted.

And, too, word of honor and, as a relative, I'll say more in re Noddy and his antecedents although this may just be repeating something you already know. Correct me if I'm wrong.

Gotta go. Am enclosing a pix; the girl on the left is a current one.

Best,
Jehu

3

Dear Rafe:

Well, sir, you take the cake *and* the icing; the words 'excuse me' are still a part of the lexicon, & I'll wait for them. And, furthermore, erase, expunge, and take away all of your *feelthy* thoughts, you cad. Strange as it may seem, to you, I *have* been known to have the very best of honorable intentions, at times. Well, enough said & amen. Keep the picture and apologize to it.

What I'd promised in re Noddy:

Noddy Perkins is a man just short of his mid-sixties; his parents were fruit tramps who showed up in the Valley just before the times of the Seditious Ones; that puts it around 1915 or so. His old man was killed by a freight train & cut up in halves or thirds, depending on who's telling the story. Some of those who say they remember, attest that 1) the old man had been drinking; 2) that he merely stumbled on the tracks on his way home. Noddy's no souse, by the way; a daily highball or two, but that's about it. He likes to be in control, you see.

Echevarría (a long time ago) told me that Noddy didn't have a pot or a down payment for one when he married Blanche Cooke; a head for business, yes, then and now. (He speaks Spanish, oh, yes, & he likes for his mexicano hands to call him *Norberto* when he dresses up like a Laredo cowboy on weekends. I keep telling you: it takes all sorts to populate Belken County. Pay attention).

He hired me (personally) some three years ago; he knew me from Klail Savings, of course (which the Ranch also owns); of course. That piece of information must come as a first-class shock to you. As you may know, we've no branch banking in Texas; not yet, anyway.

His wife, Blanche, aka Miz Noddy, Mrs. Perkins, etc. has been slightly burned by both the sun and Oso Negro gin. She's got a natural enough tan, and her voice is a bit mushy with a touch of hoarseness. The martinis get a goodly share of the blame for that, I suspect. Doesn't show up here much, but when she does or whenever she's back from her 'periodic drying out' as her dearest friends call it, she and Noddy go over to the Camelot Club or maybe to the beach to celebrate her return.

One of the V.P.'s here, he's also the Cashier, is a full-fledged member of the Cooke-Blanchard clan. Of course, of course. His name's E.B. Cooke (he's called Ibby) and he thinks Texas mexicanos were put in the Valley for the family's absolute convenience. We get along, neither well nor badly; we just get. In other words, it's 'good morning' in the a.m., and 'good evening' at closing time. And that, after my first two years here; a word to the unlearned. Noddy hired me, so I work for him is Ibby's thinking; but he's up front about it which is a blessing.

Noddy's wife gets along with Powerhouse; prob. has no option or say-so in the matter. At any rate, they share different interests, as Powerhouse says. But make no mistake: they all get along & more so when it's family v. anybody else. The spoiled darling here is Sammie Jo; two marriages, as you know, no kids, but this and that you already know. We still get along just fine, thank you.

Back to Noddy's father: he was called Old Man Raymond; Raymond was the font name, and the old mexicanos remember him as that. In English, too: Olmén Reymon.

Old Man Raymond died not only mangled but broke as well, and Noddy must've had a hard time of it for a while. (No one talks about Noddy's mother; not a word). Now, how he came to marry someone like Blanche Cooke is a mystery to me; one thing, I don't think he caused the alcohol problem, although one never knows. As you know, Sammie Jo's our age, and so NP must have married kinda late, right?

Noddy has 1) few illusions & 2) less friends. It could be that he has the type of friend the rich have, BUT! in Klail, who's rich, besides them?

One more thing, he won't rattle. To be sure, he's got more than half the deck in his hand at all times; still, you've got to see him in action. Nota Bene: you've got to watch him every second; don't turn your back on him. He's the type that'll watch your hide dry.

And that's about the book on NP.

Must close, cuz.

Best,
Jehu

4

Dear Rafe:

A short note. The sample ballots are out! The primaries will soon be with us, & from there it's the general elections in Nov. The latest gunk: Morse Terry has encountered a certain difficulty raising enough funding for his re-election. And our Ira? Very well, and thankee kindly.

I did promise over the teleph. to tell you something about the Bar-B-Q, and here goes:

They just flat-out invited everybody. A lovely woman (Anglo Texan; an atom or two on the chunky side, and somewhat myopic, I'd say) sat next to me; I was putting up with a long and fairly frayed story being told as only Mrs. Ben Timmens can tell 'em. God-it-was-long. (Chile & Peru went to war, signed a peace treaty, resumed normal relations, were up in arms again, and she still wasn't through). But, get through she did, & the arriviste piped up: "Well, just how many Mexicans *did* Noddy invite?" I was sitting the closest to her, and the others there tried to muzzle her, but she wasn't having any. She went on & on, and there was mortification & embarrassment all around until she spotted Powerhouse, yoohooed to her, & there she went.

Sighs of relief, some coughing (and hemming and hawing), anything; anything to make up, soften, a-mel-io-rate the sit-u-a-tion, don't you know.

I think it's healthy to see & hear this type of shit once in a while; it's both sobering & reassuring to know that all's not well with the world.

Oh, before I forget completely, guess who else was there? None other than María Téllez, bright, bushy-tailed, and in living color. She walks & she talks, and there's blocs and piles of votes in that purse of hers.

No secret that she and Noddy mixed business & pleasure up to a few years ago. But, now it's all business, from what I can see. They made a lovely couple

It's a bit sad, though. María's not being counted for too much on Ira's race; she's here, & she's of the company, but not *in*. Oh, she'll help in the other primary races, sure, but not in Ira's; this is something special. Everything is being handled by an advertising outfit from Jonesville. Very professional.

NP's not thinking of taking out a lease on Ira; he wants him lock, stock, and bbl. Is there any doubt? Try this one on: the sample ballots just came out, right?, but Ira's portrait was alrealy nailed to just about every telephone pole & palm tree in Belken County. You can't miss seeing him since they're on both sides of the highway. Running for *one* precinct and money is being spent from Jonesville to Edgerton and from Ruffing to Relámpago. Ho, ho!

According to those mexicanos who should know better, Morse Terry is in trouble because he's a friend to the mexicano. We never do learn, do we? Many of us still hold on for dear life to that 'friend of the mexicano' bull. Those mexicanos who've been bought & paid for and are now resting in Noddy's hip pocket, say that Ira Escobar represents The New Breed. My God! Don't they *know* what they're saying? Yes, I know what you're saying: Obviously not, obviously not.

And would you look at this: according to one of the Bank secretaries, (a Texas Anglo), she says that Sammie Jo herself sponsored Ira's wife for the Woman's Club. (The sec.'s name is Esther Bewley; she's one of the small-ranch Bewleys. Do you happen to remember some po' whites called Posey? They're all related.) Anyway, Esther says that the road had already been cleared, graded, & paved when SJ nominated Becky Escobar.

A lot of pressure, and many of Klail's first & finest fumed & cussed & spit & swore & what-all, but in the end, economic reason prevailed. Noddy has outstanding notes on *everybody,* & all it takes is a little jiggle of the rope, & that's it. There are hints, and then there are *hints* spelled with a capital $. After Sammie Jo's nominating speech (she now wears contacts, by the way), Powerhouse seconded it with a longish speech of her own, and, as a capper, Bonnie Shotwell (gotcha!) spoke in favor of Becky Escobar. Not a black ball in the lot, & now Mrs. Escobar is in the Woman's Club.

Today the Woman's Club, tomorrow the Music Club. Hut–toop–hip–fo–ah . . .

Hey! What can I tell you about Ira Escobar?

Had enough?

Best,
Jehu

5

Dear Rafe:

Lunch at the Camelot; Noddy sent me, & *sent*'s the proper word, son. It's a new piece of business: Noddy would like to shed the car agency, & the prospective buyer is to use the Bank's money for said purpose. (We sell, he borrows from us. Can't lose).

Took two hours, & I really didn't have to since I'll sic the lawyers in for most of the paperwork anyway. Still two hours away from the Bank are two hours away from the Bank, & what one learns at the Camelot, isn't learned anywhere else.

From what I hear, some recalcitrants are still somewhat unhappy about Becky Escobar's membership. All I can say to that is, T.S., girls, it's *their* town, not yours. Truth may be beauty and beauty truth, but in Klail, truth is hell absolute.

I'm telling you: the Music Club is the next target of opportunity; Noddy can do whatever he damn well pleases and whenever he well damn pleases, and what are you gonna do about it, Slick?

Sammie Jo passed by when the client and I were picking at our food, and it seemed as if everyone there stopped eating. Did I say *seemed?* I'd swear on it. She stopped, I lit her cigarette, & she walked away. She really doesn't give a damn, you know. Oh, but she's a lick, and half of the women there now brush *their* hair the way *she* does.

Care to make a bet? The day *she* stops smoking. THEY'LL STOP. I mean, she won't even have to *give* the order. ¡Viva Klail City! But:

Back to business. The client's a car dealer in Wm. Barrett & Houston; deals with his local banks, as he should, but for *this* transact., he borrows from us or it's *adiós*. Oh, he's got the money, all right, (we've checked), and, as always, the life insurance we require, for slightly more than the loan itself, in this case $700,000, he'll buy from Blanchard-Cooke Underwriters. That's no broom, son, that's an upright Hoover sucking that gold dust. He also pays the premiums for us, the beneficiaries, in case of untimely demise. The higher cost of the cars is passed on to the consumer, of c.

I'll tell you this, though, with all this talk about money, we seldom see it: one talks about resources, figures, sums, etc, but we don't soil our Christian hands with it. I was *born* to be a banker; predestined, you see.

Change of subj. Do you (happen to) remember Elsinore Chapman? (God! What a perfectly *stupid* question!) Anyway, about the time you went up to the hosp., she was back in Klail; childless & husbandless, yeah. And then she was in a wreck just east of Ruffing, and it was fairly serious. She'd been in the hosp. there for some twenty days or so and doing well, when all of a sudden, she died; just like that. (Either Pennick or Morley told me about it; I can't recall which one). I felt slightly ill; I couldn't explain it to anyone then or now, and I imagine that may be a natural enough feeling. I didn't care for her that much, but I was saddened by the news, all the same.

As per your request, I did go see Acosta about your farm land; he'll be out of town for a while, but I left word for him to call me at the Bank. Israel and Aaron have been alerted.

Best,
Jehu

6

Dear Rafe:

Glad to hear you're doing much better up there; Israel and Aaron were here yesterday, (Sun.), and we had us some beer, some meat, and much talk, & most of that was politics. You know how *that* goes. Israel's little Rafe is a Buenrostro through & through; he doesn't call me 'uncle,' it's 'Jehu this' or 'Jehu that.' And you ought to see him walk around: hands in pockets, eyes on the ground, and taking long strides. Even-tempered little guy, and he doesn't seem to give Israel or your sister-in law much trouble.

They said that on the way to town, they saw some new billboards on several country roads: IRA ESCOBAR BELIEVES IN BELKEN COUNTY. Now what the hell does *that* mean? Nothing, right? But that's what it's all about. The signs are in red, white, and blue. (I've three ball points and a slew of gofer matchbooks and some desk blotters. For ball points?)

Noddy (and the Leguizamóns, say I) are spending m u c h o d i n e r o. Ira's out and off for most of the day, and things are looking bad for Morse Terry.

Last night: another barbecue. This one was held at Raymond Perkins Field; Noddy's cowboys cooked the meat; some of them played the music, and of course we-all had us a dance. Us, by the way, means the mexicanos in this case.

I took a date along: Olivia San Esteban. (Hi, there!) I'm not letting any more grass grow around these feet, no sir. Do you remember Ollie? She returned to Austin after giving it the college try at teaching high school. She's now a pharmacist in partnership with her brother, Martin. Him you remember, and he's still a pain.

Finally met Ira's wife as a political person. Butter wouldn't melt there, kid. Right off, *she* told Ollie she'd been to school at North Texas State; a music major. And then she talked about the Woman's

Club, and, are you ready? She then asked, 'Ollie, Do you belong, Olivia? I mean, are you affiliated?'

And Ira? Smiling like a cat eating grits. Ollie then said that her mother didn't let her go out in the daytime much. Becky didn't react at all; a-tall, as she says it. Well, from there she talked of Denton, Texas, as if it were the world's own belly button which, to my way of reckoning, must be some 180-degrees off, but no matter: she's really more of a Leguizamón than they are; and that is saying a lot, ain't it?

And you guessed it, she doesn't dance *those* dances nor 'at those dances' either. Don't come telling me that Noddy didn't know what he was doing. (But with all that, she's not mean-spirited; and, she's got a great body. We get along jes' fine.)

This morning, at the bank, Ira told me that Becky enjoyed our talk and that she 'had a ball, a real ball,' and that she'll see to it that Ollie becomes a member of the Woman's Club. At times, at work, I really need a drink now and then.

After the Bar-B-Q, Ollie and I went for some coffee and coconut-pie at the Klail City Diner where we met up with Noddy, his sister-in-law, Anna Faye, and A.F.'s husband, Junior Klail. We talked about everything, but it was mostly politics; we wound up closing the place around one o'clock.

Morse Terry's name did crop up a couple of times, and despite the beating he's getting in the barbecues and on the airwaves, no one said a mean word against him. Not one. My head was spinning trying to figure out just what *that* meant, but I gave up; you go figure it.

Junior Klail, in the flesh there, sits atop some $37 million by his-self alone; this according to Noddy, and *he* should know. Let me tell you a recent story: When some national TV station said something on an editorial commentary, and junior Klail didn't like it, he (sup-posedly, now) fired off some telegrams to Paley at CBS or to some-body in NBC. According to those 'in the know' there was some sort of apology from them. As you may recall, Junior's name is Rufus T., just like our Founding Father, and Junior must be the 3rd or 4th one of the line. Although he's nudging sixty, he's still called Junior, and I imagine it's better than calling him Rufus III or Rufus IV, both of which sound a bit like a king or a racehorse or something.

Take care, and what option have you to do otherwise?

Best,
Jehu

7

Dear Rafe:

The Democratic (and only) primaries have come & gone, and the winner!!!!, Ira Escobar! Everybody adores a good loser, so Morse Terry announced he'd now run as an *independent.* An independent? In Belken? At any rate, there are three months between now and the Nov. elecs., and neither side is taking prisoners.

The change in IE is unbelievable; people can say what they want to, but seeing is *not* believing. There's radiance in that face, his eyes glaze, and then they kindle and shine. Also, he is most obliging (to his lessers), don't you know. The only thing needed now is for him to call Noddy by his first name; and this he'll try in time. (As for Noddy, he contributes to both sides of the Demo. factions; as he says: 'They're both ours.' I like that, and it further confirms what I've said about the old pirate, whatever else he may be, he's no hypocrite. Ira'd better watch himself, that's all.)

Esther Bewley tells me that Becky's a true convert to the cause: there's no more faithful adherent to the rules and regs. of the Woman's Club than B. And I like that, too, I want you to know; no half measures there, son. He who is not with me, right?

Just the other day, according to Esther, Becky spoke on patriotism, loyalty, and maternal love. Applause, and then a standing ov., followed by a joining of hands and a singing of *Texas Our Texas,* the *Star Spangled Banner* (first verse only, please) and then *The Eyes of Texas.* The *Eyes?* Oh, well.

Work here at the B., is going on as it always does: a signature there, and then Ollie and I see each other on weekends (and at other times whenever the weather and the curse permit.)

I finally got Acosta as per your inst. and took him over to the Court House. Everything's in order there: taxes all paid up, the property lines well-marked and defined, and no changes whatsoever. Of course, he'll still have the Leguizamóns as his next door neighbors, as did our grandfathers and before. I then called Israel and Aaron on this and mailed copies of the deeds, etc. by special deliv.

Now, the one who appeared at the B. this morning was Noddy's wife; she came out of nowhere, before the doors were open. She looked a bit on the trembly-wembly side and stiff-jointed. Her hair was a touch bluer than usual, and in spite of the heat, she wore long, formal gloves and had her head covered by a see-through scarf covering her sparse hair.

I told Esther to open the door, take her by the arm, and to make her comfortable; I quick-timed it to Noddy's office and himself dashed out, and we both brought her to his office. (Time for her visit to the spa, poor thing.) Her driver was at the backdoor in less than *fifteen minutes*—all the way from the Ranch, too. He's supposed to take care of her, and how she got to the Bank, no one knows. I went with her and the driver to the Ranch, & she didn't say a word to me, but it was nothing personal. She wasn't focusing too well, and she may have been thinking about her trip to Colorado where she'll stay until the next time.

Sammie Jo was at poolside as usual, and right before either of us said much, Powerhouse K., came out of nowhere and said, 'Got something to tell you, Jehu.' SJ winked, pointed at me, and dove in again.

It wasn't anything: she wanted to pass on some Valley history to me; she spoke about the time Pancho Villa came to the Valley, to Ruffing, acc. to her, and how Villa tore up tracks, held up a train, etc., She said she'd seen the dead and the burned and then that Villa etc. etc. You and I both know she's talking about the Seditionists of '15. The closest Villa came to Valley must have been 800 mi., but there she was with her 70 years in the Valley and Villa did this, and that, and the other. Why argue, right? During all of this, of course, Sammie Jo was in and out of the pool. Powerhouse finally went into the house, came out again, and drove to town. SJ walked over, smiled that smile, and I stayed for coffee.

From there to the Bank, driven back, my boy, and just in the nick to see Don Javier Leguizamón himself. What could I possibly tell you? Himself looked well and lost no time in reminding Noddy that I worked for him when I was a kid. Prob. takes credit for my job here, too, for all I know. You think he mentioned Gela Maldonado to Noddy? You take that bet, & you lose.

I swear that this may just be the very first time I've heard Himself speak English; better than avge., too.

I gave Noddy the high sign about things at home, and he understood; as I walked by, he reached out and put his hand on my shoulder. (Does care about her, doesn't he?)

Ira is beside himself (to coin a phr.) and he can taste that oh-so-sweet (and heady) wine of victory. The other day, right after work, I told him to relax, settle down. After all, we're talking about *one* precinct in *one* county out of 254 in this grand and oily state of ahs. Well, shit, he looked at me as if I had called his mother a dirty name. I'm telling you, Ira believes he may just wind up in Washington in two-three years; some hope!

The one who's even more carried away by all of this is Becky. We had some coffee this aft. in my office. Gotcha! One does need to be careful, though. She's got pretty brown eyes. Nice mouth, too. But it was business, and I kept my mind mostly on that.

Ira's convinced that he invented moveable type. And, *now,* he bends my tone-deaf ear on interest rates, points, and, *and,* the National Debt, for Christ's sake! (Sammie Jo's thrilled at the pilgrim's progress. Told me so herself.)

It's been a busy day, but here's a mild surprise for you: Don Javier Leguizamón Himself asked me about you. Ha! He wondered, he says, how our lieutenant of detectives was getting along. Our, he said. I told him you were well and enjoying life up at the V.A. hosp. No reaction. And so it goes in Klail City, son.

Best,
Jehu

NB See here, you can hardly lay the blame at my innocent feet: I sent the ball points fully expecting them to work. Now then, it turns out that they don't. Look at it this way: maybe there's something symbolic there. By the way, mine doesn't work either.

8

Dear Rafe:

Guess what? Ira, our Ira, doesn't drink; not at all. Not even a beer; allergies, he says. Now, whoever heard of a Valley boy who didn't drink beer? Damndest thing you've ever seen.

Last Sun., our cousin Santana Campoy came through with a smallish barbecue; political, what else. But just for the guys. There were also some twenty upriver Anglo Texans there.

Talk was about this & that, and old political stories, and there was Ira holding on to an RC Cola with one hand and a beefed-up tortilla on the other. He then told a joke (first in Spn. and then in Eng.) and there was polite laughter here and there. The company was a bit fast for IE, and this leads me to ask: where was he raised? Doesn't he have a sense of humor? He really isn't a bad guy, you know, but what G. Stein once said about Oakland is what you'd say about Ira.

What with the noise and the music and the beer, it wasn't long before some relatives from across the Rio came over and joined the party. Segundo de la Cruz was among the first to arrive and also among the first to ask about you. (He asked what the party was all about and who 'the nervous chubby guy' was. Segu said he hadn't heard of Ira before the primaries; talk about your low profiles.)

I left right before sundown and in time to see Ira's smiling countenance on just about every telephone pole between Santana's ranchito and Klail City. That, cuz, is no mean drive.

Tomorrow morning, early, Noddy and I are going to look over some land west of Klail; it's the old Cástulo Landín property. (The old Landín-Ledesma grant, remember?) It now belongs to Old Italo's boy, Tadeo, and we're talking of a quarter section that Noddy's interested in. Since I'm the Chief Loan Officer, I'm to handle the affair, and here's how it works: we (the Bank) buy the land, but we hand the money over to Tadeo, as a 'loan'; he pays interest on the loan twice a year (it's his money and ours, see?) Tadeo doesn't lose and the I.R.S. (one of their own fine laws) doesn't collect a penny: Why? Because Tadeo pays interest twice a year as per terms of the contract (40 payments) and then the Bank (ready?) *rents* the property (as holder of the first lien) and divides the 180-acres into 4 *labores* of 45-acres each to whomever wants to farm them. Now, Tadeo then has money in *deferred* payments as operational capital (on demand if he wants to, which he will not). To add to this, *he* can then rent the property back from the Bank, and *then* pay interest on this and on the 'loan' (both of which are deductible). What else? Well, he gets to keep his share of the Govt. money for not planting the sugar cane he wasn't going to plant in the first place. The icing: in two/three years, Tadeo can default, and the land goes to the Bank (first lien) or to some *other* interested buyer who can then submit an offer (as little as $100 over the original asking price, and so on). Small potatoes for IRS, of course, but they'll close this hole if one gets *too* greedy. So where does the money come and go and then increase? On *credit,* that's where. Ah.

It may sound bad, evil maybe, but it's perfectly legal for now and 'under the existing Tax Code' as we say.

And the Texas Mexicans? Well, we're learning a bit here and there. Since you left, for examp., at least four new Texas Mexican real estate offices have opened up from Jonesville to Edgerton.

And, some of the younger guys just out of college & law are ganging up and buying some of the old lands that had been lost years and years ago. Our Fellow Texans are sitting on top of the pile of money, but time will tell if they stay there.

With all this, however, one of Alinsky's phrases keeps coming up; now that the raza is *beginning* to wheel and deal, 'they'll all probably turn out to be shits'.

It's almost midnight, and Noddy'll be here fairly early.

Best,
Jehu

PS What happened to the photo you promised? It wasn't enclosed; send it.

9

Dear Rafe:

The photo, and thanks.

Who's the girl? A Valley type? Looks half-Mexican, half-soldier. A beauty.

The preliminaries in re the land deal are well on their way; they're now in the hands of our attorneys, as we bankers say.

The return trip with Noddy was something, though. Looking straight ahead, even-voiced, he talked of his early times in the Valley. It's the fruit tramp for a father that gets him; it isn't shame, it's more of a resentment that some people haven't forgotten where he came from. I think that most people don't even know, but *he* knows, and you know how *that* goes. Even talked about his wife; he loves her, that's plain enough. It may be that *love*'s not the right word, but he *cares*. It comes through.

He also cares about money, of c., but he likes to smell something out, haggle over it, "jew 'em down, Jehu," and then he loves to mix it in with the lawyers and such. But, first, last, and always: politics. The man lives and breathes by it.

He has no time, won't give it, really, to the Rotarians & such. 'That's bullshit,' he says, but he'll send Ned Reese as a member, and pay his dues, too. Now, if the Kiwanians or the Lions need/want something, the Bank'll buy fifty tickets and no questions asked. And, of course, a steer here and there for the occasional barbecue.

As you so well know, Viola Barragán's good and opportune word played a fair part in my moving from the Savings and Loan right to the Bank, but I do earn my daily bread and no doubt on that score. He talked a bit about Viola; admiringly, almost. My *personal* life is my *personal* life he reminded me, and although he knows lot more than he lets on, he doesn't know *everything*. And, I didn't volunteer a word.

Veering off a bit here: He says I'm a born banker; that I was made for this job. (But: To die here, on this job? Gives one pause. Beats the hell out of teaching Eng. at Klail High, though.)

Speaking of Viola, as I was just now, I spotted her at one of Noddy's parties 'ta other night. It was held near the old Relámpago property. (Do you recall that land owned by the McCoys and the Ridings? Some Malacara kin (Chuy, Neto, and Gonzalo) bought some of it back and Noddy got the other half; both halves face the River). OK, there was Viola; she sees me, gives me a big, big hug, and says, 'Howza 'bout you 'n me gettin' together, Studley?' She's incorrigible, and we both burst out laughing to the surprise of our fellow-moochers there.

Don Javier L. was there, too. He must have thirty years on her, right? Anyway, Viola nudged me again and said, 'See that old fraud? He hiked himself on over to Houston for a special operation: he had a thin plastic tube inserted in his peter-nola; helps him pee, see, and he uses it to bed whoever his latest is.'

She then mentioned Ollie and me; said it was a good thing I was thinking of settling down. She sends you her best and asked for your address; plans to send you a gift or two, I imagine.

Our old boss and now her present husband was lurking about and staying out of everybody's way; Viola B. keeps a very short rein. Rations, too, I would suspect. (*Old* Harmon *looks* old).

Viola and I mostly talked about Bank business. She's planning to buy some drive-in theaters (give 'em what they want, she says). She's a preferred customer at the Bank, but I said we'd still have to check her collateral. She winked right back and said, 'What I want to know, you sack full o' bones, is: when are you and I going to run-off together?' With this a kiss and a hug, and a reminder in re the drive-ins; she bustled off to mingle and have herself a hell of a good time. As she says, 'that's why parties were invented, goddammit.' "Go-demet" is how she says it.

What could I possibly add to VB's biog?

Olivia came up with two drinks in hand; she passed one on to me with the news that Becky wants to recommend her for the Woman's Club. (Back to *that* again). Ollie's nobody's fool, and Becky simply can't understand why someone wouldn't jump at the chance of joining the W.C. (They don't use the initials, I don't imagine.)

For the record: of all the women at the party, and there was a bunch, Becky was the only one wearing a hat. She can flat-out wear one, too. Made her even better looking, and that's saying something.

Ira joined us, and what do you think he talked about? You win. And, what if he should lose, you ask? Let me say this, One: the Valley mexicanos are convinced that Ira's their man. Two: the Anglo Texans know he's their boy. Money is bilingual, kid.

Here's a mild surprise: Morse Terry was in the bank this morn. He still does business with us. Noddy, to me, and in strictest conf., says that Morse is getting what's coming to him. Matter of factly; no heat.

(The party was the usual electioneering type of party: Anglo politics, Mexican food, Texas beer. We're both getting old, the parties and I.)

Signing off.

Best,
Jehu

10

Dear Rafe:

Primaries, primaries, o' when will they end?

The mexicano campaign manager for Ira is, need I say it?, none other than Polín Tapia. Polín slithered in quite early this a.m. to pick up 1) orders, and 2) money from Noddy: nihil novum.

Polín's still a youthful type; the years seem to pass right over him, and so do hints and direct insults, it would seem. All's well with his world, I guess.

Years ago when you and I were about twelve years old, (and I worked for Javier L. then), Bobby Campbell asked me if we considered Polín Tapia to be the Mayor of Mexican Town.

Fool that I was, I said, 'No, we don't'. What a dumb fuck I was in those days; we just weren't adept at fielding subtle insults, were we? Anyway, I remembered the 'Mexican Town' term, and I wondered what our Fellow Texans called the other mexicano neighborhoods such as Rebaje, Rincón del Diablo, Colonia Garza, etc.

Speaking of Campbell, in case you've any interest, he now works at a Sporting Goods Store in Edgerton. So much for being voted the one most likely.

Ollie and I are going to Barrones, Tamps., for the weekend. On the town. More (or less) on this at a later time.

It's a bit late, and I've got to call a halt here. Oh, before I forget: could/would you kindly call on a Wm. Barrett family for me, for old times' sake? I spent a week with them when I was getting my disch. papers at Fort Ben. They're named Gamboa and they live, or did, on Lake Street. Look 'em up.

Best,
Jehu

11

Dear Rafe:

Wednesday night.

You said there was more than met your jaundiced eye in the pre-primary goings on. Now, do you know something or is it merely our mutual paranoia? (PARANOIA: an independent disease which may be found present in the most intact of personalities.) It's poss. that I'm too close to the action to be able to sit back, to analyze, etc.

Live and learn, I say. (Yes, Señorita Parker, it *is* National Cliché Week already): Becky was in early last Monday a.m. with an invitation to dinner at *her* house. A smallish affair. We're getting along, Mrs. Escobar and I, and I do so by putting on my best manners, my best foot forward, and my best face, too.

She hasn't got a kind word for too many people, I'm sorry to report. What she needs is a bit of balance, but no complaints from this end. She'll ask a personal question now and again, and I always trot out the truth. No reason not to, I say.

Noddy knows she asks questions, of course, but Noddy also knows me and trusts me not to go telling everything we do around here. (It isn't hard to figure out old NP, by the way. All one has to do is to remember that 1) he's sharp as hell, 2) he's got a mind like a sealed box, and 3) he can nail anybody he wants to. Anytime.)

So, there you have it. Things at Chez Escobar are in order with money in the bank, friends in the street, and votes in the bag.

As for Ira, he's got Washington, D.C. on the brain. (Becky does too, I'm sure of it.) They're not even thinking of an apprenticeship up in Austin. No, sir. From Belken to Washington, but, as you say, first things first, and they are going to have to win the county election first of all. (Someone at the door.)

Sunday morning.

Sorry about the delay. Ollie came in, and we had a quiet dinner at home. On Fri., we went to the sit-down dinner at the Escobars'.

What now follows goes beyond conjecture.

From what Becky told me at the dinner, and from what I know, and from what I have been able to glue together, Morse Terry's decline and fall came about in this-here way:

It has to do with a certain business arrangement concerning FAMILY . . . Morse Terry, not here in Belken but rather in Dellis County, skinned some lands under Noddy's nose. It was a GOOD AMOUNT OF LAND, according to Becky. Morse was the broker for the opposing side; the opposing side in this case being a mexicano family from Flads right there in Dellis County. My guess is that it was the Cruz family or the Lermas or perhaps the Fischer Gutiérrez clan. Or all these, since they do work together well. At any rate, Noddy wanted that land for the Fam. What he *didn't* want, was for the land to fall into *those* mexicanos' hands. They're good, tough people and related to us on the Rincón side, right? Noddy knows this, but business is business. 'Them *cabrones* (Noddy here) are ganging up on me.' But he lost, and he lost well, I'll give him that; the anger had to wind up somewhere, and it devolved on Morse Terry.

To repeat: what I've sketched here is partly what B. said, and what I put together. She spoke rather emphatically, in confidence, and in the relative safety of her own living room. I, small time cynic that I am, asked myself, 'Why is she telling me all of this?' But, I've decided she enjoys passing information left and right. Ollie didn't say a word during all of this since she fell asleep a little after midnight. The talk went on till one or two. Becky, by the way, does have brown eyes; something like coffee sans creme. Great legs, too, or have I said that before?

Must close a bit sharply here, sorry. You're up-to-date on the latest.

Best,
Jehu

12

Dear Rafe:

Good to hear from you. Looks like you're coming along, and here's hoping you'll be home before the end of the year.

Some ticklish news here: On Sat. morn., the day after the visit to Chez Escobar, Morse Terry's wife was collared by none other than Patrolman Bowly T.G. Ponder; gave her a ticket, & a summons as well as a hard time during the writing of the citation. Yes, he did. *And,* yesterday, Mon., two of MT's accounts made an 'alienation of accounts' and transferred their business to Gaddis and Gaddis, Attys.-at-Law. Well now, MT isn't going to die of thirst or rabies on account of this, but it must be recognized that he has lost some ground here. As for his wife's arrest, why, that's just good oldfashioned harassment, pure and simple, as we know it in B. County. Judge Fikes will mete out justice there.

And looky here: yesterday, still Mon., from out of left field somewhere out there, a new political opponent v. Terry. Another independent, they say: an Anglo, of course, from either Bascom or Edgerton, and brought in for that very purpose. This comes on top of Ira Escobar's resolute opposition which means that MT's going to have to come with some more cash; what we bankers call 'an unforeseen cash flow.' (Ira, by the way, isn't sweating the new guy in the race, and that's a surprise.)

Now then, if one adds this to the big money being spent on Ira, you and I have to admit that there is more to this than meets these tired old eyes. It's too much money for one piddling county seat, son.

But, as said, it's conjecture plus facts, and I have damn little hard evidence. Still, and this you can't deny, we both know which direction the raps are coming from, and, most importantly, who's doing the knocking. What is usually not known in these cases is when and how.

And here's the final entry in this grand historical design: our mutual former employer's printing shop misspelled—misspelled, for God's sake—Morse Terry's name. No, he didn't have to pay for their error, but why go on? The man then had to wait two (most prob. three) weeks for new plates, and by then, there were some new Ira Escobar signs all over the place. To add to this, Morse then had to wait an additional two or three days over the due date due to a shortage of ink. Shortage? In a printing shop? Of course, it could all be a great-big-huge monster of a coincidence. Of course.

Noddy tells me little or noth. (it being none of my business), and, besides, I'm just a hired hand. Officially, then, I know nothing.

Must close. Take c. of y'self.

Best,
Jehu

13

Dear Rafe:

To Relámpago and to Carmen Ranch; Israel and Aaron are doing well. In Relám. I visited Auntie Enriqueta who's ailing again; introduced her to Olivia or the other way 'round. Drove over to the old lands, and I got to see Angela Vielma and your sister-in-law Delfina. We gossipped about you a bit; Delfina wanted to know when you'd be marrying again; she says that a widower at 28 yrs. of age is prime material. Your sister-in-law looks happy as well she should after shedding the splendid Rómulo a couple of years back.

In case you're interested (and I doubt this with all my heart), Rómulo is still an uncivil servant at the Jonesville International Bridge. He's no longer family, of course, but from what the girls say, he drops by now and then. I remember how well you two got along.

From Relámpago, Ollie and I followed the river road to the Y that serves as the Flora-Klail City divider. We decided to go to Flora, and, needless to say, we saw and saw and saw Ira's smiling face all the way to Flora, which is not even one of the precinct towns.

Dinner, music, a little reading, and so to bed.

Best,
Jehu

14

Dear Rafe:

Three weeks plus some days before election time and counting.

First thing this morning at the office and what do I see (comin'
to carry me home)? A note on my desk:

Jehu: As soon as you come in,
come by the Ranch. Bring your bricfcase
& mine. Tell one of the girls to call
ahead that you're on your way.
                              N.

Said and done.

Trip takes some 30 minutes, and when I got to the Big House:
nothing. Turned left by the show barn, and sho' nuff, some eight cars
and pickups in front of the long bathhouse behind the pool and the bar.

I pulled in there at quarter-to-nine or so, and the cowboys
must've been working on their third or fourth pot of coffee by then.
And guess who was there? Morse Terry, that's who.

It was all cordially correct, if not exactly warm. I didn't know if
I were there to act as pallbearer or what, but in I walked and handed
NP his briefcase, sat down, was served some coffee, and was then
offered a cigarette.

Strange. It wasn't exactly the way you described what would prob.
happen in that last letter of yours, but it came down close enough.

I'll back up. This last weekend, Ollie and I, as you know, drove
up and down on both sides of the River and so I was out of pocket.
It seems that Morse was squeezed some more between Fri. & Sun.
The upshot of that piece of *bidness is* that Morse, hat in hand, came
to see Noddy. At the Ranch, not at the Bank.

Now, as Chief Loan Officer, and thus an officer of the Bank, I usually give one of three yea/nay votes, and hence my presence here: it's a loan for MT; good-sized loan, as we say.

Mise en scéne: quiet on the set, and the only noise once in a w. is the one made by Sammie Jo's dive as she cuts through the water in that heated pool of hers. The loan is for $67,000 for six years at preferred loan risk rates, but with a king-sized collateral.

Some ass-holish hanger-on was going to be the so-called co-signer; a direct insult to MT. I suggested someone else; Noddy shot me a glance, and I pointed to Meredith Bohlen of Bohlen, Insurance. He's now the co-signer, and that was that. Papers in order & into my briefcase, and I got my second cup of coffee for being such a nice boy at the hanging.

People moved around, shuffled about quietly, and when I looked at Morse (who must be around our age), he looked ten to fifteen years older, and who wouldn't? Noddy applied the make-up, set the scene, and steered the direction. As Noddy told me later on the way to the Bank: 'It's no mystery, Jehu; it's all very simple.'

That weekend, from Fri. p.m. to Sun. night, some 48 hrs., MT rec'd twenty, count 'em 20, telephone calls from clients & friends whom he represents as an atty. They'd been thinking, they said, quite seriously as it turns out, about considering another lawyer as their legal counsel. Nothing less.

Well, at the next-to-last phone call, it was suggested that 'he would do himself and all of us a big favor if he would call Mr. Perkins'.

Cave-in time. He called NP, and that was it. (The loan is merely Noddy's way of doing business, and you *were* right about MT dropping his pants and bending o.)

And there you have it, but as you prob. suspect, there's more. There always is, isn't there? Here it is:

Noddy wants Morse Terry in Washington. Ho-ho! Just Like That.

You see, at first I thought it was Noddy's revenge for that land deal I mentioned some time back or for past deeds & misdeeds, or hate, even. But no, it's been business all the time and when will I *ever* learn?

And will you look at this:

Noddy told me to stop at Cleo's Place for a drink and this at 10:30 a.m., mind you. NP was celebrating, and he wanted to fill me in some more. Our Congressman (whom you know well and whose niece Sophie you know even better) is still Hap Bayliss. Hap (according to Noddy) is ill: 'The man is dying, Jehu. You're one of the very few who knows just how sick he is . . .'

Could be. It could be that I'm one of the few, AND it could be that Hap really is dying. But, with Noddy you never know. Now, I do know some things I shouldn't, and now I wonder if Noddy knows I know . . . no, no, no, that way lies madness.

Two beers and a snack at Cleo's, & NP talked the while. Here is the rest of the Gospel acc. to St. Noddy who, by the way, is taking a few days off 'from all this.'

1) MT is to win Hap's seat; he'll do it as write-in candidate. That's right, and it's to be announced in good time. And this, then

2) paves the way for Ira's Commissioner's post (it also gets Ira out of the way)—But,

3) none of this gets out until Ira gets the biggest scare of his life. Bring him *more* to heel, as it were

4) that, too, is Noddy's way of doing business.

While Noddy is going off on a short vac. he, naturally enough, won't be available to Ira.

Tonight, as I write this, there'll be some twenty calls to our boy (here we go again), telling him some people are planning to cross over to the independent side. Withdrawing their previous backing of I., see? Ira, of course, knows nothing of MT's recent conversion, and absolutely nothing whatsoever about Hap Bayliss and those designs. Plus, he hasn't been told of N's leaving town for a few days.

You can imagine the sucking of wind, given Ira's temperament and ASPIRATIONS. One more thing, Noddy's answering service will announce to please leave a message until Mr. Perkins can get back to the caller. (Hit me, said the masochist; I won't, said the sadist.)

So, Noddy'll be gone for the next three-four days.

New subject: am throwing away old letters, notes, papers, and the usual junk that's been piling up for yrs. and yrs. Few things will survive this purge. Not to worry, I'm fine; it's just a bit of overdue cleaning up, that's all.

Best,
Jehu

15

Dear Rafe:

Loan and Arrangement Day with Morse T. plus four. For all purposes, no official word in re the Bayliss-Perkins-Terry entente cordiale, and Ira is going out of what he is pleased to call his mind. The campaign posters are still up there, all right, and apparently nothing has changed. To top it, Ira told me yesterday morn. that Becky's gone to Jonesville for a few days (which I knew from her, of c.). But that's all Ira told me & he hasn't taken me into his confidence about the phone calls. (Neither did Becky.)

The election is now exactly two weeks off, and Ira thinks he's losing ground: he's not, but *he* thinks he is. Ira can't bring himself to ask me about Noddy, his whereabouts, or about his private line; Ira is in a bad way, and it promises to get worse. (For your information: Noddy had flown up to Wm. Barrett International to meet Hap B. Hap then flew back to Washington, and Noddy buzzed in late last night; he called and said he wanted to see me at the Ranch fairly early. He sounded happy, and that's always a bad sign.)

So, early this morning it starts again: I've been at the Ranch since 9 or so, a pile of papers for Noddy and me to sign when he stops around eleven and says (winking, mind you), 'Time to call Ira.'

He did and, believe me, I could hear Ira's heaving & breathing. Noddy begins by saying that he just got in from out of town and that there must be some one-hundred or more messages from Ira for him. Noddy's looking right at me when he says this, and he follows that with this: 'Hey, Ira, you're not thinking of dropping out of the race, are you?'

A dying groan from I., and before he can recover, Noddy the

Splendid asks about Becky (knowing full well) and then he offers to send a Ranch car to pick up Ira at the Bank.

Ira's in no condition to drive and thus he waits there for the car that'll drive him straight into the lion's den. The driver must have taken the longer way home 'cause Noddy and I talked business, signed papers, ate a snack, drank a glass of beer, and Ira *still* wasn't at the Ranch. For all I know, Noddy planned it that way.

(Don't mind me; while I may not live in Paranoiaville, *I have* bought some land out in the suburbs.)

When Ira finally showed up, Noddy was all smiles; poor Ira didn't notice that NP was using that low voice of his.

Here, let me finish this up: Noddy sounded hurt; he said he'd heard that Ira was going 'round saying that he—Ira—didn't owe a favor to anybody; that he—Ira—had gotten to where he was on his own, by his own bootstraps. And then, in that low voice, Noddy said, 'Now that's what I call downright ungrateful, Ira.'

I'd say 'Poor Ira' again, but *he* wanted the job, right? Well, he got it, all right.

Noddy sat him down (literally) and talked about the importance of water rights in the Valley. How the water was apportioned in Belken County; who manned the irrigation ditches; who assigned the watering days and the amount, and when it was to be let out. Plain as Salisbury it was. Noddy talks about water rights, but Ira sits there and nods and agrees, and he still doesn't know that what N. is really talking about is pure and simple *control.*

Last entry: Noddy offered Ira a beer, and he took it; the man's allergic to beer, for Christ's sake!

Hold it. Telephone. It was Ollie; she's coming over.

Note: I don't think I'm going to last here much longer; I don't have the tummy for it. Ira may be a perfect fool, but he's still a human being.

Best,
Jehu

Confession time: I haven't been able to do what Noddy told me to do when he first hired me at the Savings & Loan: 'You're going to have to learn not to give a damn, Jehu. When you learn *that,* you'll be successful, but not before.' Man's right.

16

Dear Rafe:

It's a good thing I've got a private office at the Bank; and yes, I do enjoy a good laugh once in a while, but do exercise a little Christian charity, cousin. Your laughing, too, was music to these old ears; anyway, thanks a lot for the call. I needed it.

I may wind up dividing this one on an hour-by-hour basis.

Tuesday. Nine days to countdown.

To begin with: the write-in campaign (via radio and tv) is well on its way for MT who, as you know, is now going after Hap Bayliss' seat on Noddy's say so. Hap announced he was ill; it was on all the wire services, etc. I, too, will be less than charitable and say he got sick at Wm. Barrett International after his meeting with NP. One more thing for your kit bag: Hap, sick as he is, is leading the write-in campaign for MT. And that's how it's done: brown or not at all, and no q.'s asked.

The paid political announcements, a euph., can be seen and heard on every Valley station: in Eng. and in Spn. both. The stations spell out Morse's name, make no mistake says the announcer. Then, it's repeated and finally spelled out a third time. And, in order not to miss anyone (the deaf shall also vote) the name comes out ever so slowly across the tv screen as if announcing a Gulf hurricane or something. (Ira? He's in like a second-story man as Comm. Precinct 3, but he's dead to the world. He had the election in his sweaty palm, then NP came and took it away, and then NP came right back and handed it to him, but it was more than our boy could take. But, as you and I laughed about it this morning, it was MT for Washington all the time and all the way. We have much to learn.)

I'm telling you, and you heard it here first, he'll win big with Morse and the strawman out of the way, but NP squeezed what juice and flavor there were in that navel orange. And, of course, Ira knows nothing about anything. And he certainly doesn't know about Beck and me. Period.

Morse, although he doesn't come 'round here much, is in contact with Noddy; NP told him not to be more than six feet away from the phone, and so our future Congressman is a prisoner in his own home. (In Washington, it'll be the same thing; as Noddy told him, in my office, 'We're just a phone call away, Morse.')

To touch lightly on what you said: Yes, you *are* right, I do know more than I should about some things, and, to repeat, you're *so* right when you say I have to take care.

One thing, though, I've no major debts to settle, nor do I have any pending accounts, to use the etymological root . . . *One* consolation is to know that NP can run me off when he wants to, but the *other* is that I, too, can walk away the same way I came here three years ago: one hand forward and one hand back, left-right-left, and right through that front door without dragging any shit behind me.

By the by, Becky doesn't rank among the very best; what she does offer is the well-known Mexican fury and flurry. No complaints, mind you, I thought it'd be a one-shot affair, but glad to report I was wrong.

Turned the radio on just now. Ho-ho! They're flooding *all* the stations again, and on both sides of the River, too.

Tonight's the last rally for the Klail mexicanos' vote. A form of insurance, let's say. There'll be further instructions on the spelling of Morse's name, although five'll get you that ten of the elec. judges will count *anything* that resembles MT's name. And, as the Father Confessor once asked; 'Is this the first time, my son?'

Mr. Polín Tapia, who else? is the head cheerleader tonight. And *that,* cousin, is how the system works around here; as if I had to tell *you* that.

Oh, and before I forget: no Texas Rangers at the polling places. A sign of the times, say the optimists, a sign from Noddy, say I.

To something else. Today, Sanford Blanchard showed up at the Bank. 'The Terror of the Female Household Staff' rushed right into

Noddy's office as I was walking out. I looked to Noddy in case he needed help, but a shake of the head got me out of there. Sanford is a Bank Director, by the by, but he always votes by proxy. Sidney (Sammie Jo's No. 2, as y. know) stayed in the car while Sanford came to see Noddy. Some trouble or another at the Ranch, I expect.

Sanford prob. can't get it up much these days, but in his younger days he was a dangerous species: he could outrun and catch any Mexican, Nicaraguan, or Guatemalan maid brought out to the Ranch; a lot of shit in that Ranch, cousin, and like it or not, I'm a part of it. But, in your heart of hearts, do you believe that some of *our* friends would give me a job if I were to need one all of a sudden? Aside from Viola, they didn't do it back then when I needed one. And now? Well, I'm not buying three pounds of shit in a two-pound bag. Neither you nor I, Rafe, owe 'em a whole hell of a lot:

'fools and knaves
at the breakfast table . . .'

You're prob. laughing, right? But that's it, son. The mexicano people can also be ass-holish when they feel like it, and I'm fresh out of brotherly love. Old-fashioned class and shame have just about played out in Belken County. Think not? Just wait for the gnashing of teeth when the word gets out that you *gave* Acosta that land for $10 total. They'll call you a fool, our friends will.

Don't pay too much attention to me, it's just me and the Curse. Look, if there's something tomorrow or the day after, I'll call or pass it along; if not, I'll wait until I hear from you.

Best,
Jehu

17

Dear Rafe:

And what has happened in the last six days or so? Noddy damn thing, as we say. The radio & tv ads are still in absolute and full swing. Morse is still at home plate (we're as near as your teleph.) and Ira is one shaken young man. (Becky called; she's now the Pres.-elect to the Woman's Club. How is *that* for a surp.? She was presented with a silver platter, she was, and with honors too numerous to mention, and *yes* I saw her again. Can't be helped when you're young, you know.)

Ira can't believe he's got the election in one of those pockets of his three-piece suit; he still thinks *something*'s going to happen. Noddy doesn't know how good a job he did on Ira. WHAT AM I SAYING? Of *course,* he knows. He just enjoys seeing Ira hop, is all . . .

The elections, and there must be another word we could use, are two days away.

On a personal note. Have not seen Ollie in 5 to 6 days; and she's not returning my calls at the pharm. It isn't as if we're formally engaged (is that still done?), but I (at least *I*) thought we had something serious there. Unless Becky blabbed; I take that back. Still, where there's smoke, right?

The phone just rang. Sammie Jo; wants to talk. In person. I'll continue this mañana.

            J.

Here I am again. SJ's worried; thinks Uncle Sanford knows about our get-togethers. She's not *that* worried, but she's thinking of me and the job at the B. About her Dad, I imagine, and what he'd do.

Told her that Sanf. had been at the Bank, but also told her not to w. Sanford Blanchard is hardly a reliable witness.

Tomorrow is election day (and I'll be glad when that's done). Bayliss (yesterday or the day before) announced he was a *vurry* sick man and gave his unconditional imprimatur and nihil obstat to MT. (Just one more time for those who didn't get it the first twenty times or so.) Bonus: we now have video tapes in many of Klail City's business estabs. & you can enjoy pro-Terry ads all you wish. We've two at the Bank, one in the coffee lounge, and one right smack in the middle of everything where Hap endorses his young, talented, and long-time friend. Endlessly. And, speaking of Morse, he called on me this morn.

Ready? He wants me to go to Washington with him. To work in his DC office! Noddy's move, I'm sure. Bribe? Could be. Spying on MT? Most prob. Anyway, I did thank MT, but no, thanks.

And so it goes 'round here. Still no word from Ollie; I call, leave my name and no., but silence reigns.

Long day tomorrow. You getting any better up there?

Best,
Jehu

18

Dear Rafe:

Election Day plus two and God's in His heaven, and Noddy's in his, regarding each other with suspicion, one would imagine.

Well, sir, it's in all the papers, and I'm not telling you something you don't already know. And now, it's simply a matter of picking up the pieces and the litter.

Our newest commissioner is more restrained, less exhuberant, *as it were.* This last is now a pet phrase. As such, he uses it at the drop of a jaw. If he's not careful, the instructed electorate will start calling him *Asitwere.* At the very least.

Two days in office, and he's saying things such as 'early on', and 'within these walls', and 'the sense of the meeting' and on and on. There just may be a little black book with all of that claptrap, and Ira may just have committed it to memory. Speaking of memory, as I just was, it would appear that Ollie has dropped me from hers. And via the U.S. Mail, too. Done struck out, Coach. And here I was, getting serious for the first time in *years.* Goes to show you.

This p.m., around closing time, Noddy came by my office. A dinner invitation to the Big House (& bring a friend, Jehu). I guess the old sumbitch knows about O. like he knows most things around here. Anyway, dinner's on for tomorrow night. Cocktails at eight; dinner at nine. Veddy formal. As you may supp., I can hardly wait.

Don't know who'll be there, but I can wager it'll be Ira and Becky, Morse, and his wife (Bedelia Boyer; grateful Bedelia, as I remember you calling her). Don't know who else will be in attendance. NP said it would be a smallish affair for a few of us. Us?

Translation: Important to all concerned.

I'll see where I fit in. Cocktails at 8 and no masks, but with Noddy, who's to know?

Hang on.

Best,
Jehu

19

Dear Rafe:

Just called you, but as always, nothing doing, and so I'll write.
(I also called you last night after *the dinner,* but no answer. May I ask
just what the hell kind of a hosp. they're running up there where no
one answers the ph.?)

Some *dinner.*

Here we go: *The table had been picked and cleared by the time
I got there.* I got there at eight, on the penny, and I spent three minutes at the Big House in all; tops.

Becky didn't raise her eyes (the whole time), the Terrys bit their
respective lower lips (no surprise there) and Ira studied the Utrillo on
the wall (an art lover, yet).

Noddy made it short: 'Jehu, I recommend that you resign as loan
officer.'

I didn't say a word; the shock, needless to say.

I also left with my tail between my legs. To home and to worry,
of which I did some on the way there. And I *did* worry, until—damn
my eyes!—I *stopped.* I was doing exactly what Noddy wanted me to
do; expected me to do. Go home and worry. About the *why.* Oh, he's
a bastard all right, I'll give him that. (Note: he said *loan officer;* not
from the *bank* itself. Now, what did the *others* hear?

Resign as loan officer and then what? Be demoted? Would I then
stay? And, if I did, would I then be cooked? If I left, I'd be out of a
job, sure, but there's always Viola. Another alternative: the Savings
& Loan, but I wouldn't go back there at the point of a gun.

Noddy, aside from being a bastard, as said, is also a very good
teacher, and I'll give him that, too. Maybe I'm his prize pupil.

Going to bed, son; tired and whether I want to admit it or not, shaky as Hell. I didn't think I'd mind leaving the Bank, but he's some kind-a bastard.

He did it in front of everybody. Ha! That's it, Rafe! He didn't do it *alone;* he *couldn't* do it alone. But that's been his pattern all along . . .

I bet, I just *bet* that Ira & Becky and the Terrys were just as surprised (shocked) as I was. They were told dinner was at six, say seven, and so, by eight . . . Jesus!

So? Look at this: day after tomorrow, to the Bank, as if nothing's happened. Monday is Armistice Day, and thus a bank holiday; I'll try to call you again and get more of this on the phone.

Good night, R.

Best,
Jehu

20

Dear Rafe:

The rub (a dub-dub) as Shakespeare and Don Victor Peláez used to say, was the coming out of anything smelling mighty but lak-a-rose. To walk out of that Bank would look (and smell) bad, and, added to which, I'd have a hell of a time explaining it; I did what I *had* to do.

I went to Noddy's office (as usual) and upon closing the door, I told him I wanted to go back to the Savings & Loan (which must've surprised him) but I needed a topic to start on.

'It's out of my hands, Jehu.'

I said it wasn't, and he said it was. I then said it'd look like hell (for me) if he let me go like that.

'You brought that on yourself, Jehu.'

I didn't argue the point 'cause if I did, we'd get into this, that, t'other, and I'd lose there, no question.

There I was, holding a Chinese straight and nothing else. Arms crossed, and looking straight on, I said: 'Does my firing have anything to do with sex, Noddy?'

Well! He squinted those faded old blues (one of his favorite ploys that squint) and *then* he exploded:

'You Mexican son-of-a-bitch!'

But I was ready. Ten, maybe even five years ago I'd-a knocked him on his ass for that, but not now, not this time. What I did, was to walk across the room, sit, look straight at him, and say: 'You may as well hear it straight from me: Becky and I had a couple of tussles, but that was it.'

'Becky? Who the hell said anything about Becky Escobar, god-dammit!'

And I: 'Then who the hell *are* you talking about? And it sure as hell better not be Ollie, 'cause that's *my* business and not the bank's, goddammit!'

'Ollie? San Esteban? I'm talking about Sammie Jo, you son-of-a-bitch!'

'Sammie Jo? You've got a-hold of some bad shit there, Noddy.'

'*Bull*shit!'

'Bull*shit*. Let's call her, better still, let's go on out there, goddammit.'

'You . . .'

'Hold on, Noddy. You *know* I'm telling the truth . . . It's something *else,* isn't it?'

The man was absolutely right, of course. But, he was bluffing; the man had aces showing, all right, but he had *shit* in the hole.

NP knows me, and he knew I was going to come over to the Bank. I swear it. But I was ready for him. This time.

And he went on:

'You gonna make a speech?'

That old fart was still swinging away, back against the wall and full of fight.

'No,' I said. 'I'm no capon, but I'm not a goddam fool, either.'

I turned to go when he said, 'You know it hurts like hell.'

'Bullshit, Noddy.'

'Okay, okay; let me start over: so you and Becky . . .'

'Sure, twice; maybe three times. I don't remember.'

'Don't *remember?*'

'No! Who the hell counts? Look, Noddy, I haven't done anything you wouldn't have done at my age. But you're wrong about Sammie and me. We're close, and we've known each other since high school, but that's it, goddammit!'

'Is that the speech?'

The old son of a bitch won't ever let you go.

'And one more goddammed thing: we'll get into that Mexican son-of-a-bitch thing at another time.'

'Oh, yeah? And what makes you think you're still working here?'

'Well, you haven't thrown me out yet.'

And with that, the old sumbitch laughed, and that's the *closest* he'll come to an apology.

So, it's settled. I'm still the Chief Loan Officer, and that's that.

Of course, he now knows about Becky and me, but I must say this: when he learns (for a fact) 'bout Sammie Jo and me, then it'll really be my ass.

Wanna bet?

Best,
Jehu

21

Dear Rafe:

Thanks for the call and thank you for the congratulations. Experimental evidence has shown that congratulations when dealing with NP must wait some five to ten years. Man's got a long arm to go with that memory of his.

Now that I think back on it, Sanford and Sidney must have put a flea in Noddy's ear. And why was Sanford the messenger boy? Because NP can't stand his own son-in-law. (And thanks for the tip.)

This a.m. (when you're hitting for extra bases, it's best to swing from the h.) I told Esther to hold all calls: I walked to the pharmacy and went to see Ollie. I had to.

It's on between us again, but on a different footing. I told her about Becky *and* about Sammie Jo, and that's how serious I am.

Things are back to normal: Ira carries on his share of the gloat by crossing each *t* and by dotting each *i;* he used to do it the other way round, but Ira is nothing if not compulsive.

Noddy's up in Colo., went to pick up Mrs. P. and taking some time off, too. The bank's rocking along and so's the work here. I'm thinking about leaving in a couple of mos. May go up to see you, may go up to Austin, may do both. Grad Sch. looks better every day, and I'm close to 30 yrs. of a.

When I do leave, though, I'm really not planning on anything def. for a bit. But I'll leave, that's sure, and under my own steam and terms. This time.

Poor Ira. Sees me here, and he doesn't know what to do or think. Talk about not believing your eyes.

In re Sammie Jo. It's over for a while. More importantly, we're still friends. As always. As for Becky: no comment. She's now busy with the Music Club, yes, that too, and now we're out of each other's hair, as it were. And, I guess that when Beck and I are both sixty years old, we'll look back on this and laugh about it. I can hardly wait.

VB then lit a cigarette and said, 'We need a business manager. Any time you want to chuck this place, let me know; pronto. Gotta go, now. Oh, before I do forget: I want a personalized wedding invitation, hear?'

No idea where she heard *that*. Not a bit of truth to it. Cross my eyes.

This much is settled: Ollie and I'll go up to see you in Wm. Barrett. That's still on.

Best,
Jehu

22

Dear Rafe:

Ein feste Burg ist unser Klail; impregnable, too. When I tell you that I see this town of ours, and I can't believe what I *do* see, then it's just too much, even for me.

The election doings provided the temporary bread and circus, of course, and people round here talk of nothing else. Complaints, mostly, but only after all has been said and done.

String's playing out, though. Came home after work, had myself a beer & went on another cleaning binge. Whatever survived the last purge, didn't survive this one.

It's funny how I've accumulated all kinds and manner of trash, and particularly since discarding is more in my line.

To the basket one and all; out, damned spots. Took some three hours, maybe more, and I did count some dozen or more grocery bags full of junk. Junk which wasn't 'junk' then, of course. Clean slates. Can't begin (may not want to, in fact) to explain how this came about. First I threw away this picture and then that letter and then that one, and it was easier every time. Therapy is what it is.

I'm up to here and there with the elections, the shit, the talk, the etc. and the etc. too. Staying in tonight and tomorrow night, and the night after that. Plan to read and re-read. Ollie may come over; I don't know. She's the best, really; but for a lifetime? Time will tell.

Also, there must be something else other than that slow, winding road to Our Lady of Mercy cemetery. There must be.

All of this on one beer? Not to worry, nothing serious. This, too, shall pass.

Don't, not for one minute, think that this has anything to do with your letter or with the visit up there. I needed that visit, and I needed to be with Ollie more than just overnight. I'll be okay.

Best,
Jehu

23

Dear Rafe:

Israel and Aaron parachuted in on me last weekend. I'm sure you put them up to it, and thanks. I didn't know I needed the company. Friends are fine and a woman is better, but you can't beat relatives.

I *was* glad to see them; they sat down, smiled, and said I was under arrest: going for a three-day sentence to Carmen Ranch for hunting and fishing, they said. I went along meekly, and I had a hell of a good time.

From my apt. window facing Hidalgo and First, I can see half of Klail, but only when I want to; I'm better now, and I'm about to decide.

This is the end of my second three-day pass away from the Bank; I'll take three days off again next week and then couple them with the weekend. O. and I are going to the beach for four or five days.

There's the phone again.

Gotta go.

Best,
Jehu

Part II

P. Galindo

24
Polín Tapia

Of the same military class as the wri, they have known each
other for years. Of Polín it was once said (by Don Abdón Bermúdez,
from most accounts) that one would do well to count one's fingers
and nails after shaking hands with Polín. Don Abdón's phrase, a bit
short on charity, may not be too far off the mark, according to the
regulars at the Blue Bar.

Tapia lives off politics and such, and thus some mexicano Klail-
ites don't care for him. On the other hand, Federico 'Chancla' Ruiz
does the same thing, and is considered *simpático*. This may be set
down as differences in style.

The wri (equality among men) is all ears: the wri, content to find
a source of information, will be happier to judge later on. For now,
equity and discretion is his motto.

"Where to start, Galindo? Are the elections as good a place as
any? Let's see . . . About the time Ira Escobar decided, definitely
decided, to run for the Commissioner's post, and by that time he'd
gotten the Ranch's and the Bank's backing, I volunteered to help in
any way, at any time. That's my style, see? You have to be on your
toes, you know. Anyway, you yourself know that I have a certain
flair, a talent, for this type of work.

"I've always got some favors to call in, and I do, and it's usually a matter of 'I'll scratch yours and you scratch mine'. But what the
hey! Why am I wasting my time telling you this? You wrote the
primer, Galindo; you know as much about this as anyone. Right?"

The wri likes to believe that he is above accepting flattery and heavy-handed compliments. Note: the wri is more than fairly ignorant about many, many things, and it's been only recently that he learned to admit how little he does know.

"Weeeeeeeeeeeeeeeeeell, Ira decides to oppose Morse Terry, a .400 hitter, Galindo, and one whom I also know quite well. Anyway, the fight's the thing, as the saying goes, but hard work and talent bring out the best in me, right?

"As you know, Ira won the generals in November; now, that Bayliss fell ill around that time, and that Morse took the Congressional seat as a write-in is something else again. I can hardly be blamed for *that;* I concentrated on the commissioner's race, right? This was my first priority, right? A-course, if I could see into the future, why, Ira'd be a Congressman by now, yes, he would. Cross my heart, Galindo. But a commissioner is a commissioner, and Belken's no down-at-the-heels county like Dellis, right? And like I always say, you got to start somewhere, hey?"

Self-corroboration is PT's strongest suit.

"The kids and the older folk at the bank worked like Trojans at election time. They stuffed envelopes, made telephone calls, raised a little money here and there, and like that. Stalwarts, all of 'em. But I'll tell you who didn't turn a lick; Jehu Malacara. I didn't *ask* him to help, but my God!, the way everyone else was hustling around there, why, you'd think he'd at least take a *hint.* God, no; thought didn't even occur to him. Hah! The only time he *said* something it sure as hell wasn't *constructive;* he told me it'd be best if I tried *working* for a living. Can you imagine that? *Him* telling *me* that? Is that what they teach 'em up in Austin? Is that the mark of an educated man?"

The wri has no idea how anyone is educated up there.

"Well! *I've* known Jehu since he was the sweep and cleanup boy at the Chagos' barbershop. Humph! Has he forgotten *that?* Ha! I sure as hell don't tell *him* how to do his job at the bank, do I?

"Ira's something else again, though. He's got a sense of humor, he knows how to laugh, knows how to show a courtesy or two, and, and, here, let me tell you this: I even drive that big Olds a-his 'n that. Ha! And Jehu? Shoot! He doesn't even *own* a car 'cause that green MG's not his, no sir: that little car belongs to the pharmacist woman friend a-his.

"Look, in my opinion, Jehu is used to having everything come his way. Everything. Made to order. It's got to be his way, or he won't play. Humph. It's time he found out what *working* is all about. That's right.

"I'm not criticizing, Galindo. In politics one learns to evaluate, rate, okay? I'm not angry, no. And no resentment, either. You, as a writer and newspaperman, know all about this."

The wri insists to the reader that the wri doesn't know much about a lot of things.

"Jehu worked at the bank, was handed a post of *some* responsibility, he had a year or two of seniority on Ira, but Ira, on talent alone earned more money than Jehu; yes, he did. Ira told me so. And what happens when you open those double-doors to the bank? The first person you see is Ira, but where is Jehu? I'll tell you where: Jehu was stuck in some small office next to Noddy Perkins' big office, that's where.

"Ira's good people, Galindo. Yes, he is. And a nice guy, to boot. Why, you won't see *him* at the *Aquí me quedo Bar* or, worse, at the Blue Bar. You'll see Jehu there, though; oh, yeah. Look, as a newspaperman *you* can go anywhere, any time. But Jehu? He's a banker! Geez! He was lowering himself, he was. And did he *care?*

"Oh, and as far as that laugh a-his, well, I'm not fooled one bit by that; no sir. That's plain old ridicule, is what that is. That's *right*. I mean, what the hell does he think he is, some sort-a royalty?

"Tell you what. My Dad, and my uncle, too, never—hear?— never hired Jehu at their place, because Jehu wasn't dependable nor serious, either. Nope. You got to work hard, polishing and wiping the furniture and the washing machines and what-all. 'A furniture store survives on shine,' my Dad used-a say. No, sir; Jehu wouldn't-a lasted a day there.

"Now, between you 'n me, I'm going to tell you something in absolute, strictest confidence: Ira may be a chubby sort, but he's All Man, yessir. Now, I know Jehu, and all I can say is that he's damn lucky he didn't set eyes on Becky or he'd-a been in big trouble, yessir. He doesn't know Ira Escobar, not like I do. Why, Ira'd made a capon out-a that boy, yes he would've. Ha! You don't think so?"

The wri, an agnostic, holds few beliefs.

"One thing for sure, people don't walk away from a cinch job every day o' the week. Nossir. I'm not saying that he was run off at the bank, but it doesn't look good his going away like that. Right? You be the judge."

The wri, no callow youth, caught himself (a time or two) with mouth agape. It'd be unnecessary to say that Polín resents Jehu somewhat, but no one's perfect, as Polín himself says. It should be understood, however, right here and now, that Polín is quite open in his assessments, in his preferences; he doesn't, then, hold anything back. That he says what he does say, may reveal the mutual confidence between PT and the wri.

But, this is what this is all about in the first place. The reader is to arrive at a personal conclusion and not wait for the wri to tie the noose round the ring to lead the reader by the nose. As it were.

25

Ira Escobar

A co-worker of Jehu's at the Klail City First National, and newly elected first-term County Commissioner, Precinct 3. Married and thus wedded to Rebecca Escobar née Caldwell, Ira was not enthusiastic to speak to the wri at the Bank, at first. But (broadminded that he is) Ira came round to give his views in the Jehu Malacara affair.

"Sure, I know him well; I've, ah, I've helped him out a couple of times, or I did. He was the ch, chief loan officer, but he, ah, he needed help once in a while. And, what are friends for, as *I* always say.

"I can't say he was much interested in politics, though he read quite a bit; at least I always had the impresson he read quite a bit. Know what I mean?

"We never, ah, ah, seldom saw each other socially except for bank parties or at political barbecues. He didn't take the barbecues seriously; he, ah, he thought they were one big joke, you know. I really don't understand why Noddy (The wri noted that the deponent looked first to his right and then to his left), Mr. Perkins, Noddy . . . I don't know why Jehu was hired. I mean, he, Jehu, had a certain flair for this type of work but ah . . . talent? Now, as to. . .

The wri waited until IE finished his sentence, but it was not to be. The sentence died on a sigh . . .

"We got along well, though. At first, my wife cried for him, but after a couple of times or so, she hardly mentioned him at all, and I don't believe she's talked to Jehu for the last eight months or so. Anyway, Becky, my wife, is, ah, usually, ah, pretty busy with her work at the Music Club, and she works late once or twice a week.

And, I was busy on my own campaign, which turned out well, as you know. So, the two of us, Becky and I, didn't exactly snub Jehu; we just simply didn't see much of him, that's all."

The wri needs to break in here: it is entirely possible that Becky Escobar works assiduously at the Woman's Club and at the Music Club as IE says. Let he who is without sin cast the very first etcetera.

"As loan officer, Jehu saw more of Mr. Per . . . of, ah, Noddy, than I did; my desk handles the smaller loans and some automobile notes, as well. I guess you know that I'd only been on the job a short while when I was asked to consider running for Commissioner for Place Three. You *must* have seen my pictures, right? I mean, they were fairly well plastered all over the place from Jonesville to Edgerton (titter) and from Relámpago on over to Ruffing (smile).

"I like politics; it's a man's responsibility, and it's also a way to do public service, don't you agree?"

The wri has precious few opinions which tend to favor politics and none whatever for politicians. This is merely one of the many faults readily admitted to by the wri.

"When Noddy, ah, (slight jerking movement of the head) informed me that Jehu was leaving, he, Mr. Per . . . Noddy, ah, didn't *exactly* offer me the senior officer's loan post, but he, Noddy, ah, did say that with my added duties at the county level, that I, ah, would be far too busy with that end of it to be *chained* to the chief loan officer's desk.

"I think I could handle both, but it could be that the Old Man (one of those rabbit-like smiles), I mean, that *Noddy*, you see, is right . . . Still, I mean, if Jehu did it, I could too, *right?*

"I'm not putting him down or anything, but I could handle the job. Sure.

"As for Jehu, again, well, he, ah . . . he had a certain difficulty of expression; an impediment. You know what I mean? His, ah, his English was a bit weak now and then, and that would've held him back had he stayed on here. Definitely.

"Look; I wouldn't mind talking to you some more on this, but I do have a luncheon date over at the, ah, the Camelot . . . right?"

Yes, the wri agrees with the reader: IE did not mention the dinner held at Noddy Perkins' some time back. The wri feels there is no need to return to IE for further information in the near future. Remains to be seen, that's all.

26

Martín San Esteban

A pharmacist; a fellow student of Rafe's and Jehu's at the University; slightly older than his sister, Olivia. Martín was born in Klail City, he grew up in Edgerton, and married one of the Ycaza girls from Ruffing. He and Olivia are co-owners of Klail City Drugs.

"We go back a long way, Jehu and I. I'm talking before Austin, and before the Army even. Yep, Jehu's always been like that. As for Ollie, I don't think they dated this much up at Austin.

"He and Rafe lived in that crazy place off Guadalupe and 26th the last two years. I roomed with my cousin at Mrs. Lundquist's.

"Do you know my cousin? Juan? Santoscoy? Well, the four of us used to run together at the University some; but neither Jehu nor Rafe were much for dances.

"I remember the time Rafe and Jehu and some other guys made some beer, some home brew. They made it *right* in the room. My God, they must have made close to ten cases of the stuff. It was dark stuff; strong, too.

"Austin wasn't that big then, you know. You could usually run into Jehu over on the West Mall. His first year there, he lived in that house by Scottish Rite; and *that* was a madhouse, and I think all the guys there were communists. Jesus! Jehu *loved* it; Rafe usually sat there, drinking his beer, talking now and then. Most of the guys who lived there were from South America or Mexico, and Jehu, 'n don't ask me why, called them The Filipinos. They didn't seem to mind it, either . . . it was strange.

"Jehu was an English major; I'm not sure he was planning to teach, though. I'll tell you this, I had no *idea* what he was going to do with *that* degree. Juan and I were both in pharmacy and we knew we had a job; and, then, later on, Mom and Dad bought this place here.

"Ollie . . . Ollie's been dating Jehu some, and now she's got it into her head about going up to Galveston. I mean, she wants to *apply* to *med* school, can you imagine? Shoot, we've got enough business *here* already. And for two more pharmacists if we wanted to.

"But Jehu's like that, you know, I mean, no sooner did he get a job at Klail High than he started thinking about something *else*.

"He's lucky, though, I'll say that. He usually manages to land some pretty good jobs; he just doesn't stick to 'em, that's all. Why, look at the job at the bank; they *liked* him there, you know.

"And now Ollie says that Jehu wants to get a Master's degree. Well, what does one *do* with a Master's in English. I mean, he's already taught at the high school, and he could probably get another job there, but to go back to *that?* Shoot. The job at the bank *pays* better, and I just hope he didn't do anything there to screw it up. No, no, don't misunderstand, I'm not saying he did; I'm just saying that it wouldn't *look* good for the mexicanos if he did, see? But Jehu's *honest.* He's *crazy,* but he's honest.

"But like I said, he and Ollie go out once in a while. He was *hell* in Austin, though. But I'll tell you this: he won't get to first base with Ollie; she's a mexicana, and raised that way.

"Have you heard from Rafe lately, Mr. Galindo? He and I were kind-a tight up at Austin, for a while, but he's just *too* damn quiet sometimes. He's steady, though. Boy, he and Jehu made quite a pair; have you ever heard Jehu sing? I'm serious, yeah. He knows some *funny* songs. In *Spanish. He* could make Rafe laugh, out loud, too.

"Do you know Rafe's, ah, of course you do. I was about to ask if you knew Rafe's sister-in-law, Delfina. Well, Delfina was here the other day, and she said that Jehu had given her her grandmother's or maybe her great grandmother's, I'm not sure which, anyway, it was a bible. An *old* one. Rafe had given it to Jehu, and Jehu, about a week or two before he left last Fall, well, he gave it to Delfina. It's a nice old book, and probably worth a lot of money, is my guess.

"By the way, I've heard that Angela Vielma and Delfina have

been talking about moving into that nice house off Palm View; the big one, the one that's kitty-corner to Hidalgo Boulevard. You know, by the old school? It's a big house. And nice, too."

The wri had not met young San Esteban prior to this; he knew of him as he knows of a lot of other things in God's Littlest Acre: by chance. The wri has no commentary to make as to the pharmacist's views and opinions on Jehu; the wri thinks he detects a slight resentment at Jehu's seemingly carefree outlook, but the wri would also like to point out that he evinced no strong criticism of Jehu's ways. It could be that Martín simply doesn't understand Jehu, his ways, his ideas, or his sister's interest in medicine and Jehu.

27

Viola Barragán

The wri is at a loss when it comes to explaining institutions, and VB is one. She's a firm believer in the *status quo ante,* of the American free enterprise system, a champion adherent of *laissez faire entre nous,* and a friend to her friends. She is also loyalty personified, an in-fighter, independent, brave, and a steady, resolute repository of all that is good and bad in the Valley. The wri (obviously, shamelessly) admires this *sui generis* personality.

"Well, Galindo! Long time and all that. Don't interrupt, I know, I know, you've been talking to people about Jehu's whereabouts, isn't that about it? Well, for starters, I can tell you right here and now, that that boy's got a job here whenever he wants one. Yessir. He's a hard worker, he's sharp, and, above everything else, a straight arrow. Plus, he's free to run my, knock on wood, many businesses here and there; they're doing well, knock with me, damn you, and that boy has a good nose for business.

"What can I tell you? You know me from way back and here I am, nudging fifty, and if you want to know something, just ask. You may not like what you hear, but the truth'll come out vanilla-clear, yessir.

"I talked to Noddy Pee-pockets about the boy not too long ago, and whatever else Noddy is, and he's a lot of things, there's no conning me: we talk shop, politics, you name it, and we talk straight. Every time. What I'm about to tell you, then, is less than a week old; I mean I talked to him then.

"He says that Jehu, some time ago, 'round election time, got to Becky Escobar. I figure that's nobody's business but theirs. And, if Noddy thought, for one damn minute, that I was going to blow *that* around here, then he sure as hell doesn't know Viola Barragán; not by a long damn chalk, hear? I'm not his goddam Western Union, nossir.

"Now, it's not that Noddy really gives a damn about that, but, what *I* didn't like then, and I still *don't,* dammit, is that Noddy said that Jehu may be in some sort of danger, or trouble, or peril, or something along that line on account of he pulled Becky's pants off. Heckfire, Galindo! They're old enough, right?

"Now then, what *I* wanted to know, and I talked to Noddy about this, what I wanted to know, was why he almost fired Jehu some time back. Oh, he tried, all right. I got this straight from Jehu. A shared confidence, you might say.

"All right, then, between you and me, too, Galindo. I'll bet, and I've no proof, okay? I'll bet Jehu got to Sammie Jo. That's right. The way I figure it, is that that's the main reason Livvie San Esteban dropped Jehu for a while. I'll tell you: the young have a lot to learn about a lot of things, and sex is one of them. Ha!

"I think, *think,* mind you, that Jehu is either at Carmen Ranch with Israel Buenrostro, and, if not there, then he's up at William Barrett with Rafe. What's wrong with ringing in the New Year with his favorite cousin? You know those kids better'n I do; trouble is, you're not going to get Israel to tell you much, and neither you nor anyone else is going to get a word out of Rafe, and that's for damn sure.

"But, to repeat, if Jehu wants a job, he's got me. And I'll pay him a hell of a lot better than Noddy, and a whole hell of a lot better than my cheapskate husband. Fair's fair, is the way I see it.

"Now, it may or it may not mean a damn thing, but I haven't seen Javier Leguizamón's hand in any of this. That's no guarantee, though. I'd pay five-hundred dollars a ticket for a front-row seat just to see that face a-his when they told him that Jehu pulled down Becky's underwe-ah, o' yeah! Pious old son-of-a-bitch; as if he hadn't diddled somebody in his day. Why . . .

"Look, Galindo, you yourself know, or you sure as hell should, that Javier himself got that dumb Ira Escobar's job for him. Yes, he did 'n I got *that* straight from Noddy; and as I told Noddy, to his face, too, 'See here, Noddy, when it comes to politics, you and I give money to all sides, and we don't much give a damn *what* party they come up with.'

"As for Ira, well, let me tell you this: Becky Caldwell married Ira Escobar for money, for the Leguizamón name, and because her Ma, Elvira Navarrete, wanted the Leguizamón union. Pure and simple. Sure, and then people talk about me whenever . . . Ha!

"Becky isn't a bad *kid;* oh, she likes a backroll now and again, and she does fool around with those Clubs and all, but she's her Ma all over again. Look who her Ma married: Catarino Caldwell, Caca. Proof enough? Do I know Elvira? Heart and soul, Galindo, heart and soul.

"And Sammie Jo? She flat likes it, and she's honest about it. An upfront kid, believe me. Married twice, you know: the first was a drunk and then the second a bit of a drunk and a pansy boy, too.

"I got that last from Jehu. Gossip? Not a bit of it, and . . . What do you mean you didn't know?

"Here, lemme tell you: Jehu, on his way over to Sammie Jo's Ranch, there on the floor itself, found a chain, and it had one of those lockets on it, see? It was right by the pool. He didn't know whose it was; he picked it up and gave it to Sammie Jo. *She* opened it; she'd given it to Sidney, see? Well, sir, she opened it up, and there they were: two a-those small pictures, you know, cut-outs. One a-them was Sidney's, the other was Hap Bayliss's. Chew on that'n awhile.

"Know what Sammie Jo did? She shrugged, and then, she and Jehu went into her room and that was that. Tell you when it was: it was one-a the times Noddy was up at Colorado or up to William Barrett; I'm not su . . . yeah, I do: around election time it was.

"Jehu told me about it, but it wasn't gossip, mind you. Now, it's my guess that *that* was when he started to think about working over here, for me. You never can tell, you know; I mean, what if Sammie Jo, a drink here and there, sort-a lets it slip out about her husband and Bayliss, or about Jehu, right? A-course, she could have told her Dad right out, about the locket, see, and left out the other part. But I don't know this, I'm just talking now.

"About that time, too, though, Jehu and Livvie San Esteban were kind-a serious, or maybe even breaking up. One-a the two.

"The Anglo Texans can damn well do what they want to, and they usually do so in the Valley. What I *didn't* want, and what I still *don't* want, is for them to get Jehu chewed up in all-a their shit. Everybody needs a friend, and I'm here to protect that boy's interests. And, if he doesn't want to work for me here in Klail, he can well go to Dellis County where, thank the Lord, I've also got some businesses.

"And that's it, Galindo. What say you and I have a drink? But only one, 'kay?"

The wri before anything else, serves notice that that *'kay* was followed by a healthy, well-meaning laugh on the part of Viola Barragán. The wri shared a tall glass of tea with VB, and the only thing he spent was time.

Difficulty: Viola Barragán does not lie, neither does she fabricate; she exaggerates very little, too, and she does stick to that which she knows. Despite these good points, the story does become somewhat complicated since Viola, with all of those good points in her favor, doesn't *know* if she knows everything. That aside, one should take what she says as gospel and not *cum granis salis.*

It's plainly evident that Viola is Jehu's champion. Affection and loyalty are to be treasured, of course, and Jehu is indeed fortunate in this regard. Fact: Jehu himself has always been straight as a die with Viola Barragán.

28
Bowly T.G. Ponder

A policeman in Klail City; he fills in as a traffic cop on occasion. Of medium build, on the thin side, a smallish flattened nose set on a ruddy face, and a shock of reddish brown hair, Ponder is a descendant of the poor whites who came to the Valley after World War I. The p.w. are on the lowest rung in the Valley's social ladder; the next to the lowest are the fruit tramps. Valley Texas Mexicans form no part in this social configuration.

Ponder was born in some of those lands bordering on the Ranch; his younger brother, Dempsey, works as a fence-rider for the Klail-Blanchard-Cooke interests; and he lives still in that same four-roomer where all nine Ponders were born; there are, then, a good number of Ponder relatives and in-laws strewn all over the Valley.

"Jehu? Sure; for years. He's a good guy; saved those two little kids on Vermont Avenue; that was about the time you was up at the V.A. hospital. He didn't tell you about that?

"Yeah, he, ah, broke the rear windows of a car and got the kids out before they suffocated to death. Damfool woman'd left 'em in there to make a phone call or something, and the kids would've fried for sure.

"That was quick thinking on his part. Lessee . . . that happened during the primaries, about the time I ran-in Congressman Terry's wife for speeding. A-course, he was a commissioner then. You didn't know about either? Sure!

"Yeah, old Bowly T.G. ran her in; old Missy Stuck-up there was speeding, and I just up and gave her a ticket for it. I wad'nt about to take any crap from her. Anyway, I was just doing my job, is all.

"Know what? She told Judge Fikes I was dis res pect ful. Little piss ant shit. I told *him* I expected the violator had been drinking some. Believe me, Galindo, I could've make that *stick* if I *needed* to.

"Know what else she said when I gave her the goddam ticket? She said I ought to go around checking on Mexican cars for state inspection tags if that was all I had to with my *time.*

"Piece of shit telling *me* how to do my *job;* well, I fixed *her* ass . . . I walked on over to my car, turned on the flashing lights, turned on the goddam car radio, loud!, and *then* I went back and *asked* her to get the hell out-a the car, to empty her purse, and wallet, too, and *then,* to open up the goddam glove compartment—from the outside—and then I made her walk around the car, too. Half-a-goddam Klail must have seen her; saw old John, you know, from the paint store? I waved to him, and then I *pointed* at her. Ol' John grinned and nodded at me.

"I don't give two hoots in anybody's hell; County Commissioner, *shit. He* speeds in Klail, *he* gets a ticket.

"And you know *what?* People round here are saying that Noddy sicced me on her; shoot! I don't mess with *his* bank, and *he* don't mess with me. Demps works for him, all right, but that's his and Demps's business—ain't none-a mine.

"And, to top it off, I had to take half a day off my vacation to go see Judge Fikes, too; and that's a fact, and she paid them twenty-two-fifty right then and there. No two ways.

"Yeh, she was put out, all right. You know *what?* Betcha she don't speed in my sector again. And that's a *fact.*"

Mighty bold talk, but it happened, and let there be little doubt, that Bowly did tighten up some loose screws in Bedelia (Boyer) Terry's case. And, don't doubt that Bowly made some heavy tracks in Knowlton Fikes' court that day.

With all that, however, the wri doth think that Bowly protests too much.

Working against Bowly's absolute credibility, and there's plenty of best evidence against him these past fifteen years, is the fact that he owes his post to Noddy Perkins (for starters). As a capper, his brother Dempsey works for the Ranch, all nephews, in-laws, relatives, etc related to the Ponders, and Bewleys, and the Watfell families, kneel at the same public trough.

That Bedelia Boyer Terry drives like a madwoman through some of Klail's streets is page-four stuff. That then, around election time, and for the first time ever, someone stopped her for speeding and then gives her a relatively hard time is too much of a coincidence.

The cat, then, pokes his head out of the bag there. The wri needs to offer this piece of information since he can't sit there with his arms crossed knowing, as he does, a good part of the facts and the actors in this little drama.

29

Olivia San Esteban

Willowy, supple and lithe all fit this mexicana beauty; looking at her, the wri calculates she's an inch or two shorter than Jehu, and not much more. Her eyes are brown as is her wavy hair; the wri hears a pleasant, clear voice, and, at twenty-nine and unmarried, she must be the envy of any number of Valley women. She laughs easily enough, but she's no giggler. The wri believes a further personal assessment of la San Esteban to be a true one: while no trimmer, she's not dog matic, either; she claims she can speak on and about Jehu with no coloration of their personal lives. (The wri does not know how the personal can be avoided in this case.)

"I knew of Jehu some time back, but didn't really meet him until we were up at Austin. He and Rafe would show up at some parties with my brother Martín and my cousin, Juan Santoscoy.

"It's no secret he was provided for by the Carmen Ranch Buenrostros. When Jehu orphaned early, they took him in; and, they're kin. Anyway, Jehu and I didn't go into that very much.

"He's headstrong about some things, but so am I; and yet, he and I agree on many things, too. One thing, though, our relationship is our relationship, and he won't take any guff from my brother Martín; right off the bat, too, he told Martín where to get off.

"He's like that.

"Now, Jehu and I do disagree on some things, as I said, but these are personal; and, speaking of personal things, just this once, Jehu is *very* much interested in my going to med school.

"I'm, ah, I'm just not *sure* he's quite ready to settle down, señor Galindo . . . Look, I'm really behind on some prescriptions and in

75

the drug inventory at the moment. Could you come back later on? This afternoon?

That afternoon.

"Hello, and thanks for coming back like this; work's like that most mornings, but I'm off for the rest of the day now. Martín'll work nights this month, and if you're willing to wait till then, he may have something to add to Jehu's whereabouts. For my part, I'll say it's no great mystery: since he isn't at the Carmen Ranch, as you say, then he's either up at William Barrett or in Austin, one. I haven't heard from him this week yet.

"I don't know where to begin 'cause there's not much to say, really.

"The last name of Malacara misses the mark, doesn't it? He's not handsome or a pretty boy, but he's sexy, señor Galindo, and don't look so shocked.

"I now realize I know little about him. He told me he worked for some holy rollers once; those were funny stories, too, but then he could always make me laugh. But he's not a clown, you know what I'm saying? He smiles and laughs and all that, but he's serious more often than not, and, ah, I, I, I'm strong for him.

"What happens is that . . . look Mr. Galindo, I'm going to say something as clearly as I possibly can: I've no proof, but Becky Escobar not only let herself be caught, she did a lot of the chasing. I just know it; Sammie Jo, too, but I already know that. From him; he walked in here one day and said so, but he also said he was through with that. I believe him, Mr. Galindo.

"I'm not a kid; I'm twenty-nine, and I am the way I am: the way I choose to be, but I don't like and I don't want to share him, and I sure as *hell,* I *sure* as hell, don't want to share him with those two. And no, it isn't because they're married or anything like that. At all. They can run around as much as they please, but not with him. That's all.

"He's no kid, I know that; but the very same day he left the bank, he came *here;* he came to *see* me, and he came to say he was leaving for a while. He came to see *me,* in person. And I'll say this, too, while I'm at it, señor Galindo, he wasn't run *off* from the bank. That's right.

"Mrs. Barragán and I have little to say to each other, and it isn't enmity or anything like that; we know each other . . . where was I? Oh, yes; Mrs. Barragán offered him any number of jobs, positions, really. Any time he wants one, too. I know this from *him,* but, I know this from her. She told me so.

"As for me señor Galindo, I want to go to med school, and Jehu will help. I'm not talking about money, but he'd be a, a, a support. A mainstay. Yes, he would, and when he comes back, and he *will,* too, he'll come for me."

"And it doesn't matter whether we get married or not; he and I have this understanding. Oh, yes, I know about *people,* and what they say or *will* say, but I understand *him,* and you know what else? He understands me. That may not be much for some, but it's quite enough for me."

The informant did not, at any time, raise her voice. A stress here, an emphasis there, and that was it. She smiled a smile that resembles Jehu's, by the way. The wri would like to add that Olivia SE has a sense of the ironic, plus, she has a clear cut idea of who she is, as well.

The wri finds no need to add anything whatsoever to OSE's views and comments on Rebecca Escobar and Sammie Jo Perkins, since la San Esteban's views are quite definite in this respect.

Opinion: If anyone knows of Jehu's whereabouts, then it must surely be OSE, the wri thinks that the person who also knows more (perhaps all) is none other than Viola Barragán.

The wri feels he has to speak with Harmon Gillette's recent widow.*

---

*Olivia San Esteban refers to Viola Barragán as Mrs. Barragán; this is an error on her part. For the record: Viola née Barragán first married the physician Agustín Peñalosa, native to Agualeguas, Nuevo León, Mexico; he died as a result of an accidental, but nevertheless lethal, prescription handed to him by the apprentice Orfalindo Buitureyra.

Viola's second husband was the German Karl-Heinz Schuler, ex-diplomat to Mexico and India, and former representative of the Volkswagen Werke in Pretoria, South Africa. Herr Schuler died of a myocardial infarction; Viola returned to Ulm (Bavaria) and tended to her rather elderly in-laws for some seven-eight years until their respective natural deaths. Her third husband, also dead, of course, was the printer Harmon Gillette, of the up-river Gillettes. His death, from what the wri has learned, was a result of pancreatic cancer.

30

Viola Barragán

Vide Nos. 27, 29.

"So good to see you again, Galindo. You're looking better these days; is it possible? Don't overdo it, now, get plenty of rest; you know how much we-all care for you.

"So? How are things going for you these days? Es ist immer das alte Lied?, as my Karl-Heinz used to say? Is it the same old tune?

"I really would like to stay and chat a while, but I'm up to my ears in work. I wouldn't be like this at all if I had a business manager like Jehu to run this for me. Here, open the door for me. That's it, thank you. Get the car door, too. (grunt) Thanks.

"Now, you be sure and call me when you hear somethin, 'kay? You really must excuse me, but I'm in a fightful hurry."

Supposition: But, is it possible that our Viola is avoiding the wri?

One answer: No, not necessarily; it could very possibly be that the multi-business affairs of this versatile woman are getting to be too much at times; too many and so much that although she would like to stop and chat, she can't.

Another: It is entirely possible that she just may be hiding something in that ample breast of hers.

Still another: She may be honor bound not to reveal Jehu's whereabouts, and thus by evasion and avoidance does not lie to the wri and thus not betray Jehu as well.

Opinion: Many of our fellow citizens do not look kindly upon Viola, and, as a consequence, they are ready to disbelieve whatever she says whether it be true or not; a baroque phrase, yes, but most people, whether they know it or not, are quite baroque themselves.

31

Rebecca Escobar

A green-eyed brunette; the wri pegs her age at twenty-six-seven; she looks younger, much younger. Her relationship with her mother-in-law, the redoubtable doña Vidala Escobar née de la Viña Leguizamón-Leyva, is, at best, tenuous; in other words, they do not get along, well or otherwise. As Jehu once said about some other people: they just get.

The wri has learned from a highly-placed source in Jonesville, that the two woman do not 'enjoy each other's company.' The wri apologizes beforehand, here, but he refuses to surrender the name of the woman friend who supplied the information; the wri, too, can keep a secret, and that's the last word on that.

Rebecca, or Becky, as she prefers, is dressed in gleaming white: hat, gloves, and linen jacket and skirt. If not exactly a beauty a la San Esteban, she does present, as the Spanish say, other *encantos;* enchantments.

She is both relaxed and assured, and the wri, who is old enough to 1) know better, and 2) be her father, is equally relaxed and assured in her presence. The wri, after a rapid first impression, finds he likes the informant. He should be ashamed of himself for taking sides here, but he isn't, and he can't: la Caldwell-Escobar is a sunny type.

"I really don't know Jehu that *well,* you know. Ira and I first met him when we first came to work at First National, I mean, when Ira became associated with the Bank. First of . . .

"You must understand that Jehu was not Ira's supervisor or anything; I mean, he wasn't even a business major like Ira who attended A&M and finished up at St. Mary's. You know what I mean, don't you?

"Anyway, I saw Jehu at some of the Bank parties and picnics; stuff like that, but not much more. *And,* he is not at *all* interested in politics. Ira told me so. But I *like* him; I find him *nice,* and he's *friendly,* okay?

"I'm usually pretty busy on my Woman's Club work, and now, more recently, this winter in fact, with the Music Club, and what with taking the Cooke kids to dance music lessons, and what-all, I really don't have much time for . . . for other social occasions, don't you know. But we, Ira and I, did meet Jehu socially; early on, anyway; I think, or maybe I've heard, that he's engaged to Ollie Sans Teben; do you know her? She's a pharmacist here.

"And you *know* about what happened at Noddy's that night. As I remember it, it was just a little after eight o'clock, and we had just finished dessert after an early sit-down dinner when Jehu came in; he saw that we were through, and he had a surprised look on his face; not for long, of course, but you could *see* that he was surprised. I mean, it was strange, and I think Sammie Jo laughed; she'd been drinking some . . .

"But that was it; Jehu came into the dining room, and he was about to pull up a chair when . . . when Mr. Perkins, and no one had said a word up to then, anyway, Mr. Perkins said or asked, demanded, I guess, that, that, ah, that Jehu resign from the Bank; there and then. Ira and I were so embarrassed, you know, after all, we're *all* of us mexicanos, right?

"Jehu looked at Mr. Perkins and nodded, but not in agreement, it didn't seem like. He looked straight at Noddy; that's all he did, and then he . . . he just *walked* out. I don't think he said good night, or anything.

"Well, one hears so many things, right? Anyway, later on, on the way home, Ira said *he* thought it might have been a question of money. But that's all Ira said. He's very discreet, you know.

"And, *then,* another surprise! Jehu was back at the *Bank!* just like that—hahahahaha—just like Jehu says, Just Like That. I mean, was it a joke on Noddy's part? Was he angry with Jehu because Jehu was late for dinner? The empty chair was there all along, you know. Ira called me first thing in the morning to tell me that Jehu was at the Bank. I was glad for Jehu; I mean, it was a bank holiday, but everyone was working inside. I mean, it was such a good job for him.

"Ira said that Jehu came in and went straight into Noddy's office just like any other Monday morning. About half-an-hour later, he was back at his own office and at work as usual. Ira says he, Jehu, worked through the noon hour, just like . . . like usual . . . and that *that* was it.

"The bank clerks couldn't have known, could they? And later, Ibby Cooke, the V.P., well, he and Jehu had their Monday afternoon meeting just like always.

"I mean: nothing had *changed*. At *all*.

"At quitting time, Jehu, on his way out, stopped by Ira's desk and said, 'Well, Mr. Commissioner, did you enjoy your dinner Saturday night?'

"I think this is probably Jehu's and Noddy's idea of a big joke. I don't mind telling you that *that* Saturday night was ruined for Ira and me, I mean, for Ira and I.

"But I still *like* Jehu. I think he's nice and the few times I've talked with him, he's been very pleasant. Anyway, that's all I know except for the fact that he was also offered a job a couple of months later by the Barragán woman. Do you know *her? She* says she knows my mother.

"Do you think that there's a connection between the Saturday night thing and Jehu being offered a job by Viola Barragán?"

The above is verbatim and seriatim, and the wri accepts what he's been told. The wri listened very carefully to Mrs. Escobar and was saddened to think that this very young girl does not know, may not have an inkling, of what sadness, happiness, or sentiment are all about. Is it really possible that this is so? The wri sincerely hopes not, but he has no contradictory evidence, sad to say.

32

Sammie Jo Perkins

Only issue of the Perkins-Cooke union; the wri sees a slender, brown-haired woman of thirty. Nothing personal, but most of those thirty have been lived on one of life's faster highways. She was divorced from Bradshaw, Theodore P. of the Dellis County Bradshaws at age twenty-three. Her present husband is Sidney Boynton; a so-called friend once said that SJ didn't have to change any initals in the bath towels, etc. Sammie Jo speaks Spanish very, very well, although this will not be evident here.

The wri would like to point out something that will be seen easily enough: speaking plainly is one of her trademarks. The wri points this for a purpose: he would not want for the reader to misjudge Sammie Jo's frankness for easy arrogance.

"Galindo, I don't *know* where he is, and I've known Jehu for a long time. He's a friend, and I don't judge friends.

"He doesn't care for Dad, you know, but he respects the way Dad runs the Bank. On the other hand, Jehu has no use for Ira, and that's no secret. But don't think that Jehu's afraid of losing his job at the Bank, 'cause Jehu could not care less about that end of it.

"Tell you *what,* Galindo: I bet you he got to Becky Escobar. Wanna bet?

"Let me add this, too: if the Mexicans across town are worried that he *stole* money, shit on 'em. They're wrong as *hell,* and they're full of it.

"I'd say he was up at at Austin, wanting to go to grad school, but I don't know. I do know that's about all he ever wanted to do. Dad thinks he's there, and I bet Olivia knows where he is.

"Ollie wants things her way, and that's fine, but I bet Jehu wants her to have her way without *him*. Have you talked to her yet? If she had *any* sense, she'd either leave him be and forget all about him, or she'd *marry* him. Provided Jehu would have her. Ha!

"I *like* him, Galindo, though Jehu can be a real shit some times. Oh, I can, too, but we're good friends.

"Why don't you call Rafe? That is, call Rafe if you can ever get him to answer the phone; he's hell too, you know.

"But, that's it, Galindo, time's up. It's time for my dip; bye, now."

And with that, Arnold and Blanche Perkins' dau. smiled, offered her hand, and walked the wri to the door.

Sammie Jo is right: the Klail City mexicanos are a suspicious lot, perhaps more than they should be. It happens, however, as the wri knows, that some of these suspicions are well-founded on historical facts: 1836, 1846, and so on.

The reader cannot help but notice that Jehu is neither all saint nor all devil. Now then, that the truth unvarnished comes bubbling out of Sammie Jo's mouth is certainly worthy of note here.

33

Arnold Perkins

The wri will borrow from Noddy Perkins's own description of himself: 'I'm a self-made man, Galindo. In some ways, ha-ha, that makes me a motherless bastard, right?'

In NP's case, the wri feels that there are enough biographical facts and data in Jehu's letters to Rafe Buenrostro. The wri, then, will not repeat what has been said. In his relationship with Belken County mexicanos, Noddy has his champions and his detractors. It's normal.

"Sure, Jehu and I have had our differences now and then, but that was to be expected; I'm not an easy man to get along with (grin with teeth showing). But it wasn't anything that couldn't be ironed out, it was business. Nothing more. You'd be surprised how well he took to banking. He has a healthy respect for money, that boy. And he's honest. Sharp, too.

"He's not much on social life, though. Oh, he dates the San Esteban girl . . . that's Emilio's girl, and I wouldn't be surprised if he also had something on the side. But, it's only natural, he's young. And, what the hell, we don't check up on our employees here. You know Klail City and the Valley, and it wouldn't take long for word like that to get around. I mean, it wouldn't take long if anything was wrong . . .

"Jehu speaks Spanish very well, you know; none of your Tex-Mex, either; I heard he'd been raised in part by a Mexican national, and that might account for it. And there ain't a thing wrong with his English, either; he's a Valley boy, and I guess the Army and the University helped there, too.

"He first started to work for us over at the Kay Cee Savings and Loan; he did mostly high risk insurance lending over there. I brought

84

him over *here* after a year's experience, and he's a natural. I mean, he *likes* banking; he knows how to smoke out a deal and see it through; but, like I said, he's not interested in the civic stuff; don't misunderstand: he knows it's important for business, and he does it. As for politics, I don't even know if he votes or not.

"He's got a sense of humor, too. It's a bit pointed at times, but I can understand that; I was born poor myself. He worked well here, and no complaints. Of any kind.

"Jehu tolerates my brother-in-law, Ibby; Ibby's been at this bank some thirty years now, almost as long as I've been here, and that's before Blanche and I were married. Now, you'd think Ibby would have picked up what the hell banking was all about in that time: you take in money and you lend it out; you charge interest, and it's always the same money, and if you know what you're doing, you wind up with more. That's all.

"I can solemnly swear that Ibby still hasn't got *that* down.

"Now, when Ira came in last year, and that boy is full a-shit, he tried telling Jehu what banking was all about; Jehu just laughed at him, as he should've. Ira's pretty thick, and this takes me to something else: Jehu's not above getting into Ol' Becky's pants and pulling 'em down. I'm not saying he did, know what I mean? Besides, it's bad for business and makes for poor employee relations. Ha!

"I'll say it again: I'm not saying it happened. But, I know Jehu; hell, I was like that myself years ago. Ask old Viola Barragán! And, ask Gela Maldonado, too; ha! I bet Ol' Javier Legui *still* doesn't know about *that*. No matter, that was over thirty years ago.

"One last thing, Jehu's got a job here whenever he wants it. When he left here, he just said he *had* to go. There was never *any* question about money. In any way. I did hear something about returning to school, but like I said, if he wants his job back, it's his."

Confession: The wri took *and* smoked one of the proffered cigars and paid for it by taking to his bed for two days afterward. The wri should know better, of course.

The wri had no idea about those old Perkins-Barragán and Perkins-Maldonado liaisons. The wri can only say that all things are possible, e.g. the *affaire* Perkins-Téllez is a matter of record.

Question: Is there any reason for giving some, any, a little or no importance to these liaisons? Do Viola and Gela Maldonado recall them as vividly? Should they? And, at this juncture, does it matter? It may be better to consider that as water flushed and under the bridge.

Of more immediate concern, of course, is Perkins' careful assessment of Jehu. It certainly coincides with Sammie Jo's high opinion and reasons for his leaving.

In re the Becky Escobar episode, father and daughter may just be trading confidences here. And this is only in part, because Sammie Jo doesn't tell her father everything.

Does Macy tell Gimbel?

34
E.B. Cooke

A widower for over a quarter of a century, this informant is the third of the six children of the Clayton and Myrna B. Cooke anschluss; of the six, four are still with us, three males and one female: the informant himself, Blanton, in his early fifties, Blanche (Noddy's wife), and Parnell, a forty-one-year old congenital idiot.

The informant is a bit curt, peevish, snappish, even; but, the wri can attest that this attitude is not directed at his person, it is merely a trait of the informant. He was baptized Everett in the Good Shepherd Episcopal Church in KC; the B. stands for Blanchard, and thus he has a foot in both camps.

"Oh, I know you've talked to Noddy, and it doesn't matter, *in the least.* I also know what he thinks of me, and I don't care about *that,* either. I don't like banking, and I never have. I wanted to be a painter, Galindo, but the Bank and the Ranch, and our other investments and interests here and abroad could not be left to . . . Well, *someone* in the *family* had to be in it at this end, and Noddy is not *family.* Sammie Jo is, but he's not. Both Grover and Andrew died young; Parnell is not equipped for it, and that leaves Blanton and me. On the Blanchard side, there's not much to pick from, if you ask me.

"And I know about Jehu. I don't care to listen or to know whatever it was that Noddy said. Jehu's been here close to four years, and he and I get along; *he* knows I don't like the business, and so he does most of the ground work; I make policy.

"I really don't know if he *likes* the business. In point of fact, it's hard to tell *what* he likes or wants. I think he enjoys it, but I can't see him buried here for the next thirty years. He won't be wasting *his* life here. I know he's got some money saved, and how much, too; and, I don't find it such a shock that he left. I do know he wants to go back to Austin, to the University, and that's all there is to *that* piece of business.

"As you know, Noddy's my brother-in-law, and we don't get along. Never have. Blanche is a sick woman and has been for years; and Noddy's been no help *a-tall*. I don't care to get into that, but I don't want you to misread my feelings on the matter.

"Noddy is a ridiculous man; he doesn't know the first thing about ranching or about the oil industry, but to hear *him* tell it, well! But, he's strong, and he's devious, and that's his due, and I may be a damned fool for coming here every day for thirty years, but *someone's* got to keep a rein on him.

"Everything is *planned* with him. He even learned *Spanish* that way. Oh, I know what you think of us, but we're from here too, you know. And Jehu and Ira won't be the last Mexicans to work here, and I can promise you that much; but, if it were up to Noddy, ha!

"Jehu's bright, but he's also impatient at times. We work well together despite what Noddy says and tells everyone. I also know that Noddy says I don't know the *first* thing about banking, but he's wrong. I take no unnecessary actions, and I always make it a practice of letting Noddy have his way up to a point, and then, only in public. I don't *care* what other people think of me; I have my own life, I have my own friends, and Noddy's not a part of either one of them. Blanche is, but she's family and so is junior Klail. And let's not get on the subject of that impossible sister of Noddy's, *please.*

"As for politics, that's what *we* are all about and *that,* Galindo, is merely farmed out to Noddy; look, we have businesses *everywhere* and Klail is but a part of it. The money started here years ago, and we started the town, from the Anglo Texan point of view, but Klail's only a part of it, and Noddy has a small part of *that.*

"I'm the Cashier here, but I'm also the Secretary-Treasurer for the Corporation. Noddy knows perfectly well what *that* means. He tries to egg Jehu on, but that young man's too sharp for Noddy, and Noddy resents it. Oh, he resents it, all right. But, giving the devil his due, Noddy's been generous with Jehu's salary.

"As for me, well, I'm a painter, Galindo. A frustrated one and perhaps not a particularly talented one, either, but I can *read* people, I can read *character* . . .

"Now, would you care for a drink? We can have one of the girls bring us something."

Well! The wri has known Ibby Cooke for years (and years), about the time of the funeral for his uncle, the centennarian judge Cooke (Walton H., Jr.), one of the founders of the Cooke-Blanchard clan. A funeral, by the way, which was excessively costly; tacky, almost. The wri, years later, learned that Noddy Perkins (married to Blanche Cooke less than a year) had been in charge of the funeral and floral arrangements.

Ibby's self-portrait does not jibe with the *role* assigned to him by Noddy; their mutual dislike may go even deeper than they realize, know, or imagine. Their opinions on Jehu differ, but only in a small degree. This may not be necessarily incompatible, it may be the same idea with two divergent points of view, that's all.

The wri must mark here that both men are steeped in the art of intrigue. They differ in method: Noddy uses spies, without their knowing they are being so used; he also uses certain base tactics: temptation (to Ira), false friendship and joviality (to the wri   Oh, yes), and a seemingly democratic chumminess (tout le monde). Cooke is more of an observer; he himself says he is, wanted to be, a painter; he is given, then, more to contemplation than to overt action. He doesn't seem to be intuitive (this may explain his failure as a painter) and by the same token, one sees him preferring pot shots to salvos. Instead of tactics, then, he prefers strategy, but this may be a semantic quibble.

The reader should consider, however, that the two in-laws have more in common than what may appear at first blush.

35

Rufino Fischer Gutiérrez

A descendant from the Cano clan. His paternal grandfather was the first Rufino Cano Guzmán, and his maternal grandmother, that grandame, was Doña Florentina Anzaldúa Cano. Rufino is the son of the late Juan Eugenio Gutiérrez Guzmán; the Fischer part comes from Don Fabián, father to Camila Fischer, who naturally enough, is RFG's mother.

A veteran of World War II as a member of the USMC, RFG was discharged in San Diego, California, returned to the Valley, passed through Klail City and Belken County and right on through Dellis County farmland; part of the 1749 Cano clan had lost some of the lands in the nineteenth century, and RFG has been buying some of them via the Texas Veterans Adms. program.

The wri has known for years that RFG and Bowly Ponder enlisted in the Marines together in 1943.

"Let's cut through here, Galindo; by the shade there. Let's see now, see that bent mesquite? The one next to that burned-up palm tree? Well, that mesquite was planted by one of the Peña boys that now lives in Barrones, Tamaulipas; no need to plant mesquites in the Valley, of course, but he went ahead and did it anyhow as called for in the grants; the mesquite's just about dab in the middle of the old Buenrostro land when the grants were first being parceled out. My cousin Israel Buenrostro has another bent mesquite on his land, and that one was planted by a Peña who lives on this side of the River. They're downriver people, as you know.

"The distance in American miles between the two mesquites is no less than forty miles, on a line. Our Fellow Texans own most of the land between the twin mesquites; that's a lot-a acreage, and I'm not saying I want it all, but I just happen to think that they've got more 'n enough, and besides that, we've already got the Leguizamóns around our necks, even here, in Dellis County.

"When we first learned that a Leguizamón from Belken was gunning for a Commissioner's post, we, the Dellis mexicanos, figured it was just one more nail in a lot-a people's coffins. And I don't think we were too far off, do you? As far as we're concerned, the water we got here in Dellis County runs, wets, and muddies up just like the one you-all've got over in Belken . . . know what I mean?

"I think that's as good a place to start as any: the land and the water.

"The last of the Ledesmas died last year; you knew Italo, didn't you? Well, ol' Jake Hendricks, the Dellis county clerk, told Arnold Perkins about it, I mean he told Perkins that the land was going to be up for sale; with this, then, Perkins had over a month's head start looking over the boundaries, the water rights, and what-all.

"By that time, the Landín family, the ones from this neck of the River, were up to their ears buying, selling, and trading off some land. One of the Landíns told us that Perkins wanted to sew up part of the Ledesma and Landín lands. That's fine with us, and business is *Geschäfte* as my German grandpa used to say. But! what we didn't like or want or *need,* was for Perkins to share that land deal with the Leguizamóns. Those bastards are plain, bad neighbors; always have been.

"I'm going to tell you how we found out about *that* piece of business.

"The Landín family came to terms with Perkins but not for all the land; what happened was that we stepped in and bought some of that land ourselves, and then we turned around and sold some part of that to the Peñas from this side o' the River, and part to the Zúñigas; the Zees are related to the Peñas, and all three of our families are part of the Cano families from Soliseño; a family thing, then.

"Here, let me show you. (Pointing) There! no, over *there,* on the *other* side o' the River. See that settlement there? They're all Canos or Zúñigas there. But the telling of it here sounds easier than it was, though.

"Who *really* helped us was Jehu; he'd been invited to a political barbecue for that Ira Escobar guy, and Jehu decided to pay a call on

Auntie Enriqueta Vidaurri before he went to the barbecue.* And it just happened that I had decided to call on Auntie Enriqueta myself; she was ailing some, and she's family . . . Jehu and I met there, and he says for me to go to the barbecue with him, and that was it.

"They had one-a those MG's, and I said the hell with that, so we followed them out there. Jehu had Livvie San Esteban with him; my wife and I baptized that girl as her godparents, but you may know this, a-course. As for Jehu, my wife and I have known him since the day he was born in the Vidaurri lands in Relámpago. All this land you and I are standing on was nothing but cotton land some time back, and it was here that that protestant minister, the one Jehu worked for, was bitten by a rattler.

"Where was I? Oh, yeh; Jehu himself told us that that Escobar guy is a Leguizamón-Leyva, and it all became clear as glass, yessir. Arnold Perkins, the land deal, that young fool running for commissioner, everything. So, using that information, then, we got on our horses to work out our *own* deal.

"I hear tell that Jehu was let go by the Bank, runoff, kind-a. Is that true? If it is, then I bet the Leguizamóns had a hand in that. Although I must admit right off that I'm willing to believe almost anything that's said against those crooks.

"Jehu worked well with Perkins; he knows the land, how much it's worth, and he knows what's good for the Bank and what's not. Now, what he told me of the Escobar-Leguizamón-Leyva plans for that land may look bad to some folk, but Jehu is family, and he was giving us a fair shake, that's all.

"And, talking about Belken County . . . I'll tell you who showed up here: Bowly Ponder; yeah, he did. Got himself a county job, no less. Oh, yeah. Celebrating he was. He was in the Marines with me way back when, y'know. Since he wears a gun in Klail, and the county now, I guess, he can't drink there. What he does is to drive on over here to Dellis County, and he hells around some of the beer joints in Flads; those joints are right on the border levee. Probably goes across, too, knowing Bowly . . .

---

*Mrs. Enriqueta Vidaurri died a month after Jehu left the Bank. She remembered him, as she should have, in her will.

"I had seen him earlier, during primary time; he'd been drinking some, and he had one or two more for old times' sake. He likes his beer, old Bowly, and when he tightens up some, he loves to talk 'n brag.

"That night he told me how he'd given some Belken commissioner's wife a hard time; a *hurd* time, don't you know. Said he'd given her a ticket, that he issued an immediate summons, too, and then, for no reason at all, Bowly said it was all politics. I didn't say anything, and then he said that Arnold Perkins was hip-deep in something. That's nothing new, and I put it to Beer and Bowly, but later on, I came to find out that the woman Bowly pulled in was married to Ira Escobar's opponent in the primary. I'm not surprised; it's typical a-those people . . .

"But a fat lot a-good it did them. That guy is now a congressman for our district, right? And the Leguizamóns can't see beyond their own damned noses, can they?

"Perkins jams a thumb full a-sugar in their mouth, and they don't even feel the dick when he sticks it to 'em. Serves 'em right.

"Well, Galindo, I'm worse than Bowly when it comes to running off at the mouth, looks like. Hey!, I haven't even offered you a beer 'r anything. Come on!

"Tell you what, seeing as to how you don't make it to this part of the Valley much, you better plan to stay and have supper with us. Got me a white-tail last Spring (wink), damned thing ran right up my front fender and tied itself there. It's dressed, frozen, and waiting for us. Here, let me get the door."

RFG and the wri talked some more after the venison supper, but there was nothing new to report.

It certainly looks as if Jehu's information to RFG on the Escobar-Leguizamón tie-ins was no accident. And, of course, Jehu didn't do it for money, either.

One conclusion: Jehu is family conscious, and he did it as a family favor.

The wri holds no opinion on whether Jehu acted in good or in bad faith by divulging that piece of information to RFG, but there is the matter of business ethics here; Jehu, of course, does know Noddy far better than most and certainly far better than the wri.

The above is not meant to exculpate Jehu, however.

36
Bowly T.G. Ponder

In a three month period, our man's economic and professional lives have improved considerably. He resigned as a policeman of the Klail City P.D., and he is now a county deputy sheriff as well as a half-partner in two convenience-type stores.

He is now on his way to becoming a minor capitalist, and the wri has also learned that Bowly's two oldest sons are sure bets for graduation from Klail High School next year.

One further note: Dempsey Ponder, Bowly's youngest brother, is now the newest member of Klail's Finest.

"Well, all of this has been in the works for some time; George Markham recommended me to Scott Daniels himself, and he, Scott, talked to Big Foot, I mean to Wallace Parkinson, and Sheriff Parkinson saw fit to appoint me as a deputy here. I know Klail, I got my contacts here, and because-a that, I didn't have to move or anything."

The wri, an unreconstructed bully, dips into sarcasm this once to say that this is Noddy's way of keeping tabs on Bowly.

"Turned out right well, don't you think? And one thing about *this* job, I've got authority in the whole county, *and* a car. And expenses, too, Galindo. All in all, things are looking pretty good here. Listen to this: just last week, in this very car, I went and picked up Congressman Terry over to Noddy's airstrip. I did, and then gave him a ride home, too. No hard feelings, either; he knew I was just doing my job a while back when I stopped his wife. Show's you what he's made of, right?"

The wri, if he were Ponder, would take care when it comes to Morse Terry. The wri cannot believe that Terry is going to sit back and do nothing about the traffic incident.

Of course, if MT is a complete cynic, as Bowly certainly pictures him to be, then the wri invites the reader to join hands with him to pray for Bedelia Boyer.

"Dempsey moved right into the radio dispatcher's job, and this means that both Bobby Bleibst and Merle Gottschalk will be out on my old car beat. Ol' Dempsey's not cut out to be no riding-around man.

"And you say you saw Rufino Eff Gee over to Flads ta-other day? You know him, do you? Did you know that he and I go back a-whiles? Yeah, and I saw him myself not too long ago. I got me some old girl friends out to Dellis County.

"I understand from the Court House gang that Lieutenant Buenrostro's due out-a the Barrett's V.A. hospital by mid-January. He sure did a good job on those murders, Galindo.

"There's the radio . . . gotta go; see you, Galindo."

From all indications, then, it does seem that Bowly Ponder is very much pleased with himself. This latest chat was not a total loss since it is now plainly evident that ex-Texas Ranger Choche Markham is still an active satellite in the Leguizamón-Perkins orbit.

The wri, without success, alas, has tried repeatedly to talk with Rep. Morse Terry: ten calls in four months (with the wri's name and teleph. no. each time) to no avail.

37
Mrs. Ben (Edith) Timmens

Edith is married to Ben Timmens, one of the ten or fifteen attorneys employed by the Ranch, and thus the Bank. She speaks Spanish, Ben does not. (He hasn't *had* to.)

Timmens's wife, Klail City born, is the dau. of the late Osgood Bayliss, D.V.M. who was in long-time service to the Ranch. She is also the sister to Hapgood Bayliss who, until recently, served as congressman (D.-Tx.) for the Valley Congressional District.

"Pure fiction, Galindo: Hap isn't sick, he's tired. He's tired of Washington, of politics, and he's tired of being away from the Valley so much. Hap says that fourteen years up there is enough, and I agree with him. Ben and I put in eight years in the State Senate up at Austin plus another eight in Washington, and I know perfectly well how Hap feels. It's time somebody out of the family went up to Washington, anyway.

"Hap had told Noddy one whole year *before* the election that he wanted out, but Noddy kept putting him off. I honestly thought he *was* going to get sick. Anyway, I think Noddy shaved it a bit too close for *anybody's* comfort. A write-in campaign, really!

"Hap's marriage ended tragically, as you know, and being an old bachelor all these years, he plain wanted to come back home. The Valley's *home* and all our friends are *here*. And besides that, Washington's no place for a normal life.

"Well, it's been, what?, three-four months since the elections? Hap looks good and he *feels* good. He and Sidney are going down to La Pesca, Mexico for a bit of fishing; I think Sammie Jo'll join them in a couple of weeks.

"Have you ever been down there? Ben and I have, and we *really* enjoy ourselves. You know, you can't help but marvel how Mexicans from down there *differ* from Valley Mexicans. Well, not *you* exactly, but you know what I mean.

"You know, Becky and Ira both are still miffed at Jehu Malacara. Jehu didn't lift a finger; I mean, he didn't lift *one* finger during the entire election. Oh, he went to some of the barbecues, but it was like pulling teeth, and he never once spoke at a barbecue. Ira was hoping Noddy would've told Jehu, and that's what Ira says; so, Ira's still miffed, and can you blame him?

"Did Jehu ever tell you about something that happened at one of the parties at the Big House? It was a, a, a silly thing, really, but you know the Valley.

"I think it was Travis DeYoung's wife, no! it was Loretta; Wig Birnham's wife. Anyway, she either told a Mexican joke, you know, one of those Beto and Lupe jokes, or . . . no! it wasn't that either. Oh, I can't remember just now, but it was something anti-mexicano, don't you know.

"Really! I don't know *what* Loretta Birnham uses for eyes or for common sense. *We* didn't know what to say; I mean, Jehu was sitting right there 'n all. But she finally got up and drifted away. My God!

"Jehu didn't say a word. He just smiled a bit and then he nodded to himself, and then the next time he spoke, it was in the most broken English imaginable. He's a terrible tease, you know. Anyway, I didn't know *what* to say. I mean, I'm not prejudiced; I'm Klail born.

"Oh, wait a minute, now. He *hummed;* yes, I remember that. Know what it was? *Texas Our Texas.* I hadn't heard *that* in *years.*

"Speaking of Jehu, Noddy says that some of the mexicanos in town are saying that Jehu stole money from the Bank! That's silly. Where do you suppose they got *that* from?

"Noddy says he won't talk to them about that piece of business. I think Noddy's right. Javier Leguizamón told Noddy not to bother explaining things to *la raza* since he, Javier, would do it. And gladly."

This conversation, as many conversations, died a natural death. The wri, as old as he is, marvels still how public opinion with a phrase here and a phrase there turns and flips and flops back again.

It isn't because Edith Timmens recommended it, but the wri is now convinced that he can no longer put off his meeting with Javier Leguizamón. It is an imperative, at this stage.

In passing: Since Edith did mention what she is pleased to call the tragic end of his brother's marriage, the wri wished to clear this matter once and for all: Hap's wife (only dau of a former Texas Secretary of State) finally eloped with an opera singer; a tenor, as the wri recalls.

Since that happened so many years ago, 1) most people don't know this; 2) many more have chosen to forget it; and 3) the majority could not care less.

The wri finds it interesting that Edith considers herself part of the KBC family, vide: the first paragraph. As interesting as it could turn out be, the wri has no time to discover what the family itself considers Edith.

38

P. Galindo, the wri

Name: P. Galindo. Profession: writer, poet, journalist. Marital status: Married, widowed; married, widowed; married, divorced. Bachelor. Age: 52, and most of them spent with friends and relatives. Health: Precarious, even when he enjoyed the best of health.

The wri has spent the last two weeks in bed, or near it. His insides, or what's left of them, served notice that he needed a rest, some time-off. The running around after this act or that one is not conducive to rest, peace, and tranquility.

The ups and down, and the comings and goings, cannot but be detrimental to one's health, to one's peace of mind. Being back in the Valley has helped the wri recover some of his good spirits, if not his health.

The X-ray machine, unfortunately, doesn't lie. The wri himself saw the telltale pictures when he was going over his notes and first drafts. The wri, or so he thinks, is on the verge of arriving at the end of this work. It's merely a matter of a few more conversations.

As is usually the case, that which was thought to be a simple piece of research turns out not to be that at all. And, in spite of what has been said, by those who would know, and by the rest, those who know less but clamor the more, everything hinders and everything helps that which the wri would like to present and make known. A paradox, but here it is.

39

Eugenio & Isidro Peralta:
Klail City Twins

Eugenio is a debt collector for the Seamon Loan Co.'s branch office in Klail City; he lives in his father's house. His father, Adrián, is called 'el coyote'. Not, by the way, a pleasant nickname to lug around. Eugenio and his wife, Hortensia (née Cáceres), have no children and they do quite well for themselves. Eugenio dabbles in politics through his father's good offices.

Isidro (aka Chirro) married Englentina Campos who died a very few years into the marriage; there was no issue. The subsequent nuptials (his father's phrase) were with María del Refugio Beristáin, who is very much alive. They have five (or six) children. (The wri did not, because he could not, give the exact no. of progeny in this case. There is, then, in this family, what is known as *un dudoso,* a doubtful one. At least this is what the wri hears bruited about.) The couple, too, lives in the same block in which Isidro was born and on the same street as his brother and father. Isidro is an electrician (he owns his own shop) and you couldn't choke him for less than $15,000 in inventory, as we say in Belken.

The two were classmates of Jehu's and Rafe's, and, they, too, are Klail High graduates.

EUGENIO: "Well, if that's the case, then, I'll start first and then you, Chirro."

The wri, since he made no mention of it, wishes to add that the twins are frighteningly identical. The wri looks upon them as decals of each other; a singular similarity in gestures, facial expressions, and in an antisocial habit of scratching: backside, crotch, sideburns, etc.

EUGENIO: "Jehu? Why I knew him before he was born, as we say. When the Korean War came up, he was among the first to be called up by the Reserve. I, by the way, have never been in the Army; failed the physical, you know. Maybe it's because I'm a ciclán; yes, that may be it.* (Turning to his brother) You failed yours, too, remember? You had TB as a child."

ISIDRO: "That wasn't the reason."

EUGENIO: "What? Everytime we talk about this, you go and change . . ."

The wri stepped in before the Brothers Peralta started to raise their voices right in the middle of Klail's mexicano downtown section.

EUGENIO: "*Okay.* I also work for the Bank, on a contract basis; they hire me to collect their bad debts. I collect for Seamon, a-course, but I farm out to the Bank, as needed, see? I don't get much from 'em, but money fits all pockets, is what I say.

"Jehu told me about the job; he explained it, too. If I collect, fine, if I don't, that's okay, too. They, the Bank, make a write-off; a bad loan, see? Now, if I do collect from a skip or somebody like that, I get a cut, and then the Bank comes out ahead, too; they get their money back and the interest or part of the collateral, right?

"Jehu also pointed out that Goyo Chapa, some time back, used to do this, but then he tried to get cute on 'em; yes, he did. Goyo reported that he couldn't collect on some of the bad debts, damfool, and then it turns out that he *had;* some of the people came to the Bank to see about their accounts 'n all, and there it was, all laid out, in black and white. Goyo'd tried to get to 'em, see? Damfool thing to do, I say.

"So what happened? Not much: Pen State, all the way! I think he was stored up for a couple-a years or something like that.

"Me, I got the job on Jehu's say-so. But, I'll tell you this, we never got along well in school; this was years ago, a-course.

"Jehu also helped me secure a loan to fix Pa's house a bit; told me *what* kind-a loan, what *terms,* too, and business like that, you know. He knows his stuff, all right.

Ciclán: A Spanish peninsular term for any male animal born but with one testicle. (From the *Dictionary of the Royal Academy.*)

"As Jehu says: 'The Bank can't lose; don't you trust us, now; we're in the business of making money.' I like the advice, all right, but the way I see it, that's no way to protect your job, giving away secrets like that. And now, I hear he's leaving or that he's left, one of the two."

ISIDRO: "Yah; and the other mexicano there'll freeze you in your tracks. Yes, he will. He doesn't even want mexicanos coming in the Bank."

EUGENIO: "Yeah, you're talking about Escobar; that's his name. I don't know him; someone said he was from Jonesville; but, nah, I don't know him at all."

ISIDRO: "Well, I don't *either,* but he's still a pain."

The wri would like to explain that the twins are speaking to each other; it's as if the wri weren't there at all; that is, they speak *with* but not *to* him. They look like two veteran actors who've been on the road so long, they know each other's lines and everybody else's, too. The wri decided not to intervene.

ISIDRO: "What I am-about-to-say-to-you, stays here; either that or nothing doing."

EUGENIO: "You got my word on that."

Isidro looked at the wri, who had no choice but to nod his assent: discretion, discretion. The wri begs forgiveness for yet another interruption, but he is a bit uncomfortable with this pair of o' jacks. The Peraltas look like two drops of water. It's amazing. (Isidro is somewhat elliptical in his descriptions; it may have to do with his profession. Who knows.)

ISIDRO: "A long time ago, a November I think it was, Sammie Jo was here in Klail on a school holiday, and Jehu, on furlough then, stuffed her like a turkey. That was years ago, okay? But another time, farther back, in high school. A summer, okay? So it wasn't the first time, you got that?"

EUGENIO: "Can you beat that, Galindo? And now, some ten years later, they're at it again."

ISIDRO: "Yah, and in the Big House, too. He's crazy."

EUGENIO: "Got-to-be, but opportunity's like getting bald, it comes by the one time. Hold it, Chirro: I said *b-a-l-d,* don't you . . ."

The wri, word of honor, attests what is here recorded was what was said, nothing less, nothing more.

EUGENIO: "Go on."

ISIDRO: "I'm an electrician, as you know."

Eugenio nods in agreement, and they both look at the wri who also nods. The wri, no fool, knows he is not of the company.

ISIDRO: "All *right,* in a subcontract I got from Tommie Kyle, a small wiring job for Ranch security, I got to see Jehu with her again; Noddy's girl. In bed."

EUGENIO: "There are five of us who know now."

THE WRI: (The wri!) "Five?"

ISIDRO: "Yah."

EUGENIO: "That's right: you, us, and them."

ISIDRO: "My turn . . ."

The wri wanted to scream as loud and as long as his failing lungs would let him, but he didn't. And then, he lusted after a drink *and* a cigarette; luckily for him, he forewent all three. The wri was both wise and fortunate in this regard.

The wri, by the way, is grateful he has no twin to dog his steps. When the Peraltas invited him to supper, the wri excused himself; he apologized, profusely, but nevertheless, he excused himself.

To avoid any, *any,* possibility of a misunderstanding, the wri affirms that he gets along well with the twins, on a one-on-one basis. The wri, on occasion, has enjoyed a mano-a-mano with one or the other, but it happens that the wri (honesty above all) finds it disquieting, unnerving almost, in dealing with xerox copies in human forms.

A weakness, true, but there it is.

40

Lucas Barrón

Dirty Barrón has owned-run-managed, whatever, some ten or so beer joints-parlors-places, whatever, in the thirty-years the wri has known him. Dirty is much older than the wri, and is, then, a member of the wri's preceding generation: the old Revolutionaries. (Guzmán, Leal, Garrido et alii.) Dirty knows the wri well; he also knows Jehu and Rafe, and with little exaggeration, half of Klail City. Mexicano Klail, that is.

He speaks English well enough, and as most Klail City mexicanos, he has and claims relatives on both sides of the northern and southern banks of the Rio Grande. Ruddy-faced and blue-eyed, Dirty has a high-pitched (almost hysterical) voice not uncommon to the Valley.

"So it's come to this, has it, Skinny? Man can't even serve a friend a free bottle-o beer. Humph! How about a Nehi orange, then? Some iced tea? Good enough; tea it is. I'll tell Crossy to bring it to us; here, we'll sit at my table.

"Cross! go across the street there and tell Noriega I want a pitcher-a tea.

"So this has got to do with Jehu, does it? Well, what can I say? I know him, and I like him. And I think highly of him, too. Now, you're not going to hear no bad mouthing from me, no sir. Knowing you, a-course, I know you want the truth, and the truth's what you're going to get, okay?

"Well, I hear a lot in here, but talking's cheaper'n knowing, as they say. Ah, here comes the tea. Two iced glasses, Crossy.

"Okay, now. Talk here, in my place, is that he was fired, kicked out, and then landed on his ass out in the street somewhere. That he was light-fingered, too, but that's bullshit. That this and that and t-other. Now, as far as I know, no one from *this* side-o town has talked to one Anglo Texan; not one. Or with any A.T. who knows anything, at any rate.

"Now, your old friend Polín Tapia blew in here and was talking up a storm, but how reliable is your old friend, I ask you? Right? And I'll tell you who else talks and talks, but talk is all he does 'cause he ain't allowed to talk at home, and that's Emilio the Gimp. That's right.

"Don Manuel Guzmán says little, you know *him,* and they should listen to what he says. Don Manuel says that if the Anglos had a case or a charge, they'd-a gotten Jehu and right quick, too. Yessir. Our fellow Texans ain't about to close their eyes to somebody making off with their money. And . . . it ain't a race thing, either. It's a money matter with them. Don Manuel says there's nothing to it, kid probably got tired, that's all. A-course, you won't hear shit about Jehu 'n all when Don Manuel Gee comes in here.

"And what can you tell me about Andrés Champion? Anybody says anything—anything—about Jehu, and Andrés'd just as soon break that expensive cue stick a-his over your head and then poke you in the eye with it. Yeah. And he ain't the only one, 'cause Jehu's got friends of all ages. You know that.

"Some other folks talk about women trouble, and that's a mite ticklish, I say. Jehu's had his share, maybe more, but the old men, the *viejitos,* they're not about to step in on *that* piece o' business.

"When it comes to the young guys, they're saying that Jehu got to one-a the girls there and you know how *that* goes. But, that too is talk, and nobody really knows anything. And they, and you, and I know *why:* Jehu's no blabber.

"And that's it, a lot-a talk, and a lotta shit, too, but nothing else. No, sir.

"And how 'bout you, Galindo? What do you hear?"

Lucas Barrón is a first-class barkeep and almost as old a listener as the wri. (He interrupts less, too.) Dirty does all right for himself: he owes no money and even less favors, as he says. The *Aquí me quedo* Bar belongs to him lock, stock, and barrels-o'-beer; and, if anyone he doesn't like begins to raise any kind of hell, he'll tell him where the door is. He'll tell him once, by the way, and no more. The second time, the bouncer, Cross-eyed Moreno, takes over from there.

Dirty didn't say so, but he won't put up with Jehu being bad-mouthed, either.

Confession: The wri wonders now and then if he has as wide a circle of friends, firm friends, as Jehu enjoys. One can't have too many good ones; no question.

The wri plans to seek out Polín Tapia for a second go-round.

41

Polín Tapia

Vide Pt. 24.

"Nothing, Galindo; I'm telling you straight; I don't know a thing, really. It isn't that I'm avoiding you. I just don't know.

"One *hears* things, but that's not *knowing, is* it?

"Oh, and don't think I've been digging here and there, either. No, sir. I have my own affairs to run, after all. I, ah, I'll be working part-time in Morse Terry's local office while he's up in Washington, don't you know. And, as for the rest of my time, I, ah, don't know; I mean, it's nothing definite, the Ranch or the Bank, MAYBE, but, ah, I, ah, I don't know in what capacity. And if not *at* the Ranch, then maybe at the Cooke Lumber Yard and Paint; you yourself know that I know about paint and such.

"And to change the subject on you: Ira is doing very, *very* well, and he'll take very good care of Klail City's interests on the county level, yes, he will, you bet. You just wait and see. Ira's got talent, yes, he does, and he knows the full meaning and definition of the word *gratitude.*

"Ira told me, just the other day, that Jehu's old job's been passed on to a relative of Morse Terry's, and I'll tell you *why:* Ira's many obligations on the County Commissioner's Court impede his progress at the Bank. Impede, Galindo. At this time. But look to this: Noddy knows and recognizes the work Ira does there, and he's not blind to Ira's talents. No, sir."

The wri does not interrupt PT: no need to. Sooner than later, PT, who knows nothing, as he says, will open up like a Rio Grande floodgate. A matter of time, that's all. The wri confesses to a certain advantage in all of this: he knows PT better than PT knows himself.

"At the Ranch, and I know little or next to nothing, everything's in order. They've all returned sunned and tanned and healthy from their trip to La Pesca, Tamaulipas. As for Sammie Jo, she decided not to go at the last minute; I think she flew up to Houston or Austin some place to see some relatives or maybe they came down to the Valley, one of the two. You know, *of course* you do, and don't shake your head, dammit, you know they own those two planes and that little jet, so those people come and go as they please and *when* they please.

"I'll tell you who was under the weather, though. Mr. E.B. Cooke; he's okay now, thanks to God. Attorney Bayliss looks fit, and he's recovered from that serious illness a-his which came over him sudden-like during the elections, remember?

"And I can't complain; I'll be at the Congressman's office here in Klail, like I said. It's Noddy's doings a-course; it's his way of showing gratitude, although I really didn't do very much, if you know what I mean."

The wri shakes his head, raises an eyebrow once in a while, crosses and uncrosses his arms, but does not interrupt the flow.

"And, there won't be a divorce, and *that's* final. Sammie Jo says that Sidney needs her, and that she'll stand by him. How about *that?* Kid's got spunk, right? She's a Perkins, yessir! No doubt-a 'bout it.

"And, and, and there's no one, anywhere, who can deny that both Noddy and the Ranch didn't do right by Jehu, 'cause they did. But what can you expect? Written in the stars, it was. If you can't show gratitude, you can't show gratitude; it's like a lack a-class, is what it is. Well . . . I better not go into that; not now, anyway."

The wri's ears perked up some, and they stayed that way until:

"But according to Ira all's well at the Bank, and one would think that Jehu'd never worked there a-tall, ha!

"And you, Galindo? How's the world treating you? You still look a mite piqued."

The wri is grateful (one must always show gratitude) to his friend's kind solicitation in re his health. And the wri is grateful, because while PT has

'a weakness or two
and rarities, too'

one does not fling and forget a thirty-year friendship, after all. Polín Tapia has damn few friends who'll listen to him for very long. The wri (a weakness and a rarity) is a first-class listener. In this case, better than that. In this case, it is of the utmost that he listen carefully and well.

A word of caution: PT isn't that damn privy to the Ranch doings. He reads the *Klail City Enterprise-News* (owned by-the-reader-knows-who) and PT, as most, reads it cover to cover every Wed. and Sun. That's all.

42

Vicente de la Cerda

Owns a Dodge truck blessed and later baptized as "Hang in There, Klail City." VdlC knows Jehu well, since Jehu was a child, he says. He approaches the wri, and he'd like to get something off his chest. He says:

"Yeah. See this truck here? Jehu loaned me the money for it. Well, no, lemme back up a bit and start off again: he fa-ci-li-ta-ted the money. He didn't sign no note, a-course, but he helped. Israel Buenrostro, and he's a good one, too, he signed the note.

"Jehu's good people, and he'll drink a beer now and again.

"Truth to tell, I don't know much about that old Leguizamón-Buenrostro feud, but I heard, and not too long ago neither, that Jehu put the old block and tackle to Becky Escobar, get me? He jacked her up, Galindo, on blocks. And you know she's married to Irineo Escobar, the one who calls himself Ah-ra. On blocks, Skinny, and that's why he had to leave the Bank.

"But what the hell! He's young, ain't he? And he ain't no capon, right?

"Well now, the one I *don't* know about is the pharmacist; don't know her either, other than she's a San Esteban. Owns that little green car, and those guys over to the Blue Bar say, but it's all talk, 'kay?, they say that if Jehu was serious, if, 'kay?, if he was serious, then it'd be with her. She's a piece—hold it, Mr. Galindo—she's a piece of class, she's educated. Just like Jehu, see? Been up to Austin, both a-them, right?

"Over to the *Aquí me quedo,* some-a the guys there say he got to Sammie Job (sic). She's Norberto Perkins' pride and joy, she is.

110

They had a, a, a arrangement, right? That's the word, right?

"It's possible, Mr. Galindo. Now some-a the guys there say that this has been going on since high school, can you imagine that? Probably nothing to it, but that's what them guys over to Dirty's 'r saying. The worst they'll say is that Norberto Perkins didn't care. That's bullshit, Mr. Galindo, that's just being mean, isn't it?

"I've also heard that Rafe Buenrostro and Sammie Job sometimes back it was, were pretty close. Ol' Cross-eyed Moreno, yeah, Crossy, he said so. But where he got that is a mystery. My guess is that Crossy knows nothing about nothing. Ha! With that right eye looking straight at his nose, what can he see, right? Cheap-ass talk, if you ask me.

"Rafe Buenrostro knows how to take care a-himself. He's . . . a, a, a, a . . ."

The wri does not believe he should put words in anyone's mouth; the wri *supposed* that the word looked for was *discreet.*

a, a, let's see, I got it: he's quiet, he can keep a secret. Yeah, that's it.

"And that's about it, Mr. Galindo. If I learn anything else, or hear anything else, or something, I'll remember . . ."

The wri wishes to go on record that he gives credit, but of that, little, to the talk at the *Aquí me quedo* Bar and the Blue Bar. But, he also recognizes that truth comes in different packages and at different weights. Thing to do, then, is to listen, to hear, to assess, and to see what truths drip out from time to time.

Vicente de la Cerda, older than Jehu and thus nearer to the wri's age, is hardly an unbiased source, obviously. Still, he volunteered, and the wri does not turn such informants away at the door.

43

Emilio Tamez

About Jehu's and Rafe's age; once a frequent barroom brawler, a marriage at age twenty-five put a halt to that way and style of life. (It isn't germane to the matter at hand, but ET's wife is one of the shortest, teensiest, women the wri has ever seen anywhere. She's shorter than short.)

Tamez still makes the rounds although not as much nor as frequent; the regulars at the Blue Bar say that the day or night that Emilio gets into another punch-up, that'll be a general announcement to the world that Esthercita Monroy, the hand that rocks the cradle, has now kicked the bucket. Emilio, instead of fighting, has now retired to safer ground: talk and little else.

He drives a pickup, as he has for some seven or eight years, sunup to sundown, picking up and driving here and there, the numerous Blanchard heirs. And they *are* numerous.

Emilio is known as The Gimp; this came about as a result of slipping on some broccoli (while running atop a refrigerator car) and breaking his knee and assorted bones. This kept him out of the Army; had this not happened, the Army would've still not got its mitts on him: Young Murillo, an otherwise peaceful youngster, once took a knife, under provocation, and sliced one of Emilio's ears off; Murillo caught it in mid-air, and handed it to Emilio, who threw up.

Many cheap shots were then hurled at Emilio after this incident.

"My brother Joaquín says that the Ranch has some seven 'r eight railroad cars on the First Street siding and all loaded up with barbed wire; it's replacement wire, and it'll be up by the end o' May. New posts, too, and all cedar. Ha! Joaquín signs for *everything* that comes there for the Ranch.

"It's a pleasure to work with that kind of people; the Blanchards may not have *all* the money in this world, but I bet they beat their relatives the Cookes, yessir.

"And look at this, now: they treat me with courtesy. Consideration, even. It's a damned shame to have to say it, and I mean what with friends here and all, Galindo, but at times, the Texas Anglos show more class than the Texas Mexicans and I'm no Anglo lover, right? But, I know what's right, and I know how to be grateful, and I'll work like a dog. And, and, and what about some of us who have a college education 'n then piss-off the job; can't hold on to it. Talking about Jehu, and a friend-a yours, I know, and no, he ain't here to protect himself, but it don't matter a bit; I'd say the same thing if he'd walk through that door, there.

"The Anglos'll put it to you, but we give 'em cause, too, you know."

Emilio Tamez talks, as the saw says, to hear himself talk. The wri finds it ridiculous that Tamez knows, or would know, what opinion, if any, the Blanchards have of the Cooke cousins, and vice versa. To add to this, he shouldn't forget that the alphabet around here begins and ends with K for Klail. As a mathematician woman friend of the wri is fond of saying: 'One should be able to distinguish between what is important and what is essential, in all things.'

"Okay, then, and what about them garage sales a-theirs? Hey? Well? They're held at the Ranch, and they're held for us, the workers. That's first-class clothing we're talking about here, clothing that's barely been used. And cheap to buy? Lemme tell you, Galindo. Yeah, and the money? Know what they do with *that?* Why, they give it to their *church,* that's what!

"They don't *need* the money; they give it to *charity.* Yeah, they do.

"All right, let's see, now, and just how long did Jehu spend with his Holy Rollers? And selling bibles, from what I hear . . . Shoot, and now look how he wound up. Making us all look bad. Yessir.

"We Tamezes are hard workers, yes, we are. And we don't take lip, neither. And Jehu? Well? Well? When has he *ever* faced anybody down in this cantina? In *any* cantina? College ruined that guy; got himself educated, and then he couldn't measure up in the street or in the Bank!"

It's entirely possible that Tamez had had more than his usual limit. The conversation/monologue jumped from here to there back again; no one at the tiller, as we say in the Valley.

The Tamez have always been hard workers, no doubt on that at all. And, favorable comment in this regard has been made elsewhere, but hard work shouldn't be worn as a special medal; other Valley mexicanos work just as hard. And as long, too.

The wri knows that Emilio says what he says relying on Common Law: What's said in a cantina stays there. If one's been drinking, more's the reason.

The law has to operate this way; life would be intolerable, otherwise.

44

Arturo Leyva

A degreed accountant; he has been married these twenty years to Yolanda (only dau. of Doña Candelaria Murguía de Salazar alias 'The Turk' and her late husband, Don Epigmenio, aka The Knight of the Woeful Hernia). Leyva is a year, perhaps two, younger than the wri; he has known Jehu for years.

"They, whoever *they* are, well, they had better not come here with stories, trumped or not, about Jehu. Not to this place, and not to this person. Ah, and if they do, they had damn well better be prepared to face Arturo Leyva head on. Right now, tomorrow morning, any day of the week, Sundays included."

The wri interrupts to say that this informant speaks of himself in the third person. Always.

"Arturo Leyva does not permit cutting remarks of any kind from anyone about himself or about his friends. If Emilio Tamez or anybody else, talks that way, away from the cantina, at the ball park or wherever, then that somebody is hereby put on call. Arturo Leyva will take matters in his own hands; Arturo Leyva says he won't stop with Tamez; it matters little or not at all whoever that whoever is or may be. Anybody deaf around here?"

The wri should like to point out that AL is not the biggest man in Klail City; he's tough enough, though, and better than that: he's a man of his word; what we call *un macho cumplidor.* He has, as such, a sense of friendship, loyalty, and he knows what they stand for.

It must also be said that Jehu, in his teens, saved AL's bacon in an *affaire de coeur;* an *affaire* that had it seen the light of day, would have been fatal for AL. The wri uses his words carefully; if Leyva's mother-in-law, The Turk, had learned, smelled out, that Arturo did, in fact, betray Yolandita, the Valley would have had one accountant less on its census rolls.

"That boy is and has been a bulwark. He'd been at the bank *one year,* and at the end of that one year, three mexicanas got jobs there; yes, they did. And he did it 'cause he hired 'em; they needed to be there, he said. And he didn't put the make on 'em, either. No sir.

"That's the way it is. Now, that he likes his fun is something else, but let he who is *without* cast the first one, right? Damn right. Hell, he's a Valley boy; he knows what to do.

"Remember Old Echevarría, whom God now graces, remember what he said about Jehu? 'Leave that boy be! What can any of you teach him that he hasn't already seen or lived? Being an orphan's a bitch, and it gives but one lesson: if you quit, you die! Leave him be, I say.' Yeah, Arturo Leyva is here to remind you all, if it bears repeating, what the Old Man said. And he said it in this cantina. 'Leave him be.'"

The wri is pleased to say that Arturo invited him to a beer; with AL, this is a sign of trust and friendship. The wri was unable to accept, sad to say. The wri is not getting any better.

45

Esther Lucille Bewley

Some four years younger than Jehu (she says so), she has worked at the Bank since graduation from KCHS. Unmarried as yet, a bit on the short side, but pretty enough, her hair is short, curly, and blond. Blue-eyed, she is a bit too thin according to the wri's own preferences. Of pleasant voice, Esther learned her Spanish out in the small ranches, fields, and cotton rows which dot the Valley and which surround Klail City, and everything else.

"Uncle Bowly said you had come 'round and talked to him a while back. You didn't know he was my Mom's older brother, did you? Well, he is, and that makes *me* a Ponder on my mother's side.

"Let's see, Jehu was a senior in high school when I was only a freshman, and I really had a crush going, let me tell you. But, that was years ago. He never knew it and didn't till I told him here at the Bank some three years ago. And when I did, he just smiled.

"Now, there *is* something I need to tell you, Mr. Galindo. It's something I know."

The voice dropped with finality but with assurance and force. When she said she knew *something,* and despite her young age, she seemed a sad old woman sentenced by some higher authority to reveal certain secrets no one else in the world is privy to.

"I do, Mr. Galindo; I really do. You see, I've *watched* Jehu. Closely. And I can add; I can put *two* and *two* together as well as anyone. But I, I, I'd *never* do anything or *say* anything to hurt him.

"He's a good person, Mr. Galindo.

117

"Not *once,* Mr. Galindo, did he ever order me around. He just asked me if I knew my job, I said I did, and he said, 'Good enough.' And then (smile) he said, 'Watch your ass, Esther; there's a lot of bastards in this world.' He's a gentleman, Mr. Galindo.

"But that *other* one! Mr. Texas A&M over there. Why, I speak better Spanish than him; and know what else? He wouldn't lift a finger to help anyone. He once told me to get him some coffee, and I told him, quiet like, but I told him to go get it hisself, *himself.* And there's a word in Spanish for guys like him, right?"

At this point, Esther turned reddish and her old age, laying in wait, passed over as a breeze by a baby's crib: light, airy, warm, calm.

"But I know something, Mr. Galindo, and I know about the fights, too. At the Big House, and at the office. And you know *what?* Mr. Perkins was righter than he *knew* and Jehu *still* beat him, Jehu beat him at his *own mean game.* Oh, I could've kissed him, Mr. Galindo.

"After the shouting in Mr. P.'s office, Jehu walked out-a there, winked at me, and then gave me that smile-a his; he then turned to Ira and pointed at him, you know, like with a toy pistol? Well, he did, and he smiled again. But it wasn't the smile he gave *me.* Know what else he did then? He called me over, and he was standing not two feet from Mr. Big-Shot's desk, he called me over 'n said, real serious like, but smiling the while: 'Esther Lucille, the world's full of sons-of-bitches, but killing's against the law, so you've got to skin 'em once in a while, just to let them know you're here.' That's exactly what he said; word for word. And then he said, 'Want to flip to see who makes the coffee?'

"See what I mean?"

The wri, who is not half the cynic he thinks he is, noticed how Esther Lucille's too-blue eyes danced and almost clouded over. No, she didn't cry, but had it come to that, the wri, yes, the wri would have dissembled and understood. (Costs little, worth a lot.)

"It's not important that I tell *how* I know, but I do. And, I know about *both* of them, Mr. Galindo. *Both* of them. You see, Uncle

Bowly knows, too, but he'd never tell Mr. Perkins. Never. He told Ma, though, and Ma told him not to say it again. To anyone. Uncle Bowly's foolish, but he's not silly; the cops, well, they *know* a lot. And, they *hear* a lot, too.

"Besides, and you don't know this; no, you don't. Jehu's cousin, the cop?, the detective?, well, he got Uncle Bowly out-a some scrap in Flads, in Dellis County. Yeah, he did. Rafe fixed it up, Mr. Galindo; whatever it was. So, you see, Uncle Bowly'd never say a word; I wouldn't either, and I won't, but, but Jehu . . ."

At this point, Esther motioned with her chin: first at Noddy's office and then at Ira Escobar's desk. Esther looked thinner still and sadder, too, but thinnish and all, Esther Lucille smiled that smile which will accompany her, taw by aggie, to her old age.

The wri, before old age comes and erodes Esther's youth, wants for Esther to be happy, and, if possible, happier for a longer time than she's ever been.

It's not too much to ask.

46

Don Javier Leguizamón

Our man has arrived at seventy-plus arduous years of fleecing his fellow man (and woman). He's religious, he's a patriot, and an inveterate user of the first-person singular.

The man, at various times, has been a merchant, a rancher, a dealer in wholesale contraband (north to south, south to north), and a faithful follower of his instincts. He was born, as the saying goes, with both eyes open. He expects to leave this valle in the same manner.

More, much more in fact, could be said about the large, vast, Leguizamón family, but the wri recognizes that one needs German patience and scholarship to cover all the Leguizamóns of the world in depth.

"Not meaning to brag, and I say this in all possible modesty since at my age now and, yes, even as a young man, have I ever sought to stoop so low as to bring attention to myself. I, then, as I was saying, I, in great part, am responsible for Jehu's position at the Bank. Accordingly, then, I, am responsible for whatever happened, señor Galindo.

"Sad to say, but I did recommend Jehu to Noddy, and there he went. A couple of years later, when another post opened up, I made sure that that one went to my niece Vidala's boy, Ira.

"I knew that Jehu was in dire, pressing, ah, need of a job and hence my recommendation to Noddy. I know Jehu, and have known him since he was a child. In point of absolute fact, he worked for me in one of our stores here in Klail."

The wri has lost count of everyone who has known Jehu since his childhood.

"I can't deny, hide the fact, that I'm somewhat disappointed that Jehu did not help us during the elections. As it turned out, he wasn't needed, but no rancor, señor Galindo, none at all. And, if the opportunity again presents itself, I'd recommend him again. Would do so, yes, and highly and gladly, too. I'm here to tell you I would; one either stands by one's word or one fails, and I, we, the Leguizamóns, are not built that way. Firm is what we are. 'You well know that . . .'"

AGHTUNG. The wri knows nothing of the kind.

". . . all of our male lineage, of those of us born in the past century, I happen to be the lone survivor. Our family, thanks and glory be to God, is flourishing, and I no longer have to see or oversee the day-to-day business affairs. No; I now leave *that* to them, to the youngsters.

"I, always, and first and foremost, have dedicated myself to family first and to business interests later. If one takes care of the first, why, the rest comes tailing right behind; an easy conscience, taking care of bringing no injury to one's neighbor, and if one finds an opportunity to do someone a favor, one does it and gladly. And I don't ask who the recipient is, no sir. All I want to know is: how can I help, when can I help, and *where* can I help. And that's it, señor Galindo; and it's said in all modesty, and if I have pride, then it's my humility that I take pride in.

"I know I have my detractors, but I'm above that. Truly. At my age, I see no reason, none, why I should worry, unnecessarily, over what is said or thought about me, as erroneous as that thinking may be.

"One isn't perfect, and I'm the first to admit it, by God. But, one's lack of perfection should not cause one to lose control or to follow the devil's ways and byways.

"Work, family, order, and progress, seriousness of purpose, sobriety, and charity to the unfortunate is the Leguizamón way of life. Not our very own personal motto, no, but we do try to follow those precepts. Assiduously.

"That favor to Jehu was not the first extended to that young man, and I stand here before you to say that it won't be the last. And, although he is a relative of the family that thinks ill of us, that may even work to destroy our good name and reputation, we, the Leguizamóns, know about favors, about extending a hand, and I am not the kind that expects payment or recognition. At any time."

Goodness! But be *that* as it may, the wri prefers that the words spoken by JL remain as a personal monument: inviolable and intact.

The wri maintains that he will not descend to the plains of irony.

47

Jovita de Anda Tamez

Married to Joaquín, the eldest of the Tamez brothers, Jovita was a bit wildish in her teens. This has passed, and the informant has given several children, and according to some, very few restless moments to her husband. Others say otherwise.*

"It's been years since I've seen Jehu Malacara. Years. And, I haven't seen Rafe for longer than that. Now, I used to see Rafe when he'd cut through here on his way to work at Lucas Barrón's place; it was one of those summer jobs, and Joaquin and I would see him go by as we sat on this porch here.

"As for Jehu, señor Galindo, as I said, it's been years. And it isn't that Klail's that big a place, but what with housework and the kids and what-not . . . You know.

"My brother-in-law, Emilio, comes by once in a while, and usually just about every Sunday for the barbecue when he and Esther come calling.** We talk about everything under the sun, a-course, but it wasn't until recently that I heard what had happened to Jehu at the Bank last year. But this is old news.

---

*The wri, and he doesn't quite know how to broach this, heard stories-rumors-base gossip, whatever, many years ago, that (sometime after the Korean War) Jovita accommodated (if that's the word), that she accommodated Jehu; others say it was Rafe. Mention is made of this (unfounded as it may be) because the rumors were not cantina-based; a woman friend of the wri, and he has a few, also mentioned it in passing years ago.

**This Esther, of course, is Esther Monroy, Emilio's wife, and not Esther Lucille Bewley, Bowly's niece. Probably no need to so identify for the careful reader, but the wri is compulsive when it comes to accuracy.

123

"Anyway, what I hear *now,* is that the pharmacist San Esteban is selling her end of the business to her brother. That she plans to *live* with Jehu; up in Houston, I hear. I heard that from Emilio, and I can't recall where else, but as far as hearing it, I did, and more'n that, too, I also hear that the pharmacist is using part of her money to pay whatever money it is that Jehu owes the bank. Emilio himself told me this.

"Can all this be true? You see, señor Galindo, I also heard that she wasn't going to help him; that Jehu has a new job in Austin, and that he sends part of his salary to the bank; a special arrangement between them, is what I hear.

"I told this to Emilio, but he says it isn't so; he also says that the pharmacist is a fool who goes around throwing her money away.

"I don't know *what* to think; I *know* Jehu, and I can't believe what people say about him. Oh! I just remembered something else I heard at Efraín Barrera's store. I heard that the Leguizamón family is helping Jehu. Joaquín says I'm a fool if I believe any part of that.

"But truth to tell, I really don't know much, and I'm telling you what I hear, and that's it. But . . . you hear it so much, see?"

The wri notes that Jovita (six kids older) is still a handsome woman; this is merely an observation on part of the wri.

The reader is free, as always, to accept or to reject whatever Emilio Tamez says.

In re Olivia San Esteban's plans, the wri, for now, does not plan to speak to OSE, or to her brother, Martín.

Part III

A Penultimate Note

The reportage mode ends with Jovita de Anda Tamez.

The wri has additional material, but it's his opinion and personal guarantee that none of it would amplify the case at hand.

That material, therefore, is considered unnecessary since writing isn't merely a case of filling in page after page of what could prove to be repetitive information.

An end has to be reached somewhere, and this is it.

Brass Tacks Are Best;
They Last Longer

Despite the unalterable fact that certain people, more or less responsible people, or others who should know, and those who do know better, and despite the many friends and backers of Jehu Malacara, and he has those who do protest friendship, (most of the Klail City mexicanos) say that Jehu is guilty.

They are not, however, precise as to what the crime may be; this is the least of their worries, they say. The wri has been witness to the tone, to the manner, and to the *how* they say it, and he thinks that if some of your basic igneous rocks were handy in Klail City, that Jehu, were he to return, would need to grow some extra eyes to dodge them all.

The wri also heard that Jehu had been dishonorably discharged from the U.S. Army, and that he was fired twice from his post at the high school. Some also said that he loafed on the job at the Bank; that he was there as a showcase. Other notes attest that because of his shady dealings, unspecified, other aspiring mexicanos will not be able to work at the Klail First in the future.

Tucker French, the local V.A. adviser, says that Jehu attended the University of Texas on the G.I. Bill, and Lauro Parás, a former assistant principal at the high school, says that Jehu left twice for better paying jobs; Mr. Parás also says that Jehu was a better-than average teacher.

The wri offers Perkins' own testimony as to Jehu's work habits and abilities.

None of the above has dented public opinion in any way. A matter of Caesar's wife, it seems.

Other voices say that Jehu hasn't married (he's now thirty years old) because of his fear of women. The running around is just a cover-up, they say.

Others say that his bachelorhood is owed to *other* preferences. The wri can only shake his head. The public is used to having its way when it comes to interesting stories that do not coincide with evident truth. Nothing new, then.

The pillars of the local churches (The Apostolic and the several Protestant branches) decry his lack of formality (sic) and seriousness. His lack of faith, too, and hint darkly at his probity at the Bank.

The wri thinks that Jehu has faith although, perhaps, not too much in his fellow Klail Citians.

The *mater familias* say that they knew all about him; they merely waited cross-armed, patiently, and with saintly resignation, one supposes. They knew, they say, that Jehu would come to a bad end. Would get his, others said.

The *pater familias, hombres machos,* nod in agreement and all agree with their consorts. The p.f. say that the majority is always right. (Originality, in Klail City, is a sin.)

The wri rests in the knowledge that someone who calls himself a friend will see to it that Jehu learns of his new reputation in Klail City. There are people in the world who love to pass on bad news in the guise of friendship.

The wri, getting down to those well-known brass tacks, is convinced that JM will return to KC someday; he is, after all, a native son.

When that day comes, he should take great care. It may be that every mutt and cur on the mexicano side of Klail City will line up to pee on him.

O tempora o mores.

Mi querido Rafa

Este trabajo se dedica a tres amigos:
Jaime Chahín
Arturo Madrid
Ricardo Romo

Introducción

Pocas obras se mueven tan a gusto en las arenas movedizas de la significación como la de Rolando Hinojosa. Desde la publicación en 1973 de *Estampas del Valle y otras obras*, título que marcaba ya la preferencia del autor por lo inconcluso y la apertura, Hinojosa ha ido añadiendo volumen tras volumen a su *Klail City Death Trip Series*, tejiendo y destejiendo líneas narrativas, incorporando a cada paso nuevas formas literarias y, sobre todo, desgranando en sus libros una amplísima galería de personajes entrañables (algunos) y execrables (otros) que nos acercan sin remedio a esa Texas de ficción apasionadamente histórica donde casi toda la acción se desarrolla.

Los catorce volúmenes que integran la serie son tal vez el experimento más ambicioso de la literatura chicana contemporánea. Se trata, nada menos, que de aunar las tradiciones hispánica y anglosajona para construir una novela total, enciclopédica . . . a sabiendas de que el efecto para el lector será el inverso del esperable a priori: cuantos más materiales aporte la serie, mayor será el grado de incertidumbre sobre el mundo narrado, como bien demuestra el ejemplo de *Dear Rafe/Mi querido Rafa*.

La trama histórica de la serie se remonta hasta 1765 y, desde ese año, nos trae hasta las postrimerías del siglo XX, abarcando unos dos siglos de intenso cambio económico, social y cultural en el sur de Texas. Como reflejo de esos cambios, en la obra de Hinojosa encontramos también intertextos variadísimos que nos llevan por los mundos de la tradición oral, las varias tradiciones escritas de las que se nutre la literatura chicana, así como el mundo de la cultura popular tecnificada (incluidos el mundo de las discográficas, la televisión, etc.). Asimismo, notamos de inmediato que las diversas entregas de la serie no suponen un avance cronológico por el mundo de los personajes; no se trata de empezar "por el principio" para traernos poco a poco hasta el presente de la narración sino, más bien, de presentar una historia sesgada, des-ordenada, en constante proceso de reconstrucción. Hasta cierto punto, podemos y debemos entender esta estrategia como un amplio comentario sobre la historia y la historiografía chicana. La serie de Hinojosa parece recordarnos a cada paso que, puesto que la experiencia de los chicanos (y sus antepasados) ha sido excluida de las historias oficiales, cualquier nueva narrativa con voluntad historiográfica debe proceder desde la conciencia de esa marginación para convertirse en una labor etnográfica y de archivo, que se guíe más por la acumulación (y articulación) de diversos materiales y voces que por la propia labor sintética del historiador.

Con ese fin, Hinojosa procede a descentralizar al máximo su narrativa, adoptando una serie de técnicas que conviene mencionar al menos brevemente. Destaca, por ejemplo, su renuncia absoluta al control autorial. A diferencia de historiadores y novelistas más tradicionales, Hinojosa opta por "dar muerte" al autor, un motivo que aparece parodiado sutilmente en *Mi querido Rafa* y *Dear Rafe* mediante los constantes recordatorios de P. Galindo sobre su precaria salud. En su lugar, la *Serie* se articula como el producto de múltiples narradores (Jehú Malacara, Rafa Buenrostro y P. Galindo, entre otros) que, a su vez, transmiten las voces y los recuerdos de otros muchos personajes, ya sea de manera oral o mediante la reproducción de cartas, diarios, y otros documentos. El resultado es una narrativa perspectivista, en la que de continuo se contrastan puntos de vista e incluso grados de conocimiento de *lo que pasó*. Además, el escalonamiento generacional de estos diversos narradores, así como de los personajes que les sirven de informantes, produce un efecto de profundidad (y continuidad) intrahistórica muy efectivo: lo que no recuerda Rafa lo puede recordar P. Galindo o el viejito Esteban Echevarría, y de la suma de sus recuerdos y de los documentos aducidos por cada uno de ellos resulta esta historia novelada a la que los personajes se refieren como el *cronicón* de Belken County. Sólo con hojear *Dear Rafe/Mi querido Rafa*, el lector se dará cuenta de cómo funciona esta polifonía de voces, narradores, generaciones y textos (las cartas, en este caso) que construyen por agregación la novela hinojosiana.

Como consecuencia, *Klail City Death Trip Series* exige no sólo una lectura atenta y cuidadosa sino también una constante relectura. Los catorce volúmenes están tan íntimamente conectados entre sí que la lectura de uno de ellos puede (y, de hecho, suele) modificar el conocimiento que como lectores tenemos hasta entonces del mundo narrativo de Belken County; más específicamente: lo que se lee en una entrega de la serie puede complementar, contradecir, o modificar en cualquier forma imaginable episodios que ya conocíamos y que, por lo tanto, tenemos que volver a considerar a la luz de la nueva información que a cada paso se nos proporciona. Así, por ejemplo, sólo al leer *Klail City y sus alrededores* (la segunda entrega de la serie, publicada en 1976) podemos entender la muerte de Alejandro Leguizamón, previamente narrada en *Estampas del Valle y otras obras*. Por supuesto, como nos avisa repetidamente P. Galindo en *Dear Rafe/Mi querido Rafa*, el lector debe tener cuidado de no creer cualquier cosa que se le cuente, ni mucho menos escuchar con la misma atención a todos los personajes.

Dentro de ese ambicioso proyecto narrativo que es la serie en su conjunto, la pareja de libros compuesta por *Mi querido Rafa* y *Dear Rafe* merece un papel especial: en ellos, como lectores, nos acercamos al umbral de lo desconocido, a esa nueva vuelta de tuerca con la que Hinojosa nos catapulta a una dimensión artística hasta entonces desconocida. Para empezar, en el mundo temático de la serie, estamos en un momento de transición entre la cultura más tradicional presentada en *Estampas del Valle* y *Klail City y sus alrededores*, por un lado, y la más reciente e integradora de libros posteriores como *Rites and Witnesses* o *Partners in Crime*, por otro. Además, *Mi querido Rafa* destaca sobremanera por explorar el mundo bilingüe del sur de Texas con más detalle y maestría que ninguna de las otras entregas de la serie, hasta el punto de que los lectores monolingües no pueden dejar de sentirse ajenos a buena parte del texto que leen. Es, sin duda, en esta obra donde Hinojosa lleva hasta el extremo el compromiso de dejar que los personajes se expresen en su idioma (o mezcla de idiomas) natural.

Tanto es así que, al publicarse por primera vez una edición conjunta de *Mi querido Rafa* con *Dear Rafe*, tenemos que huir de la tentación de calificarla como edición bilingüe, pues ¿cómo podría serlo, si ya *Mi querido Rafa* es un libro absolutamente bilingüe? Más bien, la circunstancia lingüística de estas dos obras aquí reeditadas nos obliga a reflexionar sobre el porqué de las versiones al inglés que el propio Hinojosa ha venido haciendo de sus obras a partir de *The Valley* (1983), en donde recreó en inglés el mundo de *Estampas del Valle y otras obras*; al fin y al cabo, todas las obras publicadas originalmente en español hasta esa fecha habían aparecido ya traducidas al inglés, normalmente con la traducción en el mismo volumen. La diferencia entre esas ediciones "bilingües" (con el texto original y la traducción) y la que el lector tiene ahora entre sus manos radica no tanto en una cuestión idiomática, en el más estricto sentido lingüístico, sino cultural: las versiones al inglés de Hinojosa no llevan el texto de una lengua a otra, sino de una cultura a otra.

En ese sentido, además de una cuidadosa lectura y relectura, *Klail City Death Trip Series* nos invita aquí y allá (siempre que Hinojosa se decide a regalarnos una de estas versiones) a lo que me atrevería a llamar una *translectura*, un fenómeno que los lectores de esta edición están, si leen el libro completo, a punto de experimentar. En *Dear Rafe*, como en todas las otras versiones de Hinojosa, el autor altera, reorganiza, añade o quita según sus necesidades re-creativas y lo hace, no hay duda, para comunicarse con *otro* público, uno que no lee en la lengua original de la obra y que, por lo tanto, probablemente tampoco comparte el bagaje cultural, literario e incluso social del público original. Los cambios, por tanto, además de reorganizar, sumar y restar materiales narrativos suponen una transculturación de la obra para acomodarse a las necesidades de los nuevos lectores. Nótese, por ejemplo, cómo la séptima carta de Jehú a su primo Rafa suprime (en *Dear Rafe*) un medio párrafo sobre la "raza papelera" que en el texto transculturado hubiera podido dar pie a algún que otro equívoco; o cómo la carta octava añade un párrafo sobre los parientes del otro lado del río, ausente en *Mi querido Rafa*; o cómo en la entrevista con Rufino Fischer Gutiérrez (capítulo 35 de *Dear Rafe* y 34 de *Mi querido Rafa*) se añade un parrafito sobre los mesquites, para beneficio de los lectores no familiarizados con el Valle. Los cambios, por supuesto, son mucho más amplios e incluyen también referencias culturales y literarias distintas de las que se encuentran en *Mi querido Rafa*. Con ellos, Hinojosa demuestra una nítida conciencia de que el público de la literatura chicana es un público multicultural y multilingüe, y de que para conectar con ese público es necesario moverse con soltura por varios y variados mundos y lenguajes.

Además, y como prueba de que las versiones hinojosianas son mucho más que una simple traducción, valga destacar la íntima integración orgánica que cada una de ellas entabla con el resto de la serie. Por ceñirnos al caso concreto que aquí nos ocupa, y a un ejemplo específico, el lector atento notará en *Dear Rafe* numerosas menciones a la labor de Rafa Buenrostro como detective y teniente de policía en la brigada de homicidios, ninguna de las cuales aparece en *Mi querido Rafa*. Desde un punto de vista autorial, la explicación es sencilla: entre las dos versiones de la obra que aquí se reedita, Hinojosa había estado trabajando en *Partners in Crime*, publicada (como *Dear Rafe*) en 1985, y centrada en su totalidad en esa nueva "vida" de Rafa Buenrostro desconocida para los lectores de *Mi querido Rafa*. Desde la óptica de la recepción, sin embargo, la situación se complica, pues es obvio que a causa de estos elementos añadidos *Dear Rafe*, como todas las otras versiones, se convierte en lectura obligatoria para cualquiera que quiera profundizar en el mundo narrativo de Belken County, y no sólo para aquellos lectores que se acerquen a ella por razones de idioma o cultura.

La presente reedición, por lo tanto, debe ser saludada como un hito en la historia editorial chicana, al brindarnos por primera vez (en un solo volumen) la posibilidad de embarcarnos en la lectura transcultural de una de sus novelas más significativas. En ella, los lectores encontrarán una de las mejores síntesis del estilo que ha hecho famoso a Rolando Hinojosa: la multiplicidad de narradores, la mezcla de géneros, la indefinición narrativa, la constante ironía, el contrapunto de voces populares con discursos oficiales, y muchos otros rasgos que cada cual deberá descubrir por su propia cuenta.

Como en una danza de la muerte posmoderna, el moribundo P. Galindo convoca en esta obra, uno por uno, a los principales representantes de cada estamento de la sociedad de Belken County, Texas. Junto a sus respectivas declaraciones, Galindo nos ofrece también (y de segunda mano) las cartas enviadas por Jehú Malacara a su primo Rafa Buenrostro durante la convalecencia de este último en el hospital de veteranos de William Barrett. El objetivo inmediato es adivinar el paradero del desaparecido Jehú; por el camino, y mediante un complicado juego de espejos narrativos, al lector se le ofrece una profunda reflexión sobre la vida económica, política, cultural, social, lingüística, e incluso sexual del Valle. La obra, vale repetirlo, exige atención a cada detalle, pero el lector no saldrá defraudado.

Manuel Martín-Rodríguez
University of California, Merced

Bibliografía de Rolando Hinojosa

_____. *Ask a Policeman*. Houston: Arte Público Press, 1998.

_____. *Los amigos de Becky*. Houston: Arte Público Press, 1991.

_____. *Becky and her Friends*. Houston: Arte Público Press, 1990.

_____. *Claros varones de Belken*. Tempe: Bilingual Review/Press, 1986.

_____. *El condado de Belken: Klail City*. Tempe: Bilingual Review/ Press, 1994.

_____. *Dear Rafe*. Houston: Arte Público Press, 1985.

_____. *Estampas del Valle*. Tempe: Bilingual Review/Press, 1994.

_____. *Estampas del Valle y otras obras*. Berkeley: Quinto Sol Press, 1973.

_____. *Estampas del Valle y otras obras*. Berkeley: Justa Publications, 1977.

_____. *Generaciones, notas y brechas*. San Francisco: Casa Editorial, 1978.

_____. *Generaciones y semblanzas*. Berkeley: Justa Publications, 1977.

_____. *Klail City*. Houston: Arte Público Press, 1987.

_____. *Klail City und Umgebung*. Frankfurt am Main: Suhrkamp, 1981.

_____. *Klail City y sus alrededores*. La Habana: Casa de las Américas, 1976.

_____. *Korea Liebes Lieder/Korean Love Songs*. Osnabrück, Germany: O.B.E.M.A., 1991.

_____. *Korean Love Songs*. Berkeley: Justa Publications, 1978.

_____. *Mi querido Rafa*. Houston: Arte Público Press, 1981.

_____. *Partners in Crime*. Houston: Arte Público Press, 1985.

_____. *Rites and Witnesses*. Houston: Arte Público Press, 1982.

_____. *This Migrant Earth*. Houston: Arte Público Press, 1987.

_____. *The Useless Servants*. Houston: Arte Público Press, 1993.

_____. *The Valley*. Ypsilanti: Bilingual Review/Press, 1983.

Bibliografía secundaria selecta

Akers, John C. "From Translation to Rewriting: Rolando Hinojosa's *The Valley*". *The Americas Review* 21.1 (1993): 91–102.

Bruce-Novoa, Juan. "Who's Killing Whom in Belken County: Rolando Hinojosa's Narrative Production". *Monographic Review/Revista Monográfica* 3.1–2 (1987): 288–97.

Busby, Mark. "Faulknerian Elements in Rolando Hinojosa's *The Valley*". *MELUS* 11.4 (Winter 1984): 103–09.

Gonzales-Berry, Erlinda. "*Estampas del Valle*: From Costumbrismo to Self-Reflecting Literature". *Bilingual Review/Revista Bilingüe* 7.1 (Jan–Apr. 1980): 28–38.

Illingworth-Rico, Alfonso. "Una aproximación sociolingüística a tres autores prototípico/canónicos de la literatura Chicana: Miguel Méndez, Rolando Hinojosa-Smith y Rudolfo Anaya". Diss. University of Arizona, 1994.

Lee, Joyce G. *Rolando Hinojosa and the American dream*. Denton: University of North Texas Press, 1997.

Martín-Rodríguez, Manuel M. *Rolando Hinojosa y su "cronicón" chicano: Una novela del lector*. Sevilla, España: Universidad de Sevilla, 1993.

Mejía, Jaime Armin. "Transformations in Rolando Hinojosa's 'Klail city death trip series'". Diss. Ohio State University, 1993.

Prieto Taboada, Antonio. "El caso de las pistas culturales en *Partners in Crime*". *The Americas Review* 19.3–4 (1991): 117–32.

Randolph, Donald A. "La imprecisión estética en *Klail City y sus alrededores*". *Revista Chicano-Riqueña* 9.4 (Otoño 1981): 52–65.

Rodríguez Presedo, María Begoña. "Rolando Hinojosa y su narrativa, The Klail City death trip series: hacia una reescritura de la historiografía social del Valle del Río Grande, Texas". Diss. Universidad de Deusto, España, 2000.

Saldívar, José David, ed. *The Rolando Hinojosa Reader: Essays Historical and Critical*. Houston: Arte Público Press, 1985.

Schäfer, Helmut. "Die Darstellung Der Chicanos Als Individuen Und Als Gruppe Im Erzahlwerk Rolando Hinojosa". Diss. Johannes Gutenberg Universität, Alemania, 1992.

Scholz, László. "Fragmentarismo en *Klail City y sus alrededores* de Rolando Hinojosa". *Missions in Conflict: Essays on U.S.-Mexican Relations and Chicano Culture*. Eds. Renate von Bardeleben, et al. Tübingen: Gunter Narr, 1986. 179–83.

Zilles, Klaus. *Rolando Hinojosa: A Reader's Guide*. Albuquerque: University of New Mexico Press, 2001.

Mi querido Rafa

I

Malilla Platicada*

Lo que sigue consiste de sabiendas a primera mano y de diversas opiniones, así como de comentarios, de ciertos datos y fechas, y de acontecimientos que (por un lado) se saben y que (por otro) se suponen. El escritor, el esc., piensa meter baza de vez en cuando. Advertencia: el esc. ha de ser fidedigno, ha de ser fiel. El esc., en su estado de salud, no puede proseguir de ninguna otra manera llegando, como está, casi al final del juego.

Fondo: El esc., estando internado en el hospital de veteranos en William Barrett, recibió, por manos de Rafa Buenrostro, las cartas que a éste le escribió Jehú Malacara. El esc. se encontraba en el hosp. por lo del hígado (víscera traidora) que ya no resiste ataques de frente ni emboscadas de patrullas debido al gusto (que no al vicio, señora, y repórtese usted) y —esto sigue— por lo del pulmón izquierdo: le falla el fuelle aunque no por el trago sino por su corolario: la fumadera.

Luego, para acabarla, vino el capitán médico Barney Craddock con la noticia de que el esc. también sufre de basal carcinoma; en este caso, cáncer y de la cara. Esto era lo que le faltaba al esc. para completar el dólar.

Rafa, a quien el esc. dejó en el susodicho hospital, estaba internado a causas del ojo que sigue molestándolo: esas pequeñas cicatrices que lleva en la ceja donde también perdió partes pequeñas de hueso y la otra cicatriz en el párpado del mismo lado, se deben a lo de Corea. Según los médicos, otra operación ligera y el ojo quedará como nuevo. Rafa ya lleva cosa de tres-cuatro meses en el William Barrett Veterans' Administration Hospital.

---

*Prólogo de P. Galindo a su compilación de datos que lleva por título *Mi querido Rafa*.

Explicación: Al esc. le queda poco tiempo, cosa de ocho meses, quizá nueve, o sea, relativamente, lo necesario para que nazca un ser humano, i.e., a no ser sietemesino como, a veces, suelen darse en el Valle, en el mundo, y en casas de conocidos, primos y parientes como suceso que va en suertes.

El tiempo, ya que de ello se habla, como cualquier cosa —como toda cosa, se acaba; se desmorona; se desliza; no perdona y más que marchar, cuela y corre. A veces, el tiempo se está allí quietecito y si uno no le molesta ni le pone atención, el tiempo, por su parte, desaparece. Eso, de no prestarle atención y de acabarse y de desaparecer, es muy del tiempo.

Lo dicho. Al esc., pues, le falta poco.

El esc. aquí también declara que su salud le impone que ésta sea su última contribución al cronicón del condado de Belken. No se ve que haya razón alguna por qué llorar o ponerse triste ya que la cosa no es para tanto; la salud le falla y ya.

El esc., en lo que pudo, hizo mucha caminata; reconoce, a estas alturas, que es enteramente posible que se le hayan pasado por alto ciertas verdades. Todo puede ser.

Lo que sí se asegura es que lo que sigue, hasta el momento, es todo lo que se ha podido aclarar sobre los sucesos in re Jehú Malacara, muchachohombre originario de Relámpago y, últimamente, vecino de Klail City, sede del condado de Belken en Texas.

Caveat final: ¿Sería mucho pedir que no se sorprendieran cuando los anglos texanos hablen inglés? Es su idioma natural y casero; se sabe que unos hablan español y cuando así suceda, el español saldrá por delante. Si se hablan ambos idiomas así saldrán también. También es natural que la raza del Valle hable más en español. Ahora, si la raza sale en inglés, así se reportará. (Hay que ser fidedigno, hay que ser etc.)

Jehú mismo, en las cartas que escribe a Rafa Buenrostro, nos da la pauta de ese engranaje lingüístico-social del Valle. Tal engranaje, que casi cabe llamársele levadura, es algo que mucho ha interesado a amigos de la juventud segunda del esc.: a los doctos y también doctores en filosofía, Jaime Chahín, Arturo Madrid, Ricardo Romo, y Jacqueline Toribio.

Sufficit.

Parte I

Las cartas

1

Mi querido Rafa:

Con ésta un abrazo y una esperanza de que te sientas mejor. Según Aarón, pareces uno de esos pájaros zancones que vemos en el golfo (y que tú y yo veíamos y ojalá lleguemos a ver de nuevo así que te repongas allí en el hosp.). So there.

Por acá casi sin novedad; este trabajo en el banco no es como para matar a la gente y uno, sin querer, se da cuenta de cómo cierta gente corre y maneja su vida en Klail y en buena parte de Belken. Parece mentira pero allí están las cuentas.

Ya que tienes que aguantarte en Wm. Barrett hasta el año que viene, haré lo que pueda para dejarte saber cómo anda el rol por acá. For now, las elecciones.

Ayer —y esto debe considerarse chisme ya que no tengo prueba alguna— Noddy Perkins mandó llamar a Ira Escobar a su oficina. Naturalmente, todo allí es soundproof, pero esa misma tarde, al revisar las cuentas y despedir al personal, yo le decía su good night al Perkins cuando Ira me ataja: "Que te quiero ver", dice. Me esperé y nos fuimos andando al lote que queda atrás del banco.

Ira andaba que se meaba por desembuchar; que Noddy "and some very important people, Jehú", le habían hablado seriamente, y etc. y etc. Total, que la bolillada quiere que Ira se presente, o que corra, como decimos, para comisionado del precinto núm. 4. Como lees.

Seguramente, Ira quedó decepcionado cuando me lo dijo ya que no tuve la gentileza de darle mis parabienes; lo que hice fue pedirle que me diera fuego para el cigarro que la acababa de pedir de corba. Se me quedó viendo y (Ira será bruto pero no del todo) vio que lo que yo tenía no era envidia sino solamente desinterés.

144

Se me quedó viendo un poco más y me preguntó si no sabía que qué significaba ESO: Noddy y los very imp. pers. querían postularlo (palabra mía que no de Ira) y que estaban dispuestos a verlo y a ayudarlo all the way.

Wherever that may happen to be, diría yo, pero quién soy yo para andar rompiendo ilusiones. A estas alturas tú bien sabrás que lo que Ira quería era dejármelo saber and that was it. Adelante: lo último que querría serían consejos y yo para eso tampoco sirvo. Estaba Ira que no cabía en sí y debieras haberlo visto cuando decía County Commissioner, Place Four; lo único que pensé era que qué serían los motivos de Noddy (y de la demás bolillada, although they're one and the same), ya que teniendo casi toda la tierra —AND ALL THAT MONEY, SON— allí tendría que haber gato encerrado. (If all this were true, of course.) Por ahora todo esto me tiene sin cuidado; para acabar, Ira se fue derechito a su casa a ver a su mujer para darle el notición.

Ira y su mujer llevan poco tiempo en Klail y no creo que conozcas a la muchacha; se llama Rebecca (Becky, don't you know) y es de Jonesville; Caldwell por el papá, pero raza a pesar del apellido, y Navarrete por el lado materno por no decir 'su madre' que, a veces, suena mal. La he visto pocas veces y casi siempre en ocasión de un bank party o cualquier picnic . . . (¿te acuerdas cuando íbamos a Relámpago a ver a las pelonas? ¿Se habrán casado, tú?) Anyway, no me cae mal a pesar de ser pesadita de sangre. A mí tampoco me ve mal, and there it stands.

As I said, es más bien chisme porque it could be que estén tanteando a mi Ira para que luego le den en la torre. ¡Lagarto! ¡Lagarto!

El que te manda saludos es el viejito Vielma; de la abogada ni hablar: sigue viviendo con tu cuñada y el barrio ya se cansó de hablar de "esas dos cochinas mujeres". Para qué te cuento; ya ves que seguimos tan avanzados como siempre y tú conoces este pueblo mejor que yo.

Reponte, come algo, y a ver cuándo te vemos por estas calles de Klail.

Abrazos, tu primo,
Jehú

2

Mi querido Rafa:

Primero: perdona la demora; mucho trabajo, poco tiempo, y de repente se pasan dos semanas y yo sin contestar. Segundo: Asistí al entierro del padre don Pedro Zamudio, el de Flora tan conocido. Allí conocí a dos hermanos suyos todavía mayores que él (y eso ya es decir algo). Hombres serios, nariz ganchuda como don Pedro y los tres tan calvos como la blanca de la carambola. Asistió todo mundo y por poco me río al acordarme del entierrazo que le dimos al tacaño Bruno C. Sabido es que ha llovido varias veces desde ese tiempo.

De vuelta me detuve en el cementerio mexicano cerca de Bascom viendo y leyendo nombres de gente querida y conocida. Ya sabes, todo mundo one day nearer the grave.

Item: Lo de Ira parece que va en serio: la hermana de Noddy Perkins vino al banco tres veces hoy mismo, and where there's smoke, pero por ahora no sé nada. (More on her in a minute.)

Corrección: Te equivocas y perdona; here's the story: Ira es Escobar por el padre (don Nemesio Escobar, emparentado con los Prado de Barrones, Tamaulipas. Got that?) Ahora lo fuerte y agárrate: Ira resulta ser Leguizamón —como lo oyes— por su lado materno. Leguizamón-Leyva. De la generación de tío Julián que en paz descanse. Y si vieras a Ira tú mismo lo dirías sin conocerlo; ese cabrón es Leguizamón en la pura pinta. La chamba del banco se la consiguió por eso, por lo Leguizamón pero (con todo eso) *yo* me cuidaría de Noddy P. Noddy's no fool y el pobre de Ira anda, in a word, encandilado —igual que los conejos: ojo pelón que no ve, orejas en punta que no oyen y allí está, listo para que se lo truenen con una .22; en este mundo hay gente para todo.

146

Ira mismo contó que irá a la casa de corte a pagar el filing fee. Camuco, camuco, camuco; aún sin pruebas estoy convencido que Noddy debe traer algo bajo el capote . . . I've been here three years, cousin, y apenas lo voy conociendo.

Tú, aunque no lo sepas, conoces a la hermana de Noddy. Ready? Es nada menos que Mrs. Kirkpatrick —la de typing, ¿te acuerdas?

A S D F G & don't look at the key
Q W E R T & keep your eye on me!

Sí, Power Kirkpatrick es la hermana de Noddy Perkins. La primera vez que me vio en el banco, será cosa de tres años, se me quedó viendo y me dijo, "Are you the Buenrostro boy?" Yo sabía que *ella* sabía quién era yo pero le di por su lado y los dos nos reímos; ya está veterana la Powerhouse and widowed all these twenty years, como dice ella; tiene todos los dientes más el dinero, quizá más, que le dejó su esposo. Ahora la Powerhouse se dedica al Klail City Women's Club y al KC Music Club y te juro que debe regir allí igual que lo hacía en Klail High. Dios las libre.

By the by, a Ira no le toca Place Four como le habían dicho —que feo suena eso: "como le habían dicho". At any rate, lo siguiente parece ser la jugada: Ira va a irse en contra de Morse Terry (Place Three) in the Democratic primary. ¿Te acuerdas de R.T.? Estuvo en Austin con nosotros, habla español; amigo de la raza. Ya sabes, Love's Old Sweet Song. Here goes: Parece que hubo piquete, resentimiento, perhaps a double cross or two; no sé —pero hubo algo. Y grueso. Noddy va a tratar de alinear a cierta bolillada contra Terry y en pro (así se dice) de mi Ira.

Talk about your strange bedfellows. The rundown: Ira en contra del bolillo, la bolillada en contra de éste, and so, our fairhaired boy en marcha. (Te apuesto que de noche —y solo— y quedo —y en el escusado— en frente del espejo —Ira se ve como Congressman allá en Washington; mucho es ese sueño pero cosas más extrañas se han visto, se han pensado (y si no, al tiempo.)

There is one problem, however, y por eso los viajes y trotes de la Powerhouse: Noddy quiere que la esposa de Ira sea admitida al Woman's Club. Allí te quiero ver, escopeta. More on this later.

La semana que viene este token irá a la Big House para un kick off Bar-B-Q para Ira. Una de las chicas del banco dice que se ha invitado a mucha gente —and she stressed the word *gente;* ya te contaré.

También —palabra de honor y de primo— te contaré más sobre Noddy y sus antecedentes aunque esto quizá sería repetir lo que tú ya sabes. Correct me if I'm wrong.

Me voy, me voy. Aquí te mando una foto; la bolilla que está a la izquierda trabaja en el banco.

Abrazos,
Jehú

3

Mi querido Rafa:

Estás de la mera patada y para eso son los *excuse mes;* one more thing, no seas tan mal pensado; uno, a veces, también va con buenas intenciones. Amén y he dicho.

Lo prometido in re Noddy:

Noddy Perkins es un señor de sesenta y corto pico de años; hijo de unos fruit tramps que cayeron en el Valle poco antes del tiempo de los sediciosos. Al padre me lo rebanó un tren de carga en dos o tres pedazos, según quién te cuente el cuento. Los que se acuerdan concuerdan en que andaba cuete. On the other hand, Noddy es muy medido: uno o dos farolazos diarios pero no se descompasa. Echevarría me contó —hace años— que Noddy no tenía en qué resbalarse muerto cuando se casó con Blanche Cooke; cabeza para negocios tendría y tiene porque él también les dice a los Cooke que se hagan un lado. (Habla español, natch, y le gusta que la raza le llame Norberto cuando la hace de vaquero los fines de semana. Te digo que hay gente para todo.)

A mí me ocupó hace tres años cuando me conoció en el Klail Savings; más tarde supe que también era (es) dueño of that there place, como dice él. In other words, it's owned by the Ranch. (As you know, we've no branch banking in Texas; not yet.)

Su mujer, Blanche, Miz Noddy, Mrs. Perkins, etc., está medio quemadita del sol y por el alcohol. Morenita de natural, tiene la voz pastosa y ronca debido a la ginebra que no perdona. Poco se asoma por el banco pero cada vez que vuelve from her 'periodic drying out', como dicen las malas lenguas, ella y Noddy se van al Camelot Club o a la playa para celebrar su regreso.

149

Uno de los vicepresidentes, que también es el cajero, es parte de la familia Cooke-Blanchard. Of course, of course. Se llama E.B. Cooke, le dicen Ibby y todavía cree que la raza es dejada. Te digo que se necesita tener corazón de piedra para no reírse de él. Nos llevamos que ni fu ni fa; in other words: es puro y al amanecer cigarro . . . A word to the unlearned.

La esposa de Noddy se lleva bien con la cuñada Powerhouse; probably has no option or say-so in the matter; besides, tienen distintos intereses. But make no mistake: todos se llevan bien, y más cuando it's family v. anybody else. La consentida es la Sammie Jo; two marriages, no kids, pero esto tú ya lo sabes. We still get along just fine, thank you.

Volviendo al padre de Noddy: le decían Old Man Raymond; Raymond era su nombre de pila pero la raza así lo llamaba en inglés; don't ask me why. (Tampoco me preguntes que por qué chingaos la raza llamaba Ricardo a Doyle Barston y Pedro a su hermano Neal al que también llamaban 'Catre'. ¿Quién nos entiende?)

Old Man Raymond murió con una mano adelante y otra atrás, and Noddy must have had a bad time of it there for a while. Cómo se casó con una Blanche Cooke no sé, aunque no creo que él causó el alcoholismo, but you never know. Sammie Jo's our age, and so los dos se casaron tarde, right?

Noddy tiene pocas ilusiones y menos amigos, o quizá tenga la clase de amigos que la gente rica tiene PERO en Klail who's rich, besides them?

One more thing, he won't rattle. ¿Y cómo? He's got most of the deck in his hand. Así, ¿quién no? Still, hay que verlo en acción, and above all, no perderlo de vista; not even for a second: he'll skin you and then wait to watch while your hide dries out. Hasta allí el hombre.

Aquí la mocho por ahora.

Abrazos,
Jehú

4

Mi querido Rafa:

A short note: ¡Salieron las balotas! Las primarias se llevan a cabo dentro de poco and from there las generales en nov. Según el run-rún más recién: Morse Terry ha tenido cierta dificultad en conseguir dinero para su re-elección. ¿Y mi Ira? Very well, and thank you kindly.

Te prometí contarte algo de la barbacoa y aquí va: Invitaron a medio mundo pero vinieron muchos más. Una buena señora (bolilla, regordete, y algo miope, diría yo) se sentó a mi lado; yo estaba escuchando un cuento algo largo y raído por no decir caduco (¡uco!) que contaba Mrs. Ben Timmens. Por fin acabó su cuento y casi al instante se lanza la recién llegada: "Well, just how many Mexicans *did* Noddy invite?" Éramos cinco en el grupo y yo 1) el único raza there; and 2) el más cerca a ella. Trataron de callarla pero ésta seguía dale que dale y los demás no sabían qué hacer con ella hasta que divisó a la Powerhouse y allá se fue. Well now, te puedes imaginar en lo que aquellas mujeres se vieron para disculpar o mejorar o deshacer lo que la amigaza había dicho.

Creo que todos necesitamos presenciar algo así de vez en cuando para que no se nos olvide y para que se nos quite la idea infundada de que todo va muy bien.

Ah, antes de que se me olvide. ¿Quién crees que andaba por ahí? Nada menos que María Téllez, bright, bushy-tailed, and in glorious living color, as they say. She walks and she talks: ¿y quién la calla? Que hace diez años fue querida de Noddy bien puede ser, pero ¡qué cruz, Señor!

It's sad, but a María la han hecho a un lado, aunque no lo parezca. Ayudará en las elecciones, sí, pero no en la de Ira; esto es algo especial. Very special, querido primo. Todo se hace por un advertising outfit de Jonesville. Oh, it's *very* professional; se ve que no se trata de rentar a Ira. Lo quiere lock, stock, and bbl. Y si no, allá vamos: verás el retrato de Ira en casi todo el condado. You can't miss it. Running for *one* precinct y se ha gastado dinero desde Jonesville a Edgerton y desde Ruffing a Relámpago.

Según la raza, Noddy y la bolillada de dinero le están dando contra a Morse Terry porque éste 'quiere a la raza'. Nunca aprendemos: la raza todavía sigue con eso: *porque quiere a la raza.* Lo que sí se sabe es que mucha raza (pagada, comprada y echada a la bolsa) dice que Ira Escobar es un muchacho de talento; un modelo . . . (Un modelo 'T' de los que ya no se oyen ni se ven, pero veremos qué pasa de aquí en tres meses.)

And would you look at this: según una chica del banco (otra bolilla) la Sammie Jo misma nombró a la esposa de Ira como miembro al Woman's Club; la chica (se llama Esther Bewley) es de aquellos Bewley de los ranchos. (¿Te acuerdas de aquellos po' whites, los Posey? Son parientes. ¿Ya? Okay.) Esther dice que todo el camino ya se había allanado para cuando se le nombrara a Becky. A lot of pressure; muchas of Klail's finest echaron maldiciones, escupieron, juraron, y todo el pedorrón que se debía de esperar, but, in the end, economic reason prevailed: Noddy tiene notas bancarias de todo mundo y con un leve tirón el que no es atarantado se alínea. Después de que habló la Sammie Jo (ahora usa contact lenses) —habló la tía Powerhouse— and, as a capper —la Bonnie Shotwell, qué me dices— la Bonnie Ess herself spoke in favor of Becky Escobar. No, casi nada; pura bolita blanca y allí tienes a Mrs. Escobar en el KC Woman's Club.

Today the Woman's Club, tomorrow the Music Club!

¿Qué te puedo decir ahora de Ira Escobar?

Aquí la mocho y hasta la próx. de la serie.

Abrazos,
Jehú

5

Mi querido Rafa:

Lunch at the Camelot; Noddy me mandó (& *that's* the word, son) a que fuera a look over a deal; Noddy se quiere deshacer de la agencia de carros y el buyer wants (has) to use the bank's money for said purpose. A eso se le llama barrer pa' dentro. Fue cosa de dos horas; no tenía qué ya que los abogados se encargarán —still, two hours away from the bank are two hours away from the bank y lo que se oye en el Camelot no se oye en cualquier lugar.

Some recalcitrants are still not happy re Becky Escobar's membership —pero se van a peer pa' dentro. Así se van a quedar. Te digo que the next target is the Music Club —Noddy hace lo que le dé la ch. gana & what you gone do about it, Slick?

Pasó la Sammie Jo mientras comía con el cliente y todo mundo dejó de comer; well, the women did, at any rate. Cabrona la Sammie Jo; le importa poco. She knows 'em; ¡hasta se peinan como ella!

Knows 'em? —She owns them!

Te apuesto: el día que deje de fumar, TODO MUNDO DEJA DE FUMAR. I mean, she doesn't even have to *give* an order. ¡Viva mi Klail! But:

Back to business: el cliente es un bolillo de William Barrett o de Houston; one of the two. Hard to pin down, ya sabes. Tiene negocios en los dos y trata con bancos allí, but for *this* deal he borrows from us o no hay trato. He's got the money (we've checked) pero como siempre, el life insurance policy que le sacamos, for slightly more than the loan itself, en este caso $700,000, se lo compra a Blanchard-Cooke Underwriters; that's no broom, son, it's an upright Hoover.

He also pays the premiums for us, the beneficiaries, in case of untimely demise.

I'll tell you, con todo esto de dinero y etc., casi nunca se ve: one just talks about it, but, in the long run, casi ni se ve. Nací para banquero, dejando de ch.

A otra cosa. ¿Te acuerdas de Elsinore Chapman? *What* a question! Se casó y aquí vivió por cierto tiempo; she was in a wreck up in Ruffing —choque serio y llevaba unos veinte días en el hospital and doing well, and then, de repente, se murió. Just like that. Me lo dijo Pennick o Morley; no me acuerdo cuál de los dos; me sentí mal aunque no sé por qué. I guess it's just natural; no sé.

Oye, ¿qué quieres decir con eso de que hablara con Acosta sobre tus terrenos? Fui a verlo pero no estaba allí y dejé recado, but that was over two weeks ago y hasta la fecha.

Abrazos,
Jehú

6

Mi querido Rafa:

Qué gusto saber que vas en buen rumbo; Israel y Aarón estuvieron aquí ayer, domingo. Ya sabes: carne asada, cerveza y plática. El Rafita de Israel es puro Buenrostro; a mí no me trata de 'tío', me llama Jehú. Lo has de ver cuando anda: manos en la bolsa, viendo pa' bajo, y dando largos pasos. Parece que no les da lata a tu cuñada & a Israel.

Look at this: IRA ESCOBAR: THE MAN WHO BELIEVES IN BELKEN COUNTY! ¿Y qué chingaos quiere decir eso? P's nada, right? De eso se trata, tú. Todos los rótulos están en azul y colorado con fondo en blanco; tengo tres ballpoints y un bolón de gofer matchbooks y hasta un secante para la tinta; sí, hombre, *blotters*.

Noddy (y los Leguizamón, diría yo) están gastando mucha pica. A Ira casi ni se le ve en el banco por las tardes and things are looking bad for Morse Terry.

Anoche: otra barbacoa. Ésta fue en Raymond Perkins's Field; los cocineros eran los vaqueros de Noddy; la música ídem; y hubo baile para todo mundo —mundo mexicano, of course. Invité a Olivia San Esteban (Hi, there!) Yo no me pierdo de nada, tú. ¿Te acuerdas de Oli? Se hizo farmacéutica después de enseñar dos o tres años; & now she's in partnership with good old Martín el cervecero que tan mala fama cobró cuando estaba en Austin con nosotros; as if I needed to remind *you* of *that* piece of business.

Por fin conocí a la esposa de Ira: No Quiebra Un Plato and Butter Wouldn't Melt . . . Luego luego le dijo a Oli que *ella* había ido a North Texas State: a music major. Y que era miembro del Woman's

Club. Are you ready? On the next breath, le preguntó a Oli: "Do you belong, Ollie? I mean, are you affiliated?"

¿Y Ira? Sonriendo like a cat eating shit grits. Oli le dijo que su mamá no la dejaba salir de día y por poco se me sale la cerveza por las narices. Me dio una tos de la patada.

Becky se quedó como si tal cosa. Después habló de Denton como si fuera el ombligo del mundo, lo que, a mi ver, es un error de 180°. Es más Leguizamón que los Leguizamón y eso ya es mucho decir.

And, you guessed it, ella no baila 'those dances' y también 'at those dances'. Diganme a mí que Noddy no sabía lo que estaba haciendo. (Pero, con todo eso, tiene un cuerpazo y a mí no me ve turnio la Becky.)

Esta mañana, en el banco, Ira me dijo que Becky 'had a ball, a real ball', & that she'll see to it that Ollie gets into the Woman's Club. At times, at work, I really need a drink now and then.

Después de la B B Q, Oli y yo fuimos a coffee and pie al Klail City Diner y allí nos sentamos con Noddy, su cuñada Anna Faye y el esposo de ésta: Junior Klail. Hablamos de todo un poco y cerramos el lugar a eso de la una.

Durante la plática surgió el nombre de Morse Terry varias veces y a pesar de la tunda que le están administrando en las barbacoas y en los anuncios, allí no se habló mal de M.T. Se me ocurrieron tantas ideas de por qué no se habló mal de él —en ninguna forma, ni veladamente, ni de intención— que me faltaría tiempo, papel y tinta para darte mis ideas y razones sobre el caso. And I'd probably be wrong on all counts.

La bolillada sabe más de nosotros de lo que sospechamos. Se parecen a los viejitos . . . son bilingües aunque hay mucho secreto en eso; casi como los masones.

Por ejem., sabían de los estudios de Oli y le dejaron saber que conocían a sus abuelos; nada de canchola tampoco, muy as a matter of fact; Ira no sabe en qué se ha metido . . .

El Junior Klail —allí donde lo ves— no lo ahorcas por menos de $37 millones, según Noddy, & *he* should know. Dicen que una vez que no le gustó algo que se dijo por radio o televisión (and I'm telling this badly), como sea, no le gustó lo que se dijo en un programa noticiero y mandó telegramas quejándose con los dueños or somebody. According to some there was some sort of apology from the head of CBS o NBC; según otros, que no, que no hubo nada. Count on me to get my stories right, right? Se llama Rufus T. Igual que el fundador del siglo pasado y debe ser el núm. 4 o 5 del mismo nombre. Llamarle Junior suena mejor que Rufus IV o Rufus V que huele a rey o a caballo, and it's Junior although Junior's nudging 60.

Abrazos,
Jehú

7

Mi querido Rafa:

The democratic primaries have come and gone, and the winner!!!! is Ira Escobar. Everyone loves a good loser so Morse Terry announced *he* would run as an independent. An independent? In Belken? At any rate, de aquí a noviembre son cosas de tres meses y de ahora en adelante, neither side is taking prisoners.

El cambio en I.E. es increíble; digan lo que digan, seeing is *not* believing. A lo menos yo lo veo y no lo creo. Juraría que se da shine en la cara ya que, God forbid, *eso* no puede ser sudor. Es lustre. Le bailan los ojos y es de lo más acomedido que pueda haber. Mira: sólo le falta llamar a Noddy así, Noddy, en vez de Mr. Perkins pero sabido es que hay que darle tiempo al tiempo. Of course, el descaro sigue: Reps or Dems, they're all ours, según Noddy. ¡Qué bonito, chingao!; así se evita la hipocresía.

Esther Bewley me dice que Becky es más fiel a las reglas del Woman's Club que las mismas fundadoras. Así da gusto: ¿a quién le gusta andar con medias tazas? El otro día, según Esther, habló sobre patriotismo, lealtad y amor maternal. Muchos aplausos y flores; cortó rabo y oreja, dio vuelta al ruedo y sólo faltó que la cargaran en hombros. They didn't do it, of course; fools that they are.

El trabajo va bien y sigo viendo a Oli de vez en cuando y casi siempre los fines de semana.

Una cosa no entendí de lo que dijiste sobre las tierras del Carmen. Por fin fui a la corte con Acosta y todo está en regla: contribuciones pagadas, propiedades bien demarcadas; todavía, there've been no changes, etc. Eso sí, los Leguizamón siguen siendo tus vecinos igual que antes de que nuestros abuelos nacieran. Llamé a Israel y a Aarón on this, pero no di con ellos; así que me llamen nos juntaremos. Pero tú descuida allá y ve por tu salud que por acá no hay peligro; las tierras están allí y para eso estamos Israel, Aarón y yo.

La que apareció aquí muy de mañana & apareció is the very word, fue la esposa de Noddy. Tembeleque y algo tiesecita, parece que necesita otro viaje a su spa. Llevaba el pelo un poco más azul de lo común y, a pesar del calorón, portaba guantes de salir; en la cabeza una bufanda del mismo color azul cubriendo su pelito ralo que lleva en bouffant.

Le dije a Esther que le abriera la puerta y que la atendiera; en eso fui a ver a Noddy y éste salió como bala y la condujo a su oficina. *En menos de cuarto de hora* vino el chofer; I mean, *he's* supposed to take care of her. Yo fui con el chofer para acompañarla a la casona. How she *got* to the bank no one knows. No me dijo media palabra pero no creas que lo tomé a pecho; la pobre ya andaba medio eléctrica y estaba lista para su viaje a Colorado donde la curarán hasta la próxima de la serie.

La Sammie Jo andaba por ahí y ¿qué te puedo decir yo a *ti* de ese ganado? Estábamos los dos de pie cuando de repente sale la Powerhouse: "Got something to tell you, Jehú".

No era nada; me contó de que cuando ella era joven, Pancho Villa vino al Valle —a Ruffing, tú— y que descarriló un tren, etc. Que ella vio a los muertos y quemados, y que Villa etc. y etc. Tú bien sabes que se trata de los sediciosos. Y allí estaba ella con sus setenta y pico de años y traca-que-traca que Villa aquí y Villa allá. ¿Para qué, y cómo, explicar o hablar de esto a esa pobre, indefensa, y ridícula mujer? Mientras todo esto, la Sammie Jo echando clavados en la alberca. As we both know, tiene buena pierna; take my word cuando te digo que no le gana a Oli ni a Becky who, by the by, me habla y me saluda pero de muy buena gana. Así que la Powerhouse se fue a Klail, S.J. and I had some coffee later on . . .

De ahí al banco de nuevo & just in the nick to see don Javier Leguizamón himself. ¡Qué te digo! Himself se veía bien y se apresuró a decirle a Noddy que yo, de chico, había trabajado en la tienda; si apuestas que mencionó a Gela Maldonado entre todo esto, you lose the bet.

Te juro que ésta debe ser la primera vez que oigo a Himself hablar en inglés; se defiende, I'll say that.

A Noddy le di a entender que todo bien en casa y, como siempre, con estas relaciones que tenemos con la bolillada: todo solapado.

Ira no cabe en sí; he can taste that oh-so-sweet (and I should add *heady)* wine of victory. El otro día after work, le dije que no era para tanto: que se trataba de *un* puesto en *un* condado de los 254 que tenemos en Texas. Well, shit . . . se me quedó viendo como si yo fuera un carro que se había echado a andar por sí solo . . . pobre. Lo que él trae entre mano (y entre ceja y ceja) es irse a Washington en dos o tres años. And that's what *he* says, cuz.

La que sí se ha bolado un punto es mi Becky; a veces, solamente, Beck! Parece mentira, pero cuando habla inglés hasta suena como bolilla, no del Valle, no, pero de esas de East Texas; know what I meeeeeeeean? Raza papelera; parecemos changos, hombre; donde quiera nos acomodamos y a cualquier árbol nos trepamos. Unos dirían que a eso se le llama adaptabilidad, but there must be some other word; surely. We did manage to have coffee together, though. One does need to be discreet; habla por los codos. The next time, es decir si hay repeat performance, I'll bring a bag.

Ira está convencido que ella inventó el pan rebanado ¿y para qué te cuento más? Un ejemplo: a mí me habló de réditos e intereses, de préstamos y ventas; y para acabarla, de la deuda nacional. La Sammie Jo que es una bestia (neither more nor less) aprueba todo lo que la otra dice; ¿Ira? Te podrás imaginar: encantado de la vida con su helpmate. Pero no se le quita a la Becky: 'ta buena la cabrona.

Volviendo a lo de don Javier: me preguntó por ti y le dije la verdad. No me creyó, estoy seguro, and so it goes in Klail.

Abrazos,

Jehú

Posdata: See here, no hay por qué reconvenirme: te mandé las dos ballpoints de todo corazón. Ahora, que no funcionen es otra cosa y hasta puede que haya algo simbólico por allí.

Mine doesn't work either.

J

8

Mi querido Rafa:

¿Qué crees? Ira, our Ira, ¡no toma! No; not even a beer. He must be an Eskimo, si no, entonces ¿cómo se explica?

El dom. pasado hubo tripas, cerveza y carne asada en el ranchito del primo Santana Campoy; Santana disparó derecho y parejo. Please note: hubo no menos de veinte bolillos de río arriba.

Yo también andaba de buenas y a la media hora empezaron las puntadas y las tallas, ya sabes. Allí estaba Ira con una RC Cola en una mano y taco de tripas y servilleta en la otra. Contó un chiste muy viejo y luego lo contó de nuevo, esta vez en inglés y salió mejor: esta vez se rieron unos bolillos.

Tú sabes que cuando uno se lleva —y más en ese tipo de reunión— se puede decir lo que le dé la gana ya que siempre se le va a contestar a uno de la misma forma. Why not? Somos del Valle, casi todos nos conocemos y de una manera u otra mucha raza está emparentada (malgré nous). Además, el choteo es el choteo.

Como el pobre de Ira carece de sense of humor, luego luego Santana y Segundo de la Cruz se le echaron encima, le tronaron tres o cuatro en un minuto y la risotada se oyó hasta el otro lado del Río. Seis o siete de los bolillos hablaban español igual que nosotros y no se les pasaba nada. ¿Y mi Ira? Entre azul y buenas noches.

Re la cerveza: Dijo que le daba dolor de cabeza. Santana countered que Becky le daba una paliza & from there el choteo de nuevo. Va a ganar: tiene una concha de tanque Sherman.

Al atardecer y rumbo a casa, vi su cara en casi cada poste y palma entre el ranchito y Klail, and *that,* cuz, is no mean distance.

Mañana es lunes y Noddy y yo vamos a ver unos terrenos al oeste de Klail; the old Cástulo Landín property; it belongs to Tadeo Landín now. Se trata de una cuarta sección que Noddy quiere comprar AND since I am the chief loan officer, yo hago los trámites; no parece que haya dificultad y se hará de esta manera: le compraremos el terreno, pero le pasamos el dinero en forma de 'loan'; paga los réditos del préstamo dos veces por año (it's his money and ours, ¿ves?) Tadeo no pierde, and I.R.S. (una de sus propias leyes) no recibe sorbete: el 'loan' se pagará en veinte años. Tadeo paga los réditos dos veces al año as per terms of the contract: 40 payments; y el banco, get this, *renta* la propiedad (as a lender) y divide los 180 acres en 4 labores de 45 acres each al que quiera sembrar. And, Landín has his money in deferred payments and as operational capital —on demand. To add to this, *he* can rent the property back and *then* pay interest (which is deductible) and what else? Well, he can also keep his share of Gov. money for not planting the sugar cane he wasn't going to plant in the first place.

Se oye mal, but it's all perfectly legal.

¿Y la raza? La raza va aprendiendo; con decirte que en Klail, que no es gran cosa, hay cuatro abogados raza y que dos de ellos se especializan en real estate, ¿pa' qué te cuento más?

Como ves, parte de la raza va recobrando terrenos y parcelas que se habían perdido años y años atrás; la bolillada todavía is sitting on top of the pile of money, pero el tiempo dirá.

Son casi las doce de la noche y tiempo de ir a la durmia.

Abrazos,
Jehú

Pd. ¿Qué pasó con el retrato? No venía dentro del sobre como dijiste; mándalo.

J.

9

Mi querido Rafa:

El retrato por fin & thanks.

Who's the girl? ¿Es del Valle? Tiene fachas de raza y bolilla. ¿Es mitá y mitá?

Los preliminaries del terreno en marcha; they're now in the hands of the attorneys, como decimos nosotros los banqueros.

El viaje de vuelta con Noddy fue otra cosa; es bolillo, sí, pero su procedencia (a fruit tramp for a father) le ha marcado y le ha amargado algo la vida. Lo de su mujer no le molesta; la trata con consideración y si no hay ¿hubo? amor, él ha mostrado tesón y paciencia en ese ayuntamiento. El dinero le importa mucho, sí, pero creo que le gustan los *deals* un tantito más: conseguir pista de algo, regatear, "jew 'em down, Jehú", y luego meterse con los abogados and, first, last, and always: la política. The man lives and breathes by it.

No tiene —mejor, no da— tiempo a los Rotarios. "That's bull-shit", dice, pero como quiera manda a Ned Reese como socio y le paga todo el costo; que los Kiwanis, que los Leones, nada, nada, but look here: siempre compra cien boletos de ésto y aquello and no questions asked. And, of course, a steer here and there for an occasional barbecue. . . .

A mí me ocupó por la buena recomendación de Viola B. Yo no me hago ilusión alguna, but I do earn my bread at the bank. Mi vida personal es mi vida personal aunque el muy cabrón sabe más de la cuenta. He doesn't know *everything,* of course, otherwise . . .

A decir verdad, yo nací para banquero; no doubt about it. Si hice algo bien en esta vida fue 1) to major in English and History; 2) la de dejarme de chingaderas con la enseñanza en la High; y 3) de ser recomendado por Viola Barragán en el Klail Savings. (From there, the rest is history: young Chicano is later hired at the Klail City First National and from there on to greater glories.) ¿Pero morir como trabajador en un banco? Gives one pause.

Hablando de Viola: le divisé en uno de los parties de Noddy; no aquí en Klail sino allá cerca de mi Relámpago querido. ¿Te acuerdas de las tierras de los McCoy y de los Ridings? Unos parientes Malacara (Chuy, Neto, y Gonzalo) compraron parte y Noddy la otra mitad que también da al río. Ok; allá divisé a Viola; me vio y se vino a darme un abrazo y me dijo que me tenía ganas. No se le quita.

Don Javier andaba allí —he must have thirty years on her, right?— y Viola me dijo: "¿Ves a aquel cabrón? Fue a Houston a que le pusieran un tubito en la pirinola; así mea, y cuando puede, todavía se trepa en alguien". De ahí la risa conocida de esta mujer bravía y de mucho ovario. (Lo de Olivia y lo mío lo sabrán hasta los perros porque Viola dice que ya era tiempo que me apaciguara.)

Se acordó mucho de ti; le di tu dirección y —conociéndola— te ha de mandar regalo. Our old boss, and now her present husband, andaba merodeando por ahí, pero sin chistear: Viola B. keeps a very short rein. Rations, too, I would suspect. De todos modos, Harmon se ve mal, decaído.

Viola y yo hablamos del banco, de mi trabajo y —como siempre— de business. Piensa comprar unos drive-in theaters y yo le dije (lo que ella sabe mejor que yo) that she's a preferred customer. La muy cabrona me guiñó un ojo y dijo: "Lo que quiero saber, flaco cabrón, es cuándo te casas para darte un arrejuntón la semana antes". Con esto un beso, otro abrazo y un recuerdo re los drive-ins.

¿Qué más puedo decirte de V.B.?

Olivia llegó así que acababa de irse Viola y dijo que Becky la quería recomendar para el Woman's Club; O. le dijo, "Thanks, but no thanks". O., a veces, te puede dar una sonrisa que empalaga y la pobre Becky just couldn't understand why O. didn't want to join.

For the record: de todas las mujeres, Becky era la única que llevaba sombrero. Still, se veía chula la cabrona.

El que vino a saludarnos a Oli y a mí fue Conrado Aldama, Col., U.S. Army Ret. A éste sí que se le "olvidó" el español. Allí estábamos aguantándolo cuando nos cayó Ira. Oli turned to me and said, "Somos cuatro raza juntos. I think it wise to disperse; we're too good a target". Decir esto en voz alta a esos would have been wasted on them, ¿no te parece?

¿De qué crees que habló Ira? You got it . . . Oye, ¿y si no gana? (There's been a lot of money spent, son.) Te diré esto: la raza está convencida que "Ira's their man" and the bolillada that "Ira's their boy". La bolillada sabe de dónde viene la mosca. It's in the bag.

And, speaking of Morse Terry, he still does most of his business with the bank. Noddy, to me, y en plena confianza, dice que M.T.'s getting what's coming to him. Noddy, by the way, says this very matter of factly; there's no heat in his words.

El party era lo común y corriente: party de bolillos con comida mexicana y cerveza texana. The parties and I are both getting old.

Aquí la mochila.

Abrazos, Jehú

10

Mi querido Rafa:

Elecciones, elecciones, y sigue la yunta andando.

El campaign manager raza de Ira, need I say it? es none other than Polín Tapia. Pasó por el banco esta a.m. Picking up orders from Noddy & some dinero; nihil novum. Los años no pasan por ese hombre —ni las indirectas tampoco, pero eso es harina de otro costal. Una vez, allá cuando tú y yo tendríamos unos doce años, Bobby Campbell me preguntó: "Is Polín Tapia the mayor of Mexican town?"

Le dije que no. Zonzo uno, ¿verdad? We just weren't adept at fielding subtle insults at that time. Sin embargo, a mí se me quedó eso de "Mexican town" y luego me puse a pensar que qué llamarían los bolillos al Rebaje, al Rincón del diablo, a la Colonia Garza, al Cantarranas, etc.

Hablando del cabrón de Campbell, por si te interesa, trabaja en un Sporting Goods Store si mal no recuerdo. So much for being voted the one most likely to succeed . . .

Ollie and I are going to Barrones, Tamps. for a night-weekend on the town. More (or less) on this at a later time.

Oye, ya es tarde y tengo que ponerle pare a ésto, pero, antes de que se me olvide, ¿podrías ir a visitar a una familia en William Barrett? Se portaron muy bien conmigo cuando me licencié del ejército. Se apellidan Gamboa y viven —o vivían— en la calle Lake; look 'em up.

Abrazos,
Jehú

11

Mi querido Rafa:

Wednesday night.

Tú dijiste que había gato encerrado en eso de la elección. ¿Sabes algo o se trata de la sospecha que es más el ruido que las nueces? A ver, desembucha. At times I think I'm too close to the action.

Vivir para ver y vivir para aprender. (Yes, it *is* National Cliché Week already.) Becky was in early Monday a.m. re the dinner at her house. Yo la trato poco, hasta ahora muy poco, malgré moi, aunque siempre con consideración. Mucha consideración. Lo que sí se puede decir en su favor también es que habla pestes de todo mundo y debido a su eclecticismo, ejem, a veces sale con unas puntadas casi casi originales. Ya sabes, al diablo lo del diablo y ¿para qué escatimar? Lo que le falta es sentido de equilibrio. Pero: tiene cierta sal y gracia. Desde que nos conocimos, ahora con lo de la elección, nuestra conversación más del tiempo consiste en preguntarme de asuntos personales y de contestar yo, aunque no siempre ni del todo.

Noddy knows she asks questions, of course, but Noddy also knows me. A Noddy son pocos los que le llevamos el pulso y la corriente; besides, los remos (metáfora) de Becky are too short; far too short. Para decirlo de una vez, a pesar de lo criticón que soy, me cae bien B.E.

So, en chez Escobar todo va bien; money in the bank, friends in the street, and beer in the belly; bueno, en el caso de Ira, RC Cola . . . Becky también tiene ideas de Washington, D.C. Quizá provengan de Ira; lo lindo del caso es que ni piensan en un apprenticeship en Austin; nada, nada: de Belken a Washington, but as you say: primero hay que ganarse la elección del condado.

Sin querer, por ella supe, and putting together what I already knew, algo que trata de la caída de Morse Terry; these are merely bits and pieces, pero no voy muy descaminado.

En cierto asunto de business and FAMILY, Roger T., no aquí en Belken sino en Dellis County, despojó, legalmente, unos terrenos de un conocido de Noddy; don't know the name, sorry. BUT A GOOD AMOUNT OF LAND, according to Becky. R.T. fue, as he can and should, el broker en el asunto y las tierras esas las compró una familia mexicana de Flads, right there in Dellis County. My guess es que fueron los Cruz, los Lerma, o los Fischer Gutiérrez. O todos juntos. At any rate, Noddy quería esa tierra; more than that, no quería que se vendiera a ninguna raza . . . y menos a esos que yo sospecho. They're good tough people. Parientes on the Rincón side, right? "Them cabrones (aquí Noddy) are ganging up on me." Pero perdió y perdió bien, I'll give him that; pero el rencor, and it had to go somewhere —devolved on Morse Terry.

Lo que te acabo de contar son cosas de Becky; lo dijo en su casa y en plena confianza. Yo, y viva el cinismo, me pregunté: "Why is she telling me all this?" Olivia no dijo nada; se durmió temprano porque aquello duró hasta la una o las dos. Becky, by the way, tiene los ojos color de café sin leche. Está buena la cabrona.

Still with me? Tuesday, el día despues de la visita a chez Escobar, a la esposa de Morse T. me la detuvo Patrolman Bowly T.G. Ponder; le dio su ticket *and* a citation to appear before Judge Fikes, PLUS a relatively hard time. Not much, no, but lo bastante para que le calara. And, this week, dos accounts de M.T., algo serios, hicieron un 'alienation of accounts' y se fueron con Gaddis & Gaddis, Attys.-at-Law; well now, M.T. no se va a morir ni de sed ni de rabia on account of this, but it must be recognized que se le cortó un poco de terreno. Lo de la esposa is just good old fashioned harassment, pure and simple as we know it in B. County.

And, looky here: de repente, out from left field *somewheres,* otro contrincante independiente v. Morse. Some Anglo; don't know him at all; most prob. a Bascom or Edgerton type brought in for the very purpose. (All I've seen so far are a few handbills.) This comes on top of Ira Escobar's resolute opposition and so M.T.'s going to have to come up with some more cash. (This is going to cost plenty money, Papa-san, como nos decían en **Big J**.) What we bankers call 'an unforeseen cash flow'. (Ira, by the way, isn't sweating the new guy in the race and *that's* a surprise.)

Now then, if one adds this to el dineral que se está gastando en Ira, uno tiene que decir that there's more to this than meets the jaundiced eye. I mean, *it's a lot of money for one county seat,* son.

Por ahora todo es conjecture y yo tengo poca información pero, and this you can't deny: You and I know de dónde vienen los golpes &, of course, quién los da. What is missing is the how and the when.

Here's el último clavo in the box of this grand historical design: la printing shop de nuestro viejo patrón misspelled —misspelled, for God's sake— M.T.'s name. No, no tuvo que pagar, pero para qué decirte más: se tardaron dos (quizá tres) semanas para reponer todo y para ese tiempo allí estaba Ira Escobar's smiling face all over the place; y antes de que se me olvide, Morse tuvo que esperarse dos o tres días over and above the due date por falta de tinta. Sí, y estoy contigo, todo puede ser una gran coincidencia. ¿Y si no?

Noddy me cuenta muy poco (it being none of my business) and, besides, I'm just a hired hand, as they say. So, officially, no sé nada.

Bueno, aquí la cierro. Pórtate b. que poco te cue.

Abrazos, J.

12

Mi querido Rafa:

A Relámpago y al Carmen; Israel y Aarón y las familias bien; en Relám visité las tierras y la casa vieja de doña Enriqueta; por casualidad allí andaban Angela Vielma y tu cuñada Delfina. Hablamos de ti & a good time was had by all como dicen los mejores escritores de tarjetas postales. Tu cuñada se ve de lo más contenta y quién no al deshacerse de Rómulo; una verdadera joya ese muchacho.

Por si te interesa (cosa que dudo de todo corazón) Rómulo is now a very uncivil servant at the International Bridge; trabaja y vive en Jonesville. Ya no es parte de la familia, of course, pero según las muchachas, Rómulo cae por aquí de vez en cuando. Me acuerdo que de tus concuños, éste era tu favorito. ¡Los hay con suerte!

De Relámpago, Olivia y yo le seguimos por el river road hasta el camino que se divide rumbo a Flora o a Klail; decidimos ir a Flora a cenar; needless to say, vimos y vimos Ira's smiling countenance all the way to Flora. ¿Y cómo evitar a tantos Iras Escobar?

Después a Klail, and so to bed.

A short note, but a telling one: Israel y Aarón están dispuestos a repartir tus tierras y a pasárselas a los que tú nombres. And that's it.

Abrazos,
Jehú

13

Mi querido Rafa:

Faltan tres semanas y unos días para las elecciones famosas y al llegar al banco, a sealed envelope on my desk:

Jehú:
As soon as you come in, come by the Ranch. Bring your briefcase and mine. Tell one of the girls to call ahead that you're on your way.

N.

Dicho y hecho.

El viaje es cosa de media hora; llego, no hay ningún carro en frente de la casa grande; le rodeo por la izquierda —sure enough— no menos de ocho carros y pickups in front of the bathhouse behind the pool and the bar.

Son las nueve menos diez y los cowboys han estado tomando café desde antes de las seis. De seguro. And who do I see there? A Morse Terry, that's who.

It's all stiffly cordial if not exactly friendly. No veía qué vela tenía yo en ese happy entierro pero allí andaba & ever watchful.

Strange. No. No todo lo que *tú* dijiste ni tampoco *cómo* lo describiste en tu última, but close enough.

Este fin de semana, Olivia y yo, como sabes, andábamos para arriba y para abajo pero del viernes al domingo por la noche a Morse le ajustaron unos botones y ciertos tornillos, and so, se vino a ver a Noddy. (Sooner or later todo mundo cae por aquí.) Morse vino con el sombrero en la mano.

Como chief loan officer, and thus as an officer of the bank, doy one of the three 'yea/nay' votes y por consiguiente mi presencia. My say so not needed, of course, but it looks good. Mise en scène: todo quieto y el único ruido de vez en c. era un clavado de Sammie Jo en su heated pool. En la sala todo muy formal. Un préstamo a M.T. por $67,000, por seis años, at preferred loan risk rates, y con hipoteca hasta las nalgas. (Election account, miscellaneous expense.)

Un cabrón hanger-on iba a ser el cosigner pero hasta allí el insulto a M.T. Sugerí a otra persona; yo vi mi presencia allí como un message a mí, aunque algo indirecto y me comporté como si tal cosa fuera lo más natural del mundo. (But I, too, sure as hell wasn't going to sign that note; and, anyway, it would have been against bank policy, right? As for the message, it was prob. a signal, although I'm still a bit in the blind as of right now.)

Aquello era de película; Morse debe ser de nuestra edad pero se veía mas viejo. Noddy applied the make-up, set the scene, and steered the direction. Como Noddy me dijo mas tarde: "It's no mystery . . . it's all very simple". And so it was:

Mira, del viernes al domingo por la noche, cosa de 48 horas, M.T. recibió veinte, '20 Count 'em 20' llamadas de clientes y compañías entre grandes y pequeñas que él representa como abogado. Que estaban pensando, muy seriamente, retirar su negocio. No explication, no explanation.

Entre la última o la penúltima llamada, se le sugirió que 'he would do himself and all of us a favor if he would call Mr. Perkins'.

Aflojó las corvas y lo llamó. (Lo del préstamo is just Noddy's way of doing business, and you *were* right about M.T. caving in.)

And there you have it, but as you prob. suspect, hay más. There always is, isn't there? Here it is:

Noddy quiere que M.T. vaya a Washington. Just Like That.

You see, at first I thought it was Noddy's revenge for past deeds, or hate, even, but no, no hay odio. No hay nada.

And, will you look at this:

El diputado del distrito (a quien tú conoces bien y a su sobrina Sophie un poco más) sigue siendo Hap Bayliss. Hap (según Noddy) está muy enfermo. "The man's dying, Jehú. You're one of the few who knows how sick he is . . ."

Puede ser. Puede ser que yo sea uno de los pocos AND puede ser que Hap se esté muriendo. With Noddy you never know. Now, I do know some things I shouldn't, and I now wonder if Noddy knows I know . . . no, no, that way lies madness.

Como quiera que sea, aquí está el evangelio according to Saint Noddy who, by the way, is taking a few days off "from all this". Cabrón, ¿eh?

M.T. va a ganar el puesto de Hap, and he'll do it as a write-in candidate. That's right. All of this will be announced in good time.

This, of course, paves the way for Ira to get the Commissioner's post; and it also gets Ira out of the way. Pero, PERO, none of this will be put en marcha until no se le dé un susto pesado y chingón a Ira Escobar. That, too, is just Noddy's way of doing business . . .

Esta noche, perhaps as I write this, se van a hacer veinte lla-madas a Ira (here we go again) diciendo que van a crossover to the independent side. Es decir, que no lo van a respaldar. Ira, of course, knows nothing re M.T.'s deal with Noddy & nothing whatsoever re Hap Bayliss.

You can imagine the pedorrón knowing Ira's temperament and ASPIRATIONS . . . A todo esto, el answering service de Noddy will announce to please leave a message until Mr. Perkins can get back to the caller . . .

So, Noddy'll be gone for the next three-four days.

We're up to date on this, & no tengo más que decirte.

Pasando a otra cosa: por las noches voy botando cartas, notas, papelaje and the usual junk que he venido acumulando por años. Few things will survive this purge. Not to worry; me siento bien; it's just a bit of cleaning up that needs to be done.

Abrazos,
Jehú

14

Mi querido Rafa:

Loan and Arrangements Day with M.T. plus four. For all purposes, todavía no se sabe re el convenio Bayliss-Perkins-Terry, y el pobre de Ira anda como loco loquito extraviado. Los retratos siguen en su lugar and apparently nothing has changed. To top it, ayer Ira me contó que Becky se había ido a pasar unos días en Jonesville. A todo esto, Ira hasn't taken me into his confidence re the phone calls.

The election is now two weeks off & Ira thinks he's losing ground. He's not, but *he* thinks he is. Ira no me preguntó ni por Noddy ni por el número de su private line; Ira was in a bad way, but it promised to get worse. For your information: Noddy had flown up to William Barrett International to meet Hap B. Hap then flew back to Washington, and Noddy buzzed in late last night; he called and said he wanted to see me at the Ranch fairly early. He sounded happy, and that's always a bad sign.

Hoy por la mañana a eso de las once, it starts again: I'm at the Ranch with a pile of papers for Noddy to sign and N. calls Ira. Éste, por poco, se desmaya; I mean I could *hear* the breathing! Noddy le dice que *acaba de* llegar from out of town y que tiene unos cien recados que llame a Ira. You must realize that Noddy is looking straight at me when he's talking to Ira. Para que conozcas para Noddy: "Hey, Ira, you're not thinking of dropping out of the race, are you?"

Otro soponcio de Ira y el espléndido de Noddy pregunta por Becky (knowing full well) y luego le ofrece su chofer para que vaya por él. Ira's in no condition pero aguarda el carro que lo ha de conducir a la cueva del león. The chauffeur must have taken the long way home 'cause Noddy and I talked business, and he signed papers, for over an hour and Ira still wasn't at the Ranch. For all I know, Noddy planned it that way; pero no me hagas caso; I don't live in Paranoiaville, just one of the suburbs.

Para cuando llegó Ira a la casa, Noddy was all smiles, but it looked bad: he was using that low voice of his.

Para darle fin a ésta, Noddy le dijo a Ira que Ira andaba diciendo que él no le debía favores a nadie y que había llegado a donde estaba por sus propios huevos, etc. And then, in that low voice, "Now that's what I call downright ungrateful, Ira".

Pobre cabrón, but *he* wanted the job, right?

Noddy lo sentó y entonces le explicó, en esa voz, ce por be cómo corría el agua en Belken; que quién se encargaba de las compuertas; que quién era el señor aguador; que quién decidía a cuáles acequias se les daba agua y a cuáles no; y cuánta agua y también cuándo; y etceterit y etceterot. Así. Noddy habla de agua pero hasta el más lerdo sabe perfectamente de qué se está hablando.

Aquí la mocho . . . acaba de llamar Olivia. One last thing: I don't think I'm going to last here much longer; I don't have the stomach for it.

Por pendejo que sea Ira, he's still a human being.

Abrazos,
Jehú

15

Mi querido Rafa:

It's a good thing I've got a private office at the bank, and one more thing: a little Christian charity, cousin. Escucha: si sigues riéndote, burlándote así, a carcajadas, se te va a caer al parche del ojo, y luego, ¿qué vas a hacer? Anyway, thanks for the call this morning.

Ésta no te la puedo dividir on an hour by hour's basis —que por interesante que sea— no tengo todo el tiempo del mundo, como unos que conozco, and how's that for an indirecta?

Martes: Nine days to countdown.

Para empezar: Por radio y televisión se organiza un write-in campaign for Morse Terry who, as you know, is now going after Hap Bayliss's seat on Noddy's say-so; Hap announced he was ill. I, too, will be less than charitable and say he got sick at William Barrett International after his meeting with N.P. One more thing for your kit bag: Hap himself is leading the write-in campaign for M.T. Y así se hacen las cosas: bien o no se hacen y a ver dónde se meten, right?

Los anuncios políticos pagados, as they say, se ven y se oyen en cada estación: en esp. y en ing. Cada estación hasta deletrea el nombre de Morse, luego lo repiten y lo vuelven a deletrear and, in order not to miss anyone, por fin sale escrito en la pantalla del televisor. (A todo esto, Ira's in like a second story man as Comm. Pl. 3, pero me parece que aún no sabe qué pasa o qué está pasando; the man's dead to the world. Tenía la victoria en la mano, luego NP vino y se la quitó and then NP came right back and handed it to him again; it's more than our boy can take. But, as you and I laughed about it this morning, it was Washington all the time and all the way. Tenemos mucho que aprender.)

Lo que te digo: he'll win big with Morse and the strawman out of the way, pero NP le chupó todo el jugo y sabor a esa naranja ombligona. And, of course, Ira no sabe nada de nada. De nada. Morse, aunque no asoma ni la cara ni la nariz por aquí, no se pierde de contacto con Noddy; Noddy le ha dicho que no se esté a más de seis pies del teléfono, and so, allí está Morse: prisionero en su propia casa. (En Washington casi era lo mismo; como le dijo Noddy: "We're just a phone call away, Mor".)

To touch lightly on what you said: Sí, tienes razón, sé demasiado, and sí, you're so right: me tengo que cuidar y, también de acuerdo: Noddy can run me off cuando le dé la regalada gana.

One thing, though, no tengo cuentas, ni pendientes (etymologically speaking) ni nada. Un consuelo es *saber* que NP me puede correr cuando quiera y *otro* es saber que yo bien me puedo ir igual que como entré aquí hace tres años: con una mano adelante y otra atrás, but through the front door & without dragging any shit behind me

¿Y mi Ira? Pobre cabrón —y lo digo por decir no porque lo hice cabrón ya que eso fue asunto de Becky. (Tú tenías mucha razón and, if anything, Becky era (es) más fácil de lo que tú me decías . . . you ought to consider going on the radio with la Hermana Buenaventura and tell the future . . . But, she doesn't rank among the best; lo que ofrece es la conocida furia mexicana. ¿Pero quién se queja? A one-shot affair y no espero que se repita aunque you never can tell.)

Ahí está el radio otra vez: no te digo, they're flooding *all* the stations. On both sides of the River, natch.

Esta noche el último rally pa' la raza en el parque; allí, para asegurarse un poco más, hasta habrá instrucciones en los dos idiomas de cómo deletrear el nombre de Morse Terry. (Five will get you ten that the elec. judges will count *anything* that resembles M.T.'s name . . . Y como preguntó el cura, ¿Sería esa la primera vez?)

Mr. Polín Tapia, who else, is the head cheerleader tonight. And *that,* cousin, is how the systems works around here. Sometimes.

Ah, antes de que se me olvide: no habrá rinches en el Valle para las elecciones; a sign of the times dirían los optimistas; a sign from Noddy diría yo.

A otra cosa. Hoy, en el banco, se asomó Sanford Blanchard, 'el terror de las criadas'. Tan alky como su prima Blanche; since it's a

family corp., Old Borrachín es uno de los directores; vota por proxy
y asunto concluido. Sidney (Sammie Jo's No. 2) stayed inside the car
while Sanford came to see Noddy. Se recomienda hablar por teléf.
sobre esto.

Al cabrón de Sanford ya no se le para, pero en sus días correotea-
ba a todas las criadas mexicanas, guatemaltecas y nicaragüenses que
se traían al Rancho; a lot of shit in that Ranch, cousin, y yo soy parte
de ello —pero anda tú; ¿crees, in your heart of hearts, que nuestros
amigos de la raza me ayudarían si necesitara chamba de repente?
Aside from Viola, no lo hicieron cuando pudieron, and now? No; I'm
not buying three pounds of shit in a two-pound bag. Les debemos
ceb., Rafa.

'Fools and knaves
On the breakfast table . . .'

¿Te ríes, verdad? But that's it, son. La raza es medio cabrona
cuando quiere, and I'm fresh out of brotherly love. Los has de ver;
(¿nos has de ver?). Hay poca vergüenza en este Valle.

No me pongas mucho cuidado; son cosas mías. Si hay algo
mañana, o pasado, te escribo; si no, te escribo al recibir otra tuya.
Una cosa es de seguro: aquí no pasan dos días sin acción.

Abrazos,
Jehú

16

Mi querido Rafa:

¿Y qué has pasado en los últimos seis días? Nada damn thing, as they say. Los anuncios re M.T. siguen, éste no sale de su casa (we're as close as your etc.) y mi Ira is one shaken young man. (Becky es president del Woman's Club, and how is that for a quemón? Recibió un silver plate con su nombre y toda la cosa: muchos honores. And yes, I saw her again —¿y qué?) Ira todavía no puede entender que la elección es un cinch; todavía cree que algo va a pasar. Noddy doesn't know what a good job he did on Ira . . . WHAT AM I SAYING? Of *course* he knows. He just enjoys seeing Ira hop, is all.

Las elecciones, and there must be another word for them, are two days away.

Acá entre nosotros. Llevo cinco-seis días de no ver a Oli; she's not returning my calls . . . No tenemos compromiso fijo, of course, pero yo (al menos *yo*) creía que la cosa se pondría seria —a no ser que Becky blabbed. I take that back. Still, where there's smoke, there's pedo. So . . .

The phone just rang; it was Sammie Jo; wants to talk. I'll continue this tomorrow.

J.

Here I am again.

Mañana son las elecciones (and I'll be glad when that's done). Bayliss (ayer maybe anteayer) anunció que está enfermísimo y dio su bendición just one more time a M.T. for those who didn't understand the first twenty times or so. Bonus: ahora hay videotapes y los

179

anuncios se ven en muchas tiendas de Klail City; yep, we have two monitors in the bank: one in the coffee shop and one smack dab in the middle of everything. Hap endorses his young, talented, & long-time friend, Morse Terry. Endlessly. And, speaking of which, M.T. me llamó por teléf. esta mañana y después vino al banco en pers.

Think on this y dame tu parecer: M.T. quiere que yo vaya a Washington a trabajar en su oficina. Movida de Noddy, I'm sure. Bribe? Could be. Anyway, I did thank M.T., but no thanks.

Así van las cosas —still no word from Oli; llamo y dejo recado but not even a scratch single.

Long day tomorrow. Qué te sigas mejorando y recibe un abrazo de

Jehú

17

Mi querido Rafa:

Election Day plus two and God's in his heaven and Noddy's in *his;* regarding each other with suspicion, one would imagine.

Pues sí, it's in all the papers y no te traigo noticias que tú no sepas. Ahora solamente es asunto de pick up the pieces and the litter.

Our newest commissioner is more restrained, less exuberant, as it were —eso de 'as it were' es frasecita de Ira; le gusta y la usa venga o no al caso. Sorry, no free samples. Si no se cuida, la gente le va a poner *Asitwere,* at the very least.

Dos días como comisionado y ya dice cosas como 'early on' y 'within these walls' y 'in that context' y qué sé yo; juraría que hay un librito con toda esa cagada y que Ira se lo va a aprender de memoria —hablando de memoria, it would appear that Oli has dropped me like a hot brick, to coin a phrase. Por carta, tú. I done struck out, Coach, and it do look bad.

Esta tarde antes de cerrar, Noddy came by: me invitó a una cena at the Big House (and, bring a friend, Jehú). I guess the old sumbitch knows. Anyway, la cena será mañana por la noche. Como sabrás, I can hardly wait; no sé quién más irá pero sospecho que irán, entre otros, Ira and Becky, Morse Terry and his wife (Bedelia Boyer, de gratas memorias, según tú); lo único que dijo Noddy era que it was going to be just a few of us. Of us?

Translation: It's important to all concerned.

I'll see where I fit in; there'll be no masks tomorrow night, pero con Noddy, who's to know.

Ya te contaré.

Abrazos,
Jehú

18

Mi querido Rafa:

Te acabo de llamar, and, as always, nada, and so I'll write. (Te llamé anoche, después de la *cena,* pero sin resultado. What the hell kind of a hospital are they running up there?) These may be late news, but since they're not out yet, they're as fresh and crisp and crinkly as a one-dollar bill.

Here we go: *Ya habían cenado todos para cuando yo llegué.* Llegué a las ocho (the time set for dinner by Noddy) y el asunto tomó menos de tres minutos, tops.

Becky no levantó la visita (the whole time), los Terry ni chistearon (no surprise there) & Ira was studying the Utrillo on the wall. An art lover, yet.

Noddy made it short: "Jehú, I recommend that you resign as loan officer".

I didn't say a word; the shock, needless to say.

Me salí de allí con la cola fruncida; volví a casa y de pendejo me puse a pensar que qué sería el motivo, but then realized that I was doing what Noddy *wanted* and *expected* me to do: to worry about *why.* Oh, he's a bastard all right, I'll give him that.

He's also a good teacher, and I'll give him that, too. A ver qué aprendo de esto.

Going to bed, son, cansado & whether I want to admit it or not, shaky. No creí que me doliera salir del banco. ¡Qué cabrón! Lo hizo en frente de todos. That was it! He didn't do it alone . . . he *couldn't* do it alone. Te apuesto que Ira & Becky & the Terrys were as surprised (shocked?) as I was . . . That's got to be it. ¡Qué cabrón, man!

I knew he was good, but I kept underrating him . . . but now I know: I also overrated him.

Day after tomorrow: To the Bank, as if nothing happened. Monday's Armistice Day and it's a bank holiday; I'll try to call you and get this on the phone.

Abrazos,
Jehú

19

Mi querido Rafa:

Lo quisquilloso, como decía don Víctor Peláez, era salir bien; salir disparado del banco se vería mal & I'd have a hell of a time getting another job. Anywhere around here. I did what I *had* to do.

Fui a ver a Noddy as usual y le dije que quería volver al Klail Savings and Loan. "It's out of my hands, Jehú". Le dije que no; he said yes. Le dije que yo me vería mal si él me despedía así nomás. "You brought that on yourself, Jehú". No rebatí porque de ahí nos iríamos a dimes y diretes, and I'd lose there; no question. Entonces, yo, que me agarraba de chorros de agua para detenerme, lo atajé: "Does my firing have to do with sex, Noddy?"

Se me quedó viendo por un rato larguísimo (his favorite ploy) y luego explotó:

"You Mexican son-of-a-bitch!"

But I was ready: Hace diez —quizá cinco— años le hubiera rajado la cara y la madre; esta vez no. Lo que hice fue sentarme; crucé las piernas y le dije: "You may as well hear it straight from me: Becky and I had a couple of tussles, but that was it".

"Becky? Who the hell said anything about Becky Escobar, goddammit!"

Y yo: "Then who the hell *are* you talking about? And it sure as hell better not be Ollie cause that's *my* business . . . Goddammit".

"Ollie? San Esteban? I'm talking about Sammie Jo, goddammit!"

"Sammie Jo? You've got a hold of some bad shit there, Noddy".

"*Bull*shit".

"Bull*shit*. Let's call her —better still— let's you and I go on out there. Goddammit".

"You . . ."

"Hold on, Noddy. You *know* I'm telling the truth . . . It's something *else,* isn't it?"

Of course, the man was absolutely right. But he was bluffing.

The old son-of-a-bitch *knew* I was going to come over to the bank. Me conoce. He knew I was coming over; I swear it. But I was ready for him. This time.

"You gonna make a speech?"

Mira qué cabrón . . . back against the wall but still full of fight. Me reí y estaba por irme cuando me detuvo: "You know it hurts like hell".

"Bullshit, Noddy".

"Okay, okay; let me start over: so you and Becky . . ."

"Sure; twice, maybe three times; I don't know".

"Don't *know?*"

"No! Who counts? Look, Noddy, I haven't done anything you wouldn't have done at my age. And: we'll get into that Mexican son-of-a-bitch thing at another time".

"And what makes you think you're still working here?"

"Well, you haven't thrown me out yet".

Con eso el muy hijo de su chingada madre se rio (& that's the *closest* he'll ever come to an apology).

So, it's settled; I'm back at the bank and not at the S. & L.

Of course, now he knows about Becky; eso sí, cuando sepa lo de Sammie Jo, then it'll really be my ass.

¿No te parece?

Abrazos,
Jehú

20

Mi querido Rafa:

Gracias por la llamada and for the congratulations. I think that congratulations when dealing with NP must wait some five to ten years. No te desprende tan fácilmente.

Anyway, a ver si Oli y yo hacemos ese viaje a William Barrett. It's on between us again, but on a different footing. Ya te avisaré de todo esto y del viaje.

Por acá todo bien: Ira desempeña su trabajo by crossing each 't' and by dotting every little old 'i'; antes lo hacía al revés, but Ira, if nothing else, is dutiful.

Noddy anda para Colorado; went to pick up Mrs. P. y a tomar unos días de vacaciones; el banco y el trabajo regular; pienso irme por mi propia cuenta en un par de meses. No sé qué haré inmediatamente y no quiero hacer planes luego luego. Just like that; no big announcement.

I guess I can't breathe here y si me voy, me voy por mi propia cuenta —this time.

Ira me ve y no sabe qué hacer de todo esto. Am I here or am I not?

Lo de Sammie Jo terminó, and I'm sure she won't go out & kill herself. Face it: I'm just one in a long string. Still, she's a good stick and, as we say, buena gente. De Becky ni hablar; she's now in the Club and we're both out of each other's hair. As it were.

And, I guess that when Beck and I are both sixty years old, we'll look back on this and laugh about it. ¿Tú crees?

Viola Barragán, el azote del Valle, pasó por aquí como chiflón de aire: "¿Que te casas con la hija de Emilio San Esteban? Me alegro . . ." Luego prendió un cigarro y me dijo: "Necesitamos business manager, ¿sabes? El día que te quieras largar de aquí, me avisas. Me voy, me voy . . . ah, y que no se te olvide mandarme invitación al casorio, ¿oíste?" No idea where she heard *that.* En Klail no falta. But there's not a bit of truth to it.

De todos modos, Oli y yo iremos a verte a William Barrett como quiera; that's still on.

Abrazos,
Jehú

21

Mi querido Rafa:

Ein feste Burg ist unser Klail; impregnable, too.

Cuando te digo que veo este pueblo y este condado y no lo creo, es que ya es demasiado, even for me. Lo de la elección fue un circo; la gente ya no habla de otra cosa. Después de atole, of course.

Ayer, ya tarde y después del trabajo, vine a mi cuartito con el propósito de limpiar, quemar, botar, etc. los papeles que me restan así como todo el mugrero that survived the last purge.

Es curioso el proceso de acumulación. Discarding is more in my line, though.

Al canasto con todo lo que sea: fuera. Y, si te vi y te conocí, ya no me acuerdo de ti. Who wrote that?

Me pasé tres horas, bien pueden ser más, llevando bolsas de mandado amén de los cestos y cajas de cartón. Limpia total.

Ni te podré explicar por qué lo hice o cómo me puse a hacerlo; just one of those things.

Estoy hasta aquí de las elecciones, de las pláticas, y etc. y etc. No pienso salir por dos o tres noches; siempre leo, you know me, pero ahora voy a releer más y más. I think I need that. I think I need to see, to think where it is dónde voy con mi vida. There must be something else other than el camino lento y sosegado al camposanto de Nuestra Señora de la Merced. There must be.

Not to worry; no es nada grave; se trata solamente de esas cosas que pasan y ya.

Y no creas que fue tu carta o la visita; I needed that visit, and I needed to be with Oli more than just overnight.

I'll be okay.

Abrazos,
Jehú

22

Mi querido Rafa:

Israel y Aarón me cayeron aquí la semana pasada; no les dije nada pero sé muy bien que fueron cosas tuyas. Y como casi nunca contestas el teléfono, no se te puede hablar o insultar. Como quiera que sea: gracias.

Me dio mucho gusto en verlos pero como vinieron preocupados por mí eso por poco amarga la ocasión. But we had fun, ya sabes.

Desde mi ventana veo pasar a medio Klail, but only cuando me da la gana. Pero ya estoy bien, and I am about ready to decide.

Hoy es ya el tercer día que no voy al banco; tomé otros tres días off esta semana pero mañana al desk de nuevo.

Por ahora, recibe un abrazo de tu primo,

Jehú.

Parte II

Sondas y ciertos hallazgos de P. Galindo

23

Polín Tapia

Es de la edad del esc. y se conocen desde años. De Polín se dijo, y bien puede ser que haya sido don Abdón Bermúdez, que con él conviene contarse las uñas después de saludarlo de mano. Nada caritativa la frasecita de don Abdón aunque quizá tampoco muy desviada del blanco.

Tapia vive de la política y cae mal a mucha gente; por otro lado, Federico 'Chancla' Ruiz vive de lo mismo y simpatiza. Bien puede ser que esto se deba al estilo de la persona.

El esc., equidad, equidad, es todo oídos: el esc. se contenta primero y luego se conforma con tratar de extraer la verdad; la fuente le es igual.

"¿Por dónde empezar, Galindo? ¿Con las elecciones está bien? Vamos a ver . . . Allá cuando Ira Escobar decidió definitivamente correr pa' comisionado y luego consiguió el respaldo del Rancho y del banco, yo me ofrecí para lo que fuera a su candidatura. Uno tiene que espabilarse en estos casos y tú bien sabes que yo tengo cierto talento para esto; se me deben ciertos favores y de vez en cuando los mando cobrar: hoy por ti, mañana por mí. Pa' qué te cuento a ti de esto si tú ya lo sabes y quizá mejor que yo, ¿verdad?"

Al esc. no le gusta la canchola; además, el esc. es un ignorante que hasta hace muy poco se dio cuenta de que sabe menos todos los días.

"Bueeeeeeeeeeeeeeno . . . Ira decide enfrentarse contra Morse Terry —palabras mayores— y a quien yo conozco muy bien también. Bueno, la lucha es mucha, como dice el tango, pero uno aprieta, arrima el hombro, y no se raja . . . . Como sabes, Ira ganó y ganó bien; ahora, que Bayliss se haya enfermado y que Morse haya ganado la otra elección a base de write in, eso no es culpa mía. Si uno hubiera sabido o si uno pudiera predecir el futuro ¡ja! el Ira sale Congressman en vez de comisionado. Por esta cruz. Pero comisionado es comisionado y Belken no es cualquier condado muerto de hambre, como el condado de Dellis, digamos. Además, por alguna parte se debe empezar la carrera política, ¿eh?

"Los muchachos y las muchachas del banco todos tiraron parejo y trabajaron como esclavos. El que no dio golpe fue Jehú Malacara. Como lo oyes. No le pedí que trabajara pero viendo como todos hacían el esfuerzo, ¿tú crees que tomó las indirectas? Ni por pienso. Y no creas que se hiciera el desentendido: una vez me vio en el banco y me dijo que me dejara de andar *jodiendo*. ¡Ja! P's no que fue a la universidad de Texas —¿así los educan por allá?"

El esc. no tiene la menor idea de cómo se educa por allá.

"¡Bah! A Jehú *yo* lo conozco desde que la hacía de barrendero en donde los Chagos. ¿A poco ya se le olvidó? ¡Bah! Mira, yo no le digo a él cómo haga su trabajo en el banco. ¿Pa' qué se mete conmigo?

"Ira es de lo mejor; sabe reírse y me trata con consideración y a veces hasta me deja manejar su carro. ¡Ja! Y Jehú ni carro tiene —porque lo que es ese MG verde, ése no es de él, es de la farmacéutica.

"Jehú, en mi opinión, está acostumbrado a que todo le caiga bien puesto. A la medida. Ya quisiera saber lo que es el trabajo . . .

"Esto no es crítica, Galindo. En la política uno se acostumbra a valorizar, evaluar, ¿eh? Eso no indica rencor. Tú, como periodista y escritor, sabes de eso".

Se le insiste al lector que el esc. es un ignorante, que no sabe nada.

"Jehú trabaja en el banco, tiene un puesto de más o menos responsabilidad, lleva más tiempo allí que Ira Escobar, pero Ira, por su persona, y según él me lo contó, ganaba más que Jehú. Al entrar al banco ves a Ira inmediatamente; a Jehú no; a Jehú me lo tenían en una oficina chiquita cerca de la grande de Norberto Perkins.

"Ira es buena gente; él ni se *arrima* al *Aquí me quedo* y menos al *Blue.* Jehú, sí. Mira: tú, como periodista, puedes ir a donde te dé la gana; pero ¿Jehú? Jehú era oficial de un *banco,* h'mbre. Se desprestigiaba y ni le importaba.

"Y esa risa de él a mí no me engaña; ésa es risa de burla. Como lo oyes. Ni que fuera rey, tú . . . .

"Mi papá y mi tío nunca, pero nunca, ¿me oyes?, nunca lo ocuparon en la tienda porque Jehú no era consecuente ni serio; allí hay que estar limpiando los muebles y las lavadoras y todo lo demás. 'Una mueblería vive de su brillo', decía mi Papá. No; Jehú no hubiera dado la medida en ese tipo de trabajo.

"Acá, entre nosotros, te diré algo en confianza: Ira, aunque sea gordito, es Don Pantalones; yo conozco a Jehú y bien le fue que no le puso los ojos a Becky Escobar. Bien le fue. Es que no conoce a Ira Escobar. ¡Ira lo hubiera capado! ¿Tú crees que no?"

El esc. no cree en nada.

"Hablando en plata nacional, yo no sé si lo corrieron del banco o qué. Pero esto sí te diré: uno no deja una chamba así nomás porque sí. De repente. Tú dirás".

El esc. que ya no es ningún niño, se ha quedado de una pieza. Será de más decir que Polín Tapia le cobra cierto encono a Jehú. Ahora bien, Polín también habla con plena sinceridad y con cierta soltura. De que se exprese a sus anchas revela, quizá, la confianza que le tiene al esc.

De eso se trata, de apuntar todo para que el lector llegue a sus propias conclusiones sin que el esc. lo lleve apersogado.

24

Ira Escobar

Co-trabajador en el Klail City First National con Jehú; comisionado invicto por el precinto núm. 3 y esposo y marido (para cementar) de Rebecca Escobar née Caldwell. Ira se mostró reacio de primero pero no tardó en dar su parecer en el caso.

"Sí; lo conozco bien; I've, ah, I've helped him out a couple of times, or I did . . . he was the loan officer, but he, ah, he needed help once in a while. And, what are friends for, as I always say.

"I can't say he was much interested in politics though he read quite a bit; at least I always had the impression he read quite a bit. Know what I mean?

"We never, well, seldom at any rate, we ah, seldom saw each other socially except for bank parties or political barbecues . . . He just never did take the barbecues seriously; he ah, he thought they were one big joke, you know. I really don't understand why Noddy, (El esc. notó que el declarante dobló la cara primero a la derecha y luego a la izquierda) Mr. Perkins, Noddy . . . no sé por qué lo ocupó. I mean, he, Jehú, had a certain flair for this type of work, but ah . . ."

El esc. se quedó esperando pero la oración del declarante terminó en un suspiro.

"We got along well, though. At first, my wife cared for him, but after a couple of times or so, she hardly mentioned him at all, and she hasn't talked to Jehú for the last eight months or so. Anyway, Becky my wife is, ah, usually pretty busy with her work at the Club, and she works late once or twice a week. And, I was busy on my own campaign . . . which turned out well, you know. So, the two of us, Becky and I, didn't exactly snub Jehú; we just simply didn't see much of him".

El esc. ruega que se le perdone otra interrupción pero la cree necesaria y casi de urgencia: no se debe pensar mal de la Becky ya que bien pudo estar trabajando asiduamente en el Woman's Club o en el Club, como dice I.E.

"As loan officer, Jehú saw more of Mr. Per . . . of, ah, Noddy, than I did; my desk handles the small loans and some automobile notes, as well. I guess you know that I'd only been on the job a week or so when I was asked to consider running for Commissioner for Place Three. You *must* have seen my pictures, right? I mean, they were fairly well plastered all over the place from Jonesville to Edgerton (risita) and from Relámpago on over to Ruffing (otra risita). I like politics; it's a man's responsibility, and it's also a way to do public service, don't you agree?"

El esc. tiene pocas opiniones que favorezcan a la política y ni una de sobra para los políticos. Es una de las muchas faltas del esc.

"When Noddy, ah, (otro movimiento leve de la cabeza) informed me that Jehú was leaving, he, Mr. Per . . . Noddy, ah, didn't *exactly* offer me the senior loan officer's post, but he, Noddy, ah, did say that with my added duties at the county level, that I, ah, would be far too busy with that end of it to be *chained* to the loan officer's desk.

"I think I could handle both, but it could be that the Old Man (sonrisa de conejo en plegaria), I mean, that *Noddy,* you see, is right . . . Still, I mean, if Jehú did it, I could too, *right?*

"I'm not putting him down or anything, but I could handle it . . . I'm sure, I could.

"As for Jehú again, well, he, ah . . . he had a certain difficulty of expression . . . an impediment. You know what I mean? His, ah, his English was a bit weak now and then, and that would've held him back had he stayed on here . . .

"Look, I wouldn't mind talking to you some more on this, but I do have a luncheon date over at the, ah, the Camelot . . . right?

El esc. está de acuerdo con el lector: Ira ni mencionó la cena en casa de Noddy tiempo atrás. El esc. piensa que no ha de probar esta fuente por segunda vez.

25

Martín San Esteban

Farmacéutico, estudió en Austin con Rafa y Jehú, hermano no mucho mayor que Olivia, se casó con una de las muchachas del matrimonio Pedro Ycaza, de los de Ruffing. Martín nació en Klail y se crió en Edgerton. Volvió a Klail como farmacéutico en compañía de su hermana. Como es natural dado a su edad y formación, Martín discurre mucho mejor en inglés.

"We go a long way back, Jehú and I . . . before Austin, the Army even, and Jehú's always been like that. I don't think he dated Ollie that much up at Austin . . . He and Rafa lived in that crazy place off Guadalupe and 26th the last two years; it was an awful place. I roomed with my cousin at Mrs. Bloomquist's . . . Do you know my cousin Juan? Santoscoy? Well, the four of us used to run around at the University some; but neither Jehú nor Rafa were much for dances.

"I'll tell you, one time Rafa and Jehú and a guy from Mexico —he was from some town in Coahuila— anyway, they made beer, you know, home brew? They made it *right* in the room. God, they must've made close to ten cases of the stuff. It was dark; strong, too.

"Austin wasn't that big, then, you know. You could usually run into Jehú over on the West Mall . . . and his first year there, he lived in that house over by Scottish Rite Dorm; *that* was a madhouse. I think those guys were all communists or socialists. Jesus! Jehú *loved* it; Rafa usually just sat there, drinking his beer, talking now and then. Those guys were mostly from South America or Mexicans from across. You know what we called 'em? Filipinos . . . I don't know why. I don't even know who *started* that.

"But Jehú was an English major; I'm not even sure he wanted to teach at the time. I'll tell you, I had no idea *what* he was going to do with that *degree* . . . Juan and I were both in pharmacy, and we *knew* we had a job; and then Mom and Dad helped Ollie and me here in Klail . . .

"Ollie . . . Ollie's been talking to Jehú and now she's got it into her head about going up to Galveston. I mean, she wants to *apply* to *med* school. Shoot, we've got business enough *here* already . . . and for two *more* pharmacists if we wanted to . . .

"Jehú's like that, though. I mean, no sooner did he get in at Klail High than he started thinking about something *else.* He's lucky, though, I'll say that. He usually manages to land pretty good jobs; he just doesn't stick to 'em; look at the bank, for example. Man, *allí lo apreciaban,* you know. And Ira's not a bad guy to work for even though he's an Aggie (risa de Martín) but that's a joke . . .

"Now Ollie says Jehú wants to get a Master's degree . . . What do you *do* with a Master's in English? I mean, he's already taught at the high school, and he could probably go back, but to go back to *that?* Shoot! The job at the bank *pays* better . . . I just hope he didn't do anything there to screw it up. No, no, I'm not saying he did; I'm just saying that it wouldn't look good for the mexicanos if he did, see? But Jehú's *honest.* He's *crazy,* but he's honest.

"I have no idea what he and *Ollie* talk about. He was *hell* in Austin, though. But I'll tell you, con Olivia se friega; she's a mexicana . . .

"Have you heard from Rafa? He and I were kind of tight up at Austin for a while; he's just too *goddam* quiet at times, man. ¡Jijo! He's steady, though. Boy, he and Jehú made quite a pair . . . have you ever heard Jehú sing? No, I'm serious. He knows some *funny* songs. In *Spanish . . . He* could make Rafa laugh . . . out loud, too.

"Do you know Rafa's . . . of course you do, what am I saying . . . I was going to ask if you knew Rafa's sister-in-law, Delfina . . . Well, Delfina was here the other day, and she said that Jehú had given her her grandmother's or her great grandmother's —I'm not sure which— anyway, it was a bible. An *old* one. Rafa had given it to Jehú, and Jehú about a week or two before he left last Fall, well, he gave it to Delfina. It's a nice old book; probably worth some money, too.

"By the way, I heard that Delfina and Angela Vielma were thinking about moving into that nice house just off Palm View; what they call *contraesquina* —you know, kitty corner? and, ah, just off Hidalgo Boulevard; by the old school? It's a big house. And nice".

El esc. no conocía a este muchacho; sabía de él como uno se da cuenta de muchas cosas en esta vida: al azar. No se puede colegir mucho sobre lo que se piensa o lo que se dice entre los amigos de Jehú aunque el esc. sí nota cierta curiosidad, quizá un leve resentimiento al que vive su vida libremente. Con todo eso, no se llega a la crítica fuerte ni, menos, despiadada. Es más bien un asesoramiento tibio por parte del joven San Esteban, que, en su favor, tampoco ve enteramente mal las relaciones entre su hermana y Jehú. Es que, sencillamente, no las entiende.

26

Viola Barragán

¿Qué se puede decir de este fierro sin moho? Sostenedora del *status quo ante,* del *American free enterprise system,* fiel seguidora de *laissez faire entre nous,* amiga de sus amigos, leal y luchadora, independiente, desacobardada y firme repositorio de todo lo bueno y lo malo del Valle. El esc. (obvia y descaradamente) admira a este ejemplar *sui generis.*

"Hombre, Galindo, tan caro que se te cotiza; ya ni se te ve . . .

"Ya sé, ya sé. Andas en lo de Jehú . . . alguien me lo contó.

"Bueno, pa' comenzar te diré que aquí tiene chamba y puesto cuando le dé la gana; es trabajador, listo y, sobre todo lo demás, derechito. Es más, le tengo harta confianza y ya van varias veces que le he ofrecido que se encargue de todos mis negocios. Como tú sabes, toca madera, los negocios me han salido bien, muy bien . . .

"¿Pa' qué ir más allá. Tú me conoces y yo no soy amiga del chisme y ahora a los cincuenta y pico tampoco se vale la chapuza. Mira, no hace mucho que hablé con Nori Perkins y aunque yo no le creo todo, algo se le salió que quizá sea verdad; el cabrón tiene la verdad muy enterrada y son pocas las veces que se le sale. Lo que te cuento apenas es de una semana: dice que Jehú, en un tiempo, allá por las elecciones, se echó a la Bequita Escobar. ¿Qué tal? Yo no abrí la boca y si Nori esperaba que yo desparramara ese globo, pues se fregó; no soy su mandadera.

"Y no es que Nori sea fijón . . . lo que no me gusta, y me lo dijo en español, el muy cabrón, es que también dijo que Jehú corría peligro. Ese tipo de amenaza solapada es propia de cabrones y aprovechados. Punto.

200

"Bueno, que Nori crea lo que quiera. Lo que *yo* quería saber era por qué ya mero despedía a Jehú en un tiempo atrás. Esto yo lo supe por Jehú. Cosa nuestra.

"Acá, entre tú y yo, te apuesto —y sin pruebas ni ventaja, ¿eh?— te apuesto que Jehú, flaco cabrón, se echó a la Sammie Jo *también.* Aynomás. Y creo que voy bien cuando digo que de ahí que se enojara la Livita San Esteban. ¡Ja! Estas muchachas que no saben nada de nada; creen que porque ellas no aflojan, que las demás no debiéramos tampoco. ¿Me oíste? ¡Debiéramos, tú!

"P's sí, h'mbre; si Jehú no está en el Carmen con Israel, entonces está con Rafa, allá en William Barrett; lo que te digo es que se fue a pasar el año nuevo con su primo y allí se quedó. Tú los conoces mejor que yo y si a Israel le sacas algo, cosa que dudo, ¿qué puedes esperar del Quieto chiquito?

"Ahora, si Jehú quiere trabajar, aquí estoy yo: y bien que se le pagará y no como mi Gillette que era de lo más agarrado y cabrón. Una no anda con chingaderas: se trabaja bien y se paga igual . . .

"Yo, y no es por nada ni por mucho, pero, yo, hasta la fecha, no he visto la mano de Javier Leguizamón en este asunto. Pero quién sabe. ¡Ja! y que si supiera que Jehú le bajó las pantaletas a la Beca . . . me gustaría que supiera nomás pa' verle la cara a ese viejo cabrón . . . como si él no hubiera hecho las suyas allá cuando todavía se le paraba . . .

"Mira, Galindo, tú sabes, o debes saber, que Javier le consiguió el puesto a ese cabrón-vale-pa-nada de Ira allí en el banco; Nori mismo me lo dijo. Pero es como yo le dije a Nori: 'Mira, Nori, en eso de la política, yo, igual que tú, le paso dinero a cualquier cabrón y no me importa a qué partido se agarre'.

"Ese Ira . . . mira: la Bequita Caldwell se casó con Ira por dinero y por la familia y porque su madre, Elvira Navarrete, quería liarse con los Leguizamón, o con el nombre de los Leguizamón. ¡Je! Y luego hablan de una . . . Fíjate . . .

"No es mala la Bequi; le gusta el pedo aunque lo disimule con eso de los clubes pero salió a la madre que allá —cuando éramos resistentes y de buen ver— era una chingaquedito. Que se haya casado con Catarino Caldwell es más que prueba; pero que de conocer a Elvira bien a bien, ¡vaya si la conozco!

"¿Y la Sammie Jo? Salió media güila y le gusta y pa' acabarla, le gusta la raza. Bien haya la güera. Se casó dos veces: el primero salió borrachín y el segundo algo borrachín y bastante joto. Así, como lo oyes.

"Esto último se lo saqué a Jehú. ¿Cómo que no sabías?

"Así fue la cosa: Jehú, yendo al cuarto de la Sammie Jo allá en el Rancho mismo, se encontró un broche cerca de la alberca. Jehú ni sabía de quién era. Así pasó. Jehú se encontró el *locket* ese y se lo mostró a Sammie Jo; ésta lo abrió —ella se lo había regalado a Sidney, ¿ves? P's lo abrió y allí estaban los retratitos recortados: uno del Sidney y el otro de Hap Bayliss. ¿Qué tal?

"¿Sabes lo que hizo la Sammie Jo? Jehú me dijo que la Sammie Jo encogió los hombros y que luego ella y Jehú se fueron al cuarto como si nada. Chúpate esa. A ver, eso fue allá cuando Nori andaba en Colorado por lo de la esposa o en William Barrett; no estoy . . . Ya sé; sí, fue cuando las elecciones o ayporay.

"Te diré que Jehú me lo contó pero no como chisme. Yo creo que aquí fue cuando se puso a pensar si mejor no sería venirse a trabajar conmigo . . . ya sabes, si se le sale a la Sammie Jo cuando ande en la tomada o no falta qué. Bueno, para este tiempo —aunque yo no sepa del todo— Jehú y la Livia ya andaban en serio o andaban quebrando. No sé.

"Lo de los bolillos a mí ni me interesa, Galindo. He visto mucho mundo para que me tomen sin confesar. Lo que yo no quería, ni quiero todavía, es que me pescaran a Jehú en su maquinaria. Cada quien necesita su padrino, bueno, en mi caso, madrina, y yo me he propuesto que no jodan a Jehú. Y si no quiere trabajar aquí en Klail o en este condado, bien puede irse a Dellis County que, gracias a Dios, también tengo mis negocios allá . . .

"Y eso es todo, Galindo. ¿Qué? ¿Nos echamos un trago? Pero nomás eso, ¿eh?"

El esc., antes que nada, quiere avisar que ese último *¿eh?* de Viola Barragán fue seguido por una carcajada sana y prolongada. Se asegura que lo único que se tomó con Viola fueron sendos vasos de té; el esc. también confiesa que lo único que se gastó en compañía de esa mujer sin par fue el tiempo.

Dificultad: Viola Barragán no miente, no inventa, casi no exagera y cuenta todo lo que sabe; aún así, se complica más el caso porque Viola misma, con todo eso en su favor, no *sabe* si sabe todo o no. Sin embargo, hay que tomar todo abiertamente y no *cum granis salis*.

Se ve, a veinte pasos o más, que Viola sigue siendo la firmeza personificada en su afecto y lealtad a Jehú Malacara. Tiene suerte el muchacho, pero él también se ha comportado de lo mejor con Viola.

27

Bowly Ponder

Policía general y de tránsito; flaco y mediano, nariz tirando a chato, de cara colorada y con el pelo del mismo color. Descendiente de los *poor whites* que, en la escala social de los anglos, queda en el último escalafón. El penúltimo escalafón es propiedad de los *fruit tramps*. Nosotros no contamos.

Ponder nació en unas de las pocas tierras que rodean Klail y que no son del Rancho; su hermano menor, Dempsey, que trabaja en las propiedades de los Klail-Blanchard-Cooke, aún vive en la misma casita donde nacieron todos los nueve de la prole Ponder; hay por consiguiente, un sinnúmero de parientes, primos, etc. que pululan en todo el Valle.

"Sure old Bowly T.G. ran her in; old Missy Stuck Up there was speeding, and I just up and gave her a ticket for it. I wadn't about to take any crap from her. Anyway, I was just doing my job, is all.

"Know what? She told Judge Fikes I was dis res pect ful. Little piss ant shit. I told him I expected the violator had been drinking some. Believe me, Galindo, I could've made that stick if I *wanted* to.

"Know what else she said when I gave her the goddam ticket? She said I ought to go 'round checking on Mexican cars for state inspection tags if that was all I had to do with my *time.*

"Piece of shit telling *me* how to do my *job;* well, I *fixed* her ass . . . I walked on over to my car, turned on the flashing lights, turned on the goddam car radio —loud!— and *then I* went back and asked her to get the hell out of *her* car, to empty her purse, her wallet, too, and *then,* to open up the goddam glove compartment —*from the out-*

Mi querido Rafa   205

side; made her walk around the car, too. Half-a-goddam Klail must have seen her; saw old John, you know, from the paint store? I waved at him, and then I *pointed* at her.

"I don't give two hoots in *anybody's* hell; County Commissioner, *shit. He* speeds in Klail, *he* gets a ticket.

"And you know *what?* People 'round here are saying that Noddy sicced me on her; shoot? I don't mess with *his* bank, and *he* don't mess with *me.* Demps works for him all right, but that's his and Demps' business —ain't none of mine.

"And, to top it off, I had to take half a day off my vacation to go see Judge Fikes, too; and that's a fact, and she paid them twenty-two-fifty right then and there. No two ways.

"Yeh, she was put out, all right. You know *what?* Betcha she don't speed in my sector again. And that's a *fact*".

Palabras fuertes y no se dude que Bowly le apretó ciertas tuercas a Bedelia (Boyer) Terry. Tampoco se dude que Bowly entró pisando fuerte en la corte de Knowlton Fikes. Con todo eso, el esc. cree que Bowly protesta demasiado.

En contra de Bowly, y con pruebas sobrantes estos últimos quince años, está su puesto como policía que se debe a Noddy Perkins, para comenzar, y, para seguir: el trabajo que tiene su hermano Dempsey en el Rancho; así como todas las chambas que tienen con el condado y con la ciudad los sobrinos, los cuñados, los parientes, etc. de los Ponder y de los Bewley, y los Watfell, entre otros.

Que Bedelia Boyer Terry maneje como una loca por esas calles de Klail no es ninguna novedad. Que ahora, por vez primera, se le detenga y se le abuse (relativamente) por un Bowly Ponder, es pasarse de coincidencia.

Aquí pues, el gato no está completamente encerrado. El esc. mete baza porque no puede estarse con los brazos cruzados conociendo, como conoce, buena parte de los hechos y de los actores.

28

Olivia San Esteban

Altita aunque no tanto como Jehú ni menos como Rafa Buen-rostro. De ojos cafés, cabellera también café y crespadita, la infor-mante San Esteban es a la vez seria y risueña; no es dejada ni atre-vida y lleva sus veintinueve años sin casarse; también debe decirse que no se ve en peligro de que se quede a vestir santos. Asegura, aunque no se sabe hasta qué punto, que puede hablar de Jehú evi-tando lo personal entre los dos. (El esc. no entiende eso; no com-prende cómo se podrá evitar lo personal.)

"Sabía de Jehú tiempo atrás, pero no lo conocí hasta que nos vimos en Austin. Él y Rafa salían con mi hermano Martín y con el primo Juan Santoscoy.

"Yo sé que Jehú fue protegido por los Buenrostro del Carmen antes y también después del ejército; son algo parientes, como usted sabe".

Aquí la informante se va en inglés: "Jehú and I never did go into that very much, and it doesn't matter to me. He's headstrong about some things but so am I, and yet, he and I agree on many things. One thing, *he* doesn't take any guff from Martín; he usually tells my brother where to head off.

"He's like that . . .

"Jehú and I *do* disagree on some things, but those are *personal;* and, speaking of personal things, just this once, Jehú is *very* much interested in my going on to med school . . .

"I'm, ah, I'm just not *sure* he's quite ready to settle down . . .

"Look, I'm really behind on some prescriptions and stuff here at the moment. Could you come back later on? This afternoon?"

Esa tarde: "Buenas tardes y gracias y también perdone que haya tenido que disculparme esta mañana pero el trabajo estaba agobiante —y así es de diario pero más por las mañanas.

"Martín trabaja de noche este mes y si se espera quizá él también tenga algo que decir del paradero de Jehú; de mi parte le diré que no es ningún misterio: ya que no está en el Carmen, como usted dice, entonces andará en William Barrett o en Austin.

"¿Le sorprendió a Ud. esta mañana que hablara en inglés así, de repente? Eso sucede aquí, en el trabajo . . .

"A ver, ¿qué más le puedo decir de Jehú Malacara . . . y curioso el apellido, ¿verdad? Porque . . . Jehú es bien parecido . . .

"Una vez me dijo que cuando era chico y luego cuando mayorcito también que trabajó con unos aleluyas. Mi hizo reír ese hombre . . . No tiene alma. Pero tampoco tiene miedo: detrás de esa sonrisa juguetona es más bien serio y . . . y muy hombre.

"Lo que tiene es que . . . mire, Galindo, le voy a decir claramente: a mí no me gusta andar con medias tazas. No tengo pruebas, pero yo creo que en un tiempo, y no muy atrás, que . . . que Rebecca Escobar quiso tener relaciones con Jehú. Después, alguien, y no falta quién, me dijo algo de que Sammic Jo y Jehú. Yo —y yo no soy ninguna niña— y una no es como se crió sino como se es y *yo soy así:* Jehú y yo no somos novios pero a mí me disgusta . . compartirlo y menos con esas dos; y no me importa que estén casadas; eso es lo de menos.

"Jehú ya es mayorcito pero también le diré lo siguiente, ya que estamos en eso: el día que Jehú dejó el banco, él vino *aquí;* él vino a verme a *mí;* a despedirse. De mí, y en persona. Lo único que puedo decirle es que del banco *no* lo corrieron. Una cosa más, la señora Barragán, y ella y yo no nos llevamos, ni bien ni mal, no nos llevamos y ya . . . ella, pues, le ha ofrecido trabajo a Jehú . . . cuando lo quiera. Ella mismo me lo dijo.

"De lo mío, de mi vida personal, yo quiero estudiar medicina, y Jehú, siendo como es, me ayudaría. No en dinero que eso no falta; pero Jehú sería un sostén. Cuando vuelva de donde ande, volverá por mí. Y si no para casarnos, no importa; él y yo nos entendemos. Ya; ya; sé que me creen engreída o ensimismada pero solamente *yo* sé *cómo* soy y Jehú me entiende. Es el único que me ha entendido".

La informante no alzó la voz ni una sola vez; es más, se notó una que otra sonrisa (parecida a la de Jehú) y también se hace constar que Olivia San Esteban tiene un sentido de humor así también como una idea propia de cómo es y de cómo se ve ella misma.

El esc. no cree que debe hacer comentarios hacia la actitud demostrada vis á vis Rebecca Escobar y Sammie Jo ya que no hay duda que la informante se explica perfecta y claramente. Lo suyo son sospechas, según lo que colige el esc.

Opinión: Si alguien sabe del paradero de Jehú, O.S.E. debe saber más de lo que dice; también hay que decir que la que también sepa más (quizá sepa todo) parece ser Viola Barragán.

El esc. tiene que hablar nuevamente con la recién viuda de Gillette, nuestra amiga Viola Barragán.

29

Viola Barragán

Lo dicho anteriormente; ver #26.

"Dichosos los ojos, Galindo; te ves algo repuesto. Tú sigue cuidándote, ya sabes que se te aprecia.

"¿Y cómo va lo tuyo? ¿En las mismas? Quisiera hablar más pero ando atareada con tanto trabajo; como te digo, si tuviera un business manager como Jehú, no anduviera como ando. Mira estos paquetes, a ver, ábreme la puerta, por favor. Eso; gracias. Llámame cuando oigas algo. Perdona, pero ando de prisa".

Suposición: Pero, ¿será posible que nuestra Viola trate de evitar trabar conversación cerrada con el esc.?

Una respuesta: No necesariamente; bien puede ser que los negocios múltiples de esta mujer versátil se agolpen tanto que le corten tiempo y terreno.

Otra: Es enteramente posible que esconda algo bajo su amplio escote.

Opinión: Mucha gente (la raza) no ve bien a Viola y por consiguiente está lista a creer que cualquier cosa que ella diga no sea verdad. Frase algo barroca que también refleja el pensamiento de gente conocida.

El esc. adopta su actitud de siempre para con Viola: V.B. dice la verdad hasta que se pruebe lo contrario. Siendo así, el esc. ha pedido cita con Arnold Perkins. Esto, quizá, ha de tomar cierto tiempo.

30

Rebecca Escobar

Algo morenita, tampoco mucho, el esc. le atina que tiene unos veintiocho años de edad; representa menos a pesar de tener ya dos nenes curiosines. Las relaciones con su suegra, doña Vidala Leguiza-món-L. née de la Viña son de lo más tenue, vamos, se quiere decir que no se llevan bien. Esto se sabe gracias a los buenos oficios de una amiga del esc. que vive en Jonesville. El esc. lo siente pero rehusa dar el nombre de esta amiga.

El español de Becky es algo mocho y ella prefiere el inglés; el esc., de lo más ecuánime, señala que (en pos de la verdad) no tiene reparo alguno y que los informantes pueden, deben explayarse en el idioma que más les convenga.

"I really don't know Jehú that *well,* you know; isn't he related to Rafe Buenrostro . . . do you know *him?* Rafe, I mean?

"Well, Ira and I first met Jehú when we first came to work at the bank, you know; I mean, when Ira became *associated* with the bank. You understand that Jehú was not Ira's supervisor or anything; I mean, he wasn't even a business major like Ira who attended A&M and finished up at St. Mary's. You know what I mean, don't you?

"Anyway, I saw Jehú at some of the bank parties and picnics; stuff like that, but not much more. *And,* he's not at *all* interested in politics . . . Ira told me so. But I *like* him; I find him *nice,* and he's *friendly* . . . okay?

"Well, anyway . . . I'm usually pretty busy on my Woman's Club work, and now, more recently, this winter in fact, with the Music Club . . . and what with taking the kids to dance lessons, and what all, I really don't have much time for . . . for other social occasions, don't you know. But we, Ira and I, did meet Jehú socially, early on anyway; I think, or maybe I've heard that he's engaged to Ollie Sans Teban; do you know her? She's a pharmacist here . . .

"And you *know* about what happened at Noddy's that night . . . Well, as I remember it, it was just a little after eight o'clock, and we had just finished dessert after an early sit-down dinner when Jehú came in; he *saw* we were through, and he had a surprised look on his face; not for long, of course, but you could *see* that he was surprised. I mean, like he wasn't expecting *us* —the Terrys were there, too— like he wasn't expecting *us* to be there. It was strange . . . I think Sammie Jo laughed; she'd been drinking . . .

"But that was it; Jehú came into the dining room, and he was about to pull up a chair when . . . when Mr. Perkins . . . and no one had said a word up to then . . . Anyway, Mr. Perkins said, or asked, demanded, I guess, that, that, ah, that Jehú resign from the bank; there and then. Ira and I were *so* embarrassed, you know, after all we're all mexicanos, right?

"Jehú looked at Mr. Perkins and nodded but not in agreement, it didn't seem. He looked straight at Noddy; that's all he did, and then he . . . he just *walked* out; I don't think he said good night or anything.

"Well, one hears so many things . . . Anyway, later, on the way home, Ira said *he* thought it might have been money, you know. But that's all Ira said . . . He's very discreet, you know.

"And *then, another* surprise! Jehú was back at the *bank!* Just like that —hahahaha— just like Jehú says: Just Like That . . . I mean, was it a joke on Noddy's part? Was he angry with Jehú because Jehú was late for dinner? The empty chair was there all along, you know. Ira called me first thing in the morning to tell me that Jehú was there . . . I was glad for Jehú; I mean, it was a bank holiday, but everyone was working inside . . . I mean, it was such a good job for him . . .

"Ira said that Jehú came in and went straight into Noddy's office like any other Monday morning. About half an hour later, he was back at his own office and at work as usual. Ira says he —Jehú— worked through the noon hour just like . . . ah . . . like usual . . . and that *that* was it.

"Nothing to it, and the bank clerks couldn't have known a *thing*. *And,* Ibby Cooke, you know, the V.P., well, he and Jehú had their Monday afternoon meeting just like always.

"I mean: nothing had *changed.* At *all.*

"Later in the day, Jehú, on his way out, stopped by Ira's desk and said, 'Well, Mr. Commissioner, did you enjoy your dinner Saturday night?' It was probably Jehú's and Noddy's idea of a big joke. I don't mind telling you that *that* Saturday night was ruined for Ira and me . . . Ira and I.

"But I still *like* Jehú. I think he's nice, and the few times I've talked with him, he's been very pleasant. Anyway, that's all I know except for the fact that he was also offered a job a couple of months later by the Barragán woman. Do you know *her?*

"I don't know *what* to think, but do you think that there's a connection between the Saturday night thing and Jehú being offered a job by Viola Barragán?"

Lo susodicho, pues, es lo que dijo la señora Escobar y el esc. lo acepta. El esc. escuchó con mucho cuidado a la señora Escobar y le dio cierta tristeza pensar que esta muchacha ni sospecha (en lo más fondo de su corazón) qué cosas son esas que nosotros llamamos *tristeza, alegría, sentimiento,* etc.

31

Sammie Jo Perkins

Hija única del matrimonio Perkins-Cooke, esbeltita, pelo crespo y oscuro; tiene unos treinta años de edad que bien se notan. Propiamente divorciada de Bradshaw, Theodore P., y, actualmente, esp. de Sidney Boynton, habla bastante español aunque aquí se demuestre muy poco; no tiene pelos en la lengua, por decirlo así.

"Galindo, I don't know, and I've known Jehú for a long time —I don't know if Jehú even *likes* people. I mean, I believe that Jehú doesn't judge people by how much he *likes* 'em or not.

"He doesn't care for Dad at all, you know, but he respects the way Dad operates now and then. But *that's* about it. Jehú has no use for Ira, and that's no secret. But it isn't fear about the bank job; I mean, Jehú could not care less about that end of it.

"Tell you *what,* Galindo: I bet you he got to Becky Escobar. Wanna bet?

"As for now . . . I know where he's *at.* And if the Mexicans across town are worried: shit on 'em. And, if they're so goddam worried he stole *money,* then they're wrong, and they're *full* of it.

"He's up in Austin; he wants to go to grad. school. That's all, and that's all he's ever wanted to do. I know he's there, *Dad* knows he's there, and I bet that *Olivia* knows he's there. And, as for Ollie, *she* wants things her way. And that's fine, and Jehú is willing to let her have her way. Thing is, Jehú wants her to have her way without *him.* That's all. Have you talked to her yet? If she had *any* sense, she'd either leave him and forget him or she'd *marry* him. If Jehú would have her . . . ha!

"I *like* him, Galindo, though Jehú can be a real shit sometimes. Oh, I can, too, but we're *good* together and *that's* what counts with me.

"But they're wasting their time. *Gente pendeja,* they won't believe what you tell them, but they're ready to believe the worst about him. Call Rafe, That is, call Rafe if you can ever get him to answer the phone; he's hell, you know . . .

"Boy, now there's a couple of *primos* for you . . . Well, time's up, Galindo; it's time for my dip. Bye, now".

Y así, la única heredera de Arnold y Blanche Perkins se despidió del esc.

La Sammie Joe tiene razón: la raza es suspicaz; quizá demasiado suspicaz. El esc., por su parte, piensa que la raza tiene razón de serlo por aquello de tantas veces que se lleva el cántaro al agua.

El lector no puede dejar de notar que Jehú no es ni santo ni diablo. Ahora, que la verdad salga de la boca de Sammie Jo es la más grande de las ironías. El esc. piensa que Sammie Jo sabe que Rafa no contesta teléfonos así, casualmente, por medio de Jehú. No ve ninguna otra conexión.

32
Arnold Perkins

El famoso 'Noddy' y, entre la raza, 'Norberto'. El esc. describe a Noddy usando las palabras de Noddy en su autoidentificación: *A self-made man.* En las cartas de Jehú a Rafa Buenrostro se ven los datos biográficos de Noddy; el esc. no ha de repetir lo dicho. Cabe decir que Noddy, entre la raza, tiene sus campeones y sus detractores. Lo normal.

"Sure, Jehú and I have had our differences now and then, but that was to be expected; I'm not an easy man to get along with (risa ligera y de diente pelón). But it wasn't anything that couldn't be ironed out, it was business . . . nothing more . . . You'd be surprised how well he took to banking. He has a healthy respect for money, and he's honest . . . Sharp, too.

"He's not much on social life, though. Oh, he dates the San Esteban girl; you know, Emilio's daughter? I wouldn't be surprised if he also had something on the side. But, it's only natural . . . he's young. But what the hell, we don't check up on our employees here. You know Klail City and the Valley, and it wouldn't take long for word like that to get around . . . I mean, if anything was wrong . . .

"Jehú speaks Spanish very well, you know; none of your Tex-Mex either; I heard he'd been raised in part by a Mexican national and that might account for it. And there's nothing wrong with his English either; he's a Valley boy, and I guess the Army helped there, too.

"He first started to work for us —the Ranch— over at the KC Savings and Loan; he did mostly high risk insurance lending over there. I brought him over *here* with barely a year's experience; but, he's a natural. I mean, he *likes* banking; he knows how to smoke out

215

a deal and see it through, and he's not interested in politics or the civic stuff; don't misunderstand: he knows it's important for business . . . I don't even know if he votes or not.

"He's got a good sense of humor, though. It's a bit pointed at times, but I can understand that; I was born poor myself . . . He worked well here . . .

"Jehú tolerates my brother-in-law, Ibby; Ibby's been at this bank some thirty years now, almost as long as I've been here, and that's before Blanche and I were married. Now, you'd think Ibby would have picked up what the hell banking was all about in that time: you take in money and you lend it out; you charge interest, and it's always the same money, but you usually wind up with more. That's all. I can solemnly swear that Ibby still hasn't got *that* down. But Ibby's too easy a target, and so Jehú won't go after *him;* so, he tolerates him. Puts up with him, don't you see? Now, when Ira came in last year, and that boy is full of shit, he tried telling Jehú what banking was all about —Jehú let him; still does. Or did 'til he left. At times the humor was so sharp Ira didn't feel the pin pricks —I mean, he's *that* thick. Old Jehú would ask the dumbest questions you ever heard, and Ira would stumble over *that.* Well, I didn't care as long as it didn't affect the work here . . . but this takes me to something else: Jehú's not above getting into old Becky's pants and pulling 'em down. Know what I mean? Well now, that's where I come in —hold it, Galindo, I mean that *that* is bank business; we can't have that going on. It's bad for business. Right?

"I'm not saying it happened. But I know Jehú; hell, I was like that myself, years ago. Ask old Viola Barragán; shoot! ask Gela Maldonado, too; ha! I bet old Javier Legui *still* doesn't know about *that* . . . no matter, that was over thirty years ago . . .

"One last thing: Jehú's got a job here whenever he wants it. When he left here he just said he *had* to go. There was never *any* question about money. In any way. I heard something about graduate school, but that's probably just a thought on his part".

Confesión: El esc. se fumó uno de los puros ofrecidos y pagó por ello con dos días de cama tan malo así se puso y se sintió.

El esc. le avisa el lector que él no sabía ni tenía noticia de los viejos enlaces Perkins-Barragán y Perkins-Maldonado. El esc. sólo se permite decir que todo puede ser.

Pregunta: ¿Habrá razón alguna para darle importancia (debida/indebida) a los susodichos enlaces? ¿Acaso se acordarán Viola y Gela? ¿Acaso importa que se acuerden? Se le advierte al lector que quizá mejor será dejar lo del agua al agua.

33

E.B. Cooke

Viudo por más de cuarto de siglo, este informante es el tercero de seis hijos que tuvieron Clayton y Myrna B. Cooke; de los seis, restan tres hombres y una mujer: el informante, y luego le siguen Parnell, idiota congénito; Blanton, cincuentón que ahora vive en New York; y Blanche, la esposa de Noddy Perkins.

El informante es algo displicente pero el esc. ve que lo desabrido no viene con él; es decir, no es nada personal, es solamente parte del carácter del informante. Su nombre de pila es Everett; la inicial *B* es por lo Blanchard que explica el parentazgo de estas dos familias.

"Oh, I know you've talked to Noddy —and it doesn't matter . . . *in the least.* I also know what he thinks of me, and I don't care about *that* either. I don't like banking, and I never have. I wanted to be a painter, Galindo, but the bank and the Ranch and the stores, and the land, and the rest . . . well, *someone* in the *family* had to be in it here, at this end, and, Noddy is not *family.* Sammie Jo is, but *he's* not. Both Grover and Andrew died young; Parnell is not equipped for it and that leaves Blanton and me. On the Blanchard side, there's not much to pick from, if you ask me.

"And I know about Jehú —and I don't care to listen or to know whatever it was that Noddy said. Jehú's been here close to four years, and he and I get along; *he* knows I don't like this business, and so he does most of the ground work; I make policy.

"I really don't know if he *likes* the business. In point of fact, it's hard to tell *what* he likes or wants. I think he enjoys it, but I can't see him here for the next thirty years . . . he won't be wasting *his* life here. I know he's got some money saved; how much, too; and I don't

218

find it such a shock that he left or wants to leave. I don't know where *that* stands at the moment. I know he wants to go back to Austin, to the University, and that's all there is to *that* piece of business.

"As you know, Noddy's my brother-in-law, and we don't get along. Never have. Blanche is a sick woman and has been for years; and Noddy's been no help *at-tall*. I don't care to get into that, but I thought you should know . . .

"As for Noddy . . . Noddy doesn't like the way I talk, maybe even the way I walk . . . And that's just too damn bad; I'm *family*. And I'm not queer, whatever Noddy may wish and hope for.

"Noddy is a *ridiculous* man; he doesn't know the first thing about ranching or about the oil industry, *but* to hear *him* tell it, well! But he's strong, and he's devious; that's his due, and I may be a damned fool for coming here every day for thirty years, but *someone's* got to keep a rein on him.

"Everything is *planned* with him. He even learned *Spanish* that way. Oh, I know what you think of us, but *we're* from here, too, you know. And Jehú and Ira won't be the last Mexicans to work here —and I can promise you that much; but, if it were up to Noddy . . . ha!

"Jehú's bright; he's also impatient, at times. We work well together despite what Noddy says and tells everyone. I also know that Noddy says I don't know the *first* thing about banking, but he's *wrong*. I take no unnecessary actions, and I always make it a practice of letting Noddy have his way. Up to a point. And, then, only in public. I don't *care* what people think of me: I have my own life, I have my own friends, and Noddy's not a part of either one of them. Blanche is, but she's family and so is Junior Klail. And let's not get on the subject of that impossible sister of Noddy's, *please.*

"As for politics, that's what *we* are all about and *that,* Galindo, is merely *farmed* out to Noddy; look, we have businesses *everywhere,* and Klail is but a part of it; the money started here years ago, and we started the town . . . from the Anglo point of view, anyway. But Klail's only a part of it, and Noddy has a small part of *that.*

"I'm the cashier here, but I'm also the Secretary-Treasurer for the Corporation; Noddy knows perfectly well what *that* means. He tries to egg Jehú on, but that young man's too sharp for Noddy, and Noddy may even resent that.

"As for me, well, I'm a painter, Galindo. A frustrated one, and perhaps not a particularly talented one either, but I can *read* people. I can read *character* . . . Now, would you care for a drink? We can have one of the girls bring something in".

Donde menos se piensa salta la liebre. El esc. conoce a Ibby desde años y años atrás casi desde el entierro de su tío, el centenario Judge Cooke (Walton H., Jr.) el fundador de los clanes Cooke-Blanchard. Entierro que fue un escándalo de derroche. Más tarde se supo que Noddy tuvo mano en los arreglos funerarios.

El autorretrato de Ibby Cooke discrepa con el papel que Noddy le asigna y el rencor quizá sea más hondo de lo que los mismos cuñados piensen o se imaginen. Las opiniones de los cuñados también discrepan acerca del valor o del conocimiento que puedan tener de Jehú. Esto no es innecesariamente incompatible sino más bien la misma idea con dos divergentes puntos de vista.

El esc. no puede dejar de calcar que ambos señores conocen el juego de la intriga. Difieren solamente en sus métodos: Noddy, a base de espías, sin éstos saber que son espías, y también a base de tácticas conocidas: la tentación (a Ira), la falsa amistad y jovialidad (al esc.) y el trato aparentemente democrático (con todo mundo). Cooke es más observador; él mismo dice que es —quiso ser— pintor; es más dado a la contemplación de las personas y de las acciones. No parece ser intuitivo (quizá su fracaso como pintor se deba a esto) pero tampoco anda dando tiros sin puntería; en vez de tácticas, se podrá decir que prefiere la estrategia que, a su vista, es un campo mayor y elevado. Se invita al lector que considere que los cuñados tienen más en común de lo que parece.

34

Rufino Fischer Gutiérrez

RFG también es Cano, es decir, es Gutiérrez por su padre, Fischer por su madre, y dos veces Cano: por su abuelo paterno, el primer Rufino Cano Guzmán, y por su abuela materna, doña Florentina Anzaldúa Cano. Rufino es hijo del difunto Juan Eugenio Gutiérrez; lo Fischer le viene por don Fabián, el padre de Camila Fischer que viene siendo madre de RFG.

Veterano de la Segunda Mundial como miembro de la USMC, RFG se licenció en San Diego, Cal, volvió al Valle, pasó por Klail y se enterró en esas tierras de Dellis County para recobrar parte de la que perdieron sus antepasados.

El esc. sabe que RFG y Bowly Ponder se presentaron como voluntarios a la USMC allá en el año 1943.

"Le damos por aquí, ¿a la sombra, Galindo? A ver, ¿ves aquel mezquite doblado, el que está cerca de la palmera? Bueno, ese mezquite lo plantó un Peña de los que ahora viven en Barrones, Tamaulipas; queda casi en el medio de la merced que les tocó a los Buenrostro allá cuando las repartieron. Mi primo Israel Buenrostro tiene otro mezquite que también plantó otro Peña pero de los de este lado. De Río abajo, ya sabes. La distancia entre los dos mezquites llega a no menos de cuarenta millas americanas en línea. Tú bien sabes que entre los dos mezquites la bolillada tiene la mayoría de la tierra; uno no querrá toda pero tampoco queremos que acaparen más. Bastante tenemos con los Leguizamón encima.

"Cuando acá se supo que un Leguizamón iba a correr pa' comisionado allá, los mexicanos de este condado vimos eso como maniobra pa' agarrar más tierra. No andábamos descaminados. Aquí en

Dellis County el agua corre, moja y enloda igual que la de ustedes en Belken . . . Sí, me parece que sería mejor empezar por allí, con la tierra y el agua.

"El año pasado murió el último Ledesma. Tú conociste a Italo, ¿verdad? Bueno, el county clerk de Dellis —Hendricks— le avisó a Arnold Perkins —a Nore Poike, como le decía el viejito don Esteban Echevarría. Bueno, Hendricks le avisó a Perkins que la tierra se iba a poner en venta, y así fue que Perkins tenía correntía de más de mes. Para ese tiempo, los Landín de acá ya andaban vendiendo y comprando tierra. Uno de los Landín nos avisó que Perkins quería juntar parte de la tierra de los Ledesma y los Landín. Está bien; el negocio es el negocio, pero lo que no nos cayó bien fue que Arnold Perkins quería compartir la tierra con los Leguizamón. Eso lo supimos por otro lado, como tú verás.

"Los Landín hicieron trato con Perkins pero no por toda la tierra; entonces nosotros también compramos parte a los Landín y ésa se la vendimos, parte también, a los Peña de este lado del Río y parte a los Zúñiga, parientes de éstos —los Zúñiga, Galindo, son de los Cano del Soliseño. Bueno, mira, allí, mira, allí mismo, al otro lado del río; ¿ves ese caserío? Puro Cano y Zúñiga allí. Como te cuento la cosa parece bien fácil y como nos las puso Perkins también.

"Lo que nos ayudó fue una visita de Jehú después de una barbacoa política que le hicieron a ese pendejo de Ira Escobar. Yo había ido al Relámpago a ver cómo andaban los negocios de la tía difunta Enriqueta Vidaurri; estando allí, vi a Jehú y fuimos a la barbacoa.

"Jehú andaba en compañía de Livita San Esteban . . . mi mujer y yo somos sus padrinos de confirmación, y a Jehú lo conocemos desde que nació. En esta labor donde estás, aquí, precisamente en ésta, fue donde le picó la cascabel a un ministro protestante; un ministro a quien Jehú ayudaba. Bueno, por boca de Jehú supimos que ese Escobar es Leguizamón-Leyva y allí vimos la jugada de Arnold Perkins; a base de esa información —y sin que Perkins lo supiera— hicimos los tratos.

"Ahora me dicen que despidieron a Jehú del banco; en eso yo sigo viendo la mano de los Leguizamón. Aunque te diré francamente que estoy dispuesto a creer cualquier cosa de esa gente cabrona.

"Jehú obró bien con Perkins: conoce algo de tierra, conoce el valor y sabe qué le conviene al banco y qué no. Lo que nos dijo de la parentela de Escobar quizá no se vea bien pero esto es asunto de familia y para mí que Jehú lo vio así.

"Mira, hablando de Belken County . . . Al que vi de allá fue a Bowly —a Bowly Ponder, el que estuvo en los Marines conmigo. Como carga pistola en Klail, él no toma allá y se viene acá a Dellis County y lo has de ver en Flads, tomando en las cantinitas cerca del bordo.

"Me topé con Bowly cuando él ya andaba en trago. Andaba a medio chile; es muy tetera el cabrón, y cuando anda cuete, se la recarga.

"Esa noche estuvo hablando de cómo le había hecho la vida pesada a la esposa de un comisionado de Belken. Que le dio un boleto y que la citó con el juez de paz; esto quizá no venga al caso pero dijo que tenía que ver con la política del condado; sin decirlo, dijo que Perkins andaba por ahí metido en eso. Ahora resulta que esa mujer es la esposa del que fue contrincante de Ira Escobar. Una jugada típicamente cochina de esa gente cabrona. ¡Ja! Pa' lo que les sirvió esa cochina jugada a esos cabrones: el otro salió de diputado a Washington para este distrito. Qué cortos alcances tienen esos Leguizamón . . . Perkins les mete el dedo en la boca y no sienten la picha en el culo . . .

"Hombre, a ver si pasas más seguido por acá; que no se te olvide esta parte del Valle. ¿Qué? ¿Te quedas a cenar? Dale, hombre, a ver qué más me sale".

RFG y el esc. hablaron un tanto más después de la cena pero no fue gran cosa. De lo que dice RFG se deduce que Jehú no dio la información sobre los parentazgos Escobar-Leguizamón por accidente. Tampoco se puede decir que lo hizo por dinero.

Una conclusión: Lo hizo por su conciencia de familia.

El esc. no juzga si obró bien o mal, aunque sí le parece que Jehú violó la confianza de Arnold Perkins en alguna manera. También es preciso notar que Jehú conoce a Noddy mejor que el esc.

Lo dicho no es para disculpar a Jehú.

35

Bowly Ponder

En cosa de tres meses han cambiado, para lo mejor, las vidas económicas y profesionales de nuestro hombre. Renunció al puesto de policía (que se traspasó a su hermano Dempsey) y ahora es diputado al sheriff del condado y, del día a la noche, es medio propietario de una de esas tiendas que llaman Seven-Eleven. Lo vemos, pues, en su marcha como pequeño capitalista y ahora hasta habla de cómo sus dos hijos mayores van a acabar y a recibirse de la secundaria de Klail.

"Well, this has been in the works for some time; George Markham recommended me to Scott Daniels himself, and then the sheriff saw fit to appoint me as a deputy here; I know Klail, I got my contacts here, and I didn't have to move or anything".

El esc., aprovechado que es, se baja al sarcasmo para decir que así Noddy Perkins lo tendrá a la vista.

"Turned out right well, don't you think? And one thing about *this* job, I've got authority in the whole county, *and* a car. And expenses, too, Galindo. All in all, things are looking pretty good; here, listen to this: just last week, in this very car, I went and got Congressman Terry over to Noddy's airstrip. I did, and then gave him a ride home. No hard feelings either; he knew I was just doing my job a while back. Show's you what he's made of, right?"

El esc., si fuera Ponder, se cuidaría de Morse Terry. El esc. no puede creer posible que Morse Terry sea tan irresoluto como parece a no ser que M.T. sea aún más cínico de lo que pinta Bowly. Si así es, entonces el esc. y el lector deben apiadarse de Bedelia Terry.

"Dempsey moved right into the radio dispatcher's job, and this meant that both Bobby Bleibst and Merle Gottschalk will now be out on my old car beat. Ole Dempsey's not cut out to be a riding-around man.

"And you say you saw Rufino Eff Gee over to Flads the other day . . . You know him, do you? Did you know that he and I go back a-whiles . . . I saw him not too long ago myself. I got some old girl friends out to Dellis County".

Por lo visto, Ponder está muy satisfecho de sí mismo. La plática no fue una pérdida total: se ve que Choche Markham todavía vuela y gira en la órbita Leguizamón-Perkins.

El esc. trató varias y repetidas veces de hablar con Morse Terry pero sin éxito: diez llamadas en cuatro meses, con su recado en cada llamada.

36
Mrs. Ben (Edith) Timmens

Edith es esposa de uno de los diez o quince abogados empleados por el Rancho y de ahí, el banco; ella habla español, él no. Se puede ver que él no ha tenido que usarlo. La señora de Timmens, originaria de Klail City, es hija del dif. Osgood Bayliss, veterinario que fue del Rancho, y es, por consiguiente, hermana de Hapgood Bayliss, hasta hace pronto, Diputado (D.-Tx.) por el distrito que abarca todo el Valle.

"Pure fiction, Galindo: Hap isn't sick, he's tired. He's tired of Washington, of politics, and he's tired of being away from the Valley so much. Hap says that fourteen years up there is enough, and I agree with him; Ben and I put in six years in the State Senate up at Austin plus another eight in Washington, and I know perfectly well how Hap feels.

"He had told Noddy one whole year *before* the election that he wanted out, but Noddy kept putting him off. I honestly thought he *was* going to get sick. But! *This* time, I think Noddy shaved it a bit too close for *anybody's* comfort.

"Hap's marriage ended tragically as you know, and being an old bachelor all these years, *well,* he just wanted to come back home. The Valley's *home,* and all our friends are *here;* Washington's no place for a normal life.

"Well, it's been . . . what? Three-four months since the elections? Hap *looks* good, and he *feels* good. He and Sidney are going down to Mexico, La Pesca, I think, and then Sammie Jo's to join them in a couple of weeks. Have you ever been down there?

"Ben and I have, and we *really* enjoy ourselves. You know, you can't help but marvel how Mexicans from down there *differ* from the Mexicans from up here. Well, not you exactly, but *you* know what I mean. . . .

"The last time we went to La Pesca was during pre-election time, so Becky and Ira couldn't come, but there'll be other times, we told them.

"You know, Becky and Ira both are still miffed at Jehú Malacara. Jehú didn't lift a finger; I mean he didn't lift *one* finger during the entire election. Oh, he went to *some* of the barbecues, but he never once spoke at a barbecue. You'd think *Noddy* would've *told* Jehú —that's what Ira says; so, Ira's still miffed, and can you honestly blame him?

"Did Jehú ever tell you about something that happened at one of the parties at the Big House? It was silly, but you know the Valley . . . I think it was Travis DeYoung's wife . . . No. It was Loretta; Wig Birnham's wife. . . . Anyway, she either told a Mexican joke, you know one of those Beto and Lupe jokes, or . . . no, it wasn't that either. Oh, I can't remember just now, but it was something anti-mexicano, don't you know . . . Really! I don't know *what* in the hell Loretta Birnham uses for eyes or for common sense. My God! Well, *we* didn't know what to say or do and then she finally just drifted away.

Jehú didn't say a *word* . . . I remember that . . . Oh, yes: he smiled a bit, and he nodded, to himself, and then the next time he spoke, it was in the most broken English imaginable . . . He's terrible, you know. Anyway, I didn't know *what* to say.

"Oh, wait a minute, now. He *hummed;* yes, I remember that. Know what it was? 'Texas Our Texas' . . . I hadn't heard *that* in *years*.

"Speaking of Jehú, Noddy says that some of the mexicanos in town are saying that Jehú stole money from the bank! That's silly. Where do you suppose they got *that* from?

"Noddy says he won't even talk to them about that piece of business. I think Noddy's right. Javier Leguizamón told Noddy not to bother explaining things to *la raza* since he, Javier, would do it. And gladly".

Esta conversación, como muchas conversaciones, murió una muerte natural. El esc., a su edad, aún se maravilla de cómo con una frase aquí y otra allá, la opinión pública gira y torna, que es un encanto.

No porque lo sugirió Edith Timmens, sino porque el reportaje lo exige, el esc. está convencido de que ya no puede prorrogar su visita con don Javier Leguizamón.

De paso: ya que Edith mencionó lo que ella se dispone a llamar el trágico fin del casamiento de su hermano, el esc. desea aclarar eso con lo siguiente: la esposa de Hap (hija única de un ex-gobernador del estado) se huyó con un cantante, tenor por cierto, de una compañía de ópera.

Como de esto hace mucho, 1) muchos ni saben ni se acuerdan; 2) a muchos más ni les importa.

37

P. Galindo: El Esc.

Nombre: P. Galindo. Estado civil: Soltero. Edad: 52 años de edad vivida la mayoría de ella entre gente conocida. Estado de salud: precario aún cuando estaba rebosante de salud.

El esc. se ha pasado dos semanas en cama o cerca de ella. Los órganos le dieron aviso que se acostara, que era mucho el trote del macho.

Tanto trajín, si no peligroso, no deja de ser nocivo. Parece que el Valle le ha ayudado al esc. a recobrar parte de la salud; también puede ser que esté en error y que lo que verdaderamente ocurra es que ve a tanta gente conocida que eso lo hace *sentirse* mejor.

Los rayos equis, desgraciadamente, no mienten. El esc. los estuvo revisando a la par que repasaba sus notas y borradores. El esc. cree vislumbrar el fin de su búsqueda; se trata de unas cuantas conversaciones más.

Como siempre, lo sencillo no resultó serlo. A pesar de lo que digan los que deben saber y los otros, los que saben menos y chillan más, *todo* impide y *todo* ayuda a esclarecer lo que se quiera traer a luz. Una paradoja, pero así lo es.

Para el esc., el paradero de Jehú era importante, tangencialmente. Lo que más importaba era tratar de averiguar lo ocurrido y lo que de eso se pensaba en ambos lados de la ciudad.

Por ahora se puede decir que dejó el puesto por su propia voluntad dígase lo que se diga entre la raza hasta ahora. Lo que sigue tocará sobre lo mismo y se aconseja que tampoco hay que irse con ideas preconcebidas.

Otros hechos y datos así como varios rasgos de información, a veces no siempre halagadores para nadie ni para todos, se incluyeron tal y como se oyeron; el esc. en lo que pudo, trató de evitar, a veces hasta con cierto éxito, trató de evitar, se decía, la sátira y el sarcasmo.

El esc. avisa además que sigue estando de acuerdo con Roberto Arlt: "En realidad, uno no sabe qué pensar de la gente".

Nota final: los médicos, como cada hijo de vecino, y no por vez primera ni última se han equivocado un poco. El esc. está para acabar el mes noveno y cree que tiene parque para un poco más, pero el hígado no perdona y aquí no se valen las ilusiones: realidad, realidad, realidad.

38

Eugenio & Isidro Peralta, Cuates

Eugenio es cobrador de cuentas para la Seamon Loans aquí en Klail, y vive en la casa de su padre, Adrián, por mal nombre "El Coyote". Eugenio y su mujer Hortensia (Cáceres) no tienen familia y la pasan bien; Eugenio también le entra a la política por vía del padre.

Isidro se casó con Englentina Campos y enviudó a los pocos años; no hubo sucesión. En segundas se casó con Mª. del Refugio Beristáin y tienen cinco (o seis) de familia. (El esc. no puede dar el número exacto en este caso. En esa familia hay un dudoso; bueno, eso es lo que dicen.) Vive en la misma manzana que lo vio nacer y en la misma calle donde también viven su hermano y su padre. Isidro trabaja como electricista (dueño propio) y va saliendo.

Ambos se recibieron en Klail High con Rafa y Jehú.

EUGENIO: Bueno, si así lo quieres, yo empiezo y después tú, Chirro.

El esc., ya que no lo dijo anteriormente, consta que los cuates son de lo más idéntico que pueda haber: el parecer, los ademanes, la facha y hasta en el modo de rascarse los cabellos.

EUGENIO: A Jehú lo conozco desde el año de la hebra. Cuando lo de Corea, Jehú fue uno de los primeros que mandó llamar la reserva. Yo no fui al ejército; no pasé el examen físico y creo que se debe a que soy ciclán; lo más probable. Tú tampoco pasaste el examen en San Antonio; tuviste tis de chico.
ISIDRO: No fue por eso.
EUGENIO: ¿Entonces? Cada vez que hablamos de esto cambias . . .

El esc. se interpuso antes de que los gemelos Peralta se hicieran de palabras.

EUGENIO: A mí me contrata el banco, de vez en cuando, para ir a cobrar a las malas pagas. Soy cobrador de la Seamon pero hay veces que hago corretaje por el banco también. No es mucho, no lo creas, pero todo cabe en la bolsa.

Jehú me explicó que el banco no pierde: si cobro, bien, y si no, también. Ellos hacen un write-off; un bad loan. Si cobro, pues, me dan mi corretaje y ellos también salen bien: recobran su dinero, ¿ves?

Jehú también me explicó que Goyo Chapa, en un tiempo, hacía esto pero se pasó de listo: Goyo reportó que no pudo cobrar a varios —el muy pendejo— y luego resultó que sí, porque la gente vino a ver sus cuentas al banco y allí se vio que Goyo se había clavado parte de la feria.

Casi nada: Pintoville. Estuvo alzado por dos años y medio o algo así . . .

Jehú me recomendó porque me conoce por mucho tiempo, aunque, por cierto, te diré que en la escuela nunca nos llevamos bien . . . pero de eso hace años.

Jehú también me ayudó a conseguir el dinero para arreglar la casa de Papá; que qué clase de préstamo, que qué plazos tomara, etcétera.

Me costó mucho menos. Si lo hubiera tomado con la Seamon Loans: ni hablar, aquí te matan.

Como dice Jehú: "el banco no pierde y no le tengan ni confianza ni compasión". Me gusta el consejo pero como yo lo veo, ése no es modo de proteger la chamba . . . y ahora me dicen que se va o que se fue definitivamente . . .

ISIDRO: Sí, y el otro mexicano que trabaja allí te congela con la mirada; no quiere ni que la raza entre en el banco, h'mbre.

EUGENIO: Hablas de Escobar; así se llama. A ése no lo conozco; dicen que es de Jonesville. Como te digo, no lo conozco.

ISIDRO: No, ni yo, pero como quiera me cae mal.

El esc. hace saber que los gemelos se hablan uno al otro. Es como si el esc. no estuviera allí; es decir, hablan con él pero no a él.

Más bien parecen actores que conocen todos los papeles de memoria. El esc. decide dejarlos hablar.

EUGENIO: Lo que te voy a decir se queda entre nosotros o no digo nada.
ISIDRO: Sabes que soy discreto.

Isidro entonces vio al esc. y éste asintió con la cabeza: discreción, discreción. El esc. pide perdón por todavía otra interrupción pero es que está algo incómodo con este par. Los Peralta *no* se parecen a dos gotas de agua, *son una sola gota*. Lo que sigue fue algo confuso pero se aclaró por sí solo.

ISIDRO: Un verano mentado, la Sammie Jo andaba aquí de vacaciones y Jehú le dio pa' los dulces . . . De eso hace mucho. Y *esa,* Galindo, no fue la primera vez; una vez, hace mucho, cuando la secundaria, en otro verano . . . no la primera vez, ¿*okay?*
EUGENIO: Fíjate, y ahora años más tarde, en las mismas otra vez.
ISIDRO: Pero en la misma casa, tú. 'Ta loco.
EUGENIO: P's sí, tienes razón, pero las ganas no perdonan.

El esc. asegura que lo dicho es lo que se dijo y cómo se dijo; para los cuates, el esc. *debía* saber o pepenar de *qué* se hablaba.

EUGENIO: Síguele.
ISIDRO: Ya sabes que soy electricista.

Eugenio asienta con la cabeza. El esc. hace ídem. Nada, nada: se hablan uno al otro y el esc. que se vaya a freír hongos.

ISIDRO: En un subcontract que tuve con Tommie Kyle, pa' componer una alambrada en el Rancho, me tocó ver otra vez a Jehú con la hija de Noddy Perkins. En la cama, ¿eh?
EUGENIO: Somos cinco los que sabemos.
EL ESC.: (¡Sí, el esc.!) ¿Cinco?
ISIDRO: Sí.
EUGENIO: Tú, nosotros y ellos dos . . . .
ISIDRO: Ahora voy yo . . . .

El esc. tuvo la enorme tentación de gritar larga y prolongadamente. No lo hizo. También suprimió la tentación de echarse un trago y de fumarse un cigarro. Con suerte que no lo hizo. El esc. se siente agradecido que él no tiene un doble. Los Peralta lo invitaron a cenar pero se disculpó; dio las gracias, sí, pero se disculpó.

Para evitar cualquier mal entendimiento: el esc. se lleva bien con estos jóvenes, pasa que eso de las calcomanías lo encuentra sobrecogedor.

39

Lucas Barrón

El Chorreao, cantinero viejo y dueño del *Aquí me quedo,* es mucho más mayor de edad que el esc.; es, pues, de la camada de los viejos revolucionarios (Guzmán, Leal, Garrido, et alii). Conoce bien al esc. y a Jehú, a Rafa y, con poca exageración, a medio Klail. Klail mexicano, se entiende.

Habla inglés bien y como mucha de la raza de Klail, tiene parientes en ambos lados del río. De cachetes chapeados y de ojo cristalino, el Chorreao tiene esa voz alta, algo histérica, que se oye en el Valle de vez en cuando.

"A lo que hemos llegado, Flaco; ahora resulta que ni te puedo servir una cerveza de hoquis. ¿Una naranjada? ¿Un té helado? ¿Sí? Ahorita le digo a Turnio que te lo traiga; mira, nos sentamos aquí en mi mesa. A ver, ¡Turni!

"Turni, ve a cruzar la calle y dile a Noriega que quiero un jarro de té helado.

"Conque se trata de mi Jehú, ¿eh? ¿p's qué quieres que te diga? Lo conozco y lo quiero y lo aprecio; todo junto. De mí no oirás nada malo de ese muchacho y conociéndote sé que buscas la verdad. P's bien; aquí se habla mucho pero se sabe poco y no te recomiendo a nadie. Ni a mí, fíjate.

"Ahí viene el té; a ver, Turnio, dos vasos.

"Aquí se oye que lo botaron, que lo pusieron de patitas y de ojete en la calle, que robó, que si esto y que si aquello . . . Que yo sepa, nadie de este lado del pueblo ha hablado con un bolillo; bueno, a lo menos con un bolillo que sepa algo.

"El que viene aquí y habla y dice y que fue y que vino y lo que tú quieras, es Tapia. Pero Polín es fuente muy dudosa. Otro que habla por hablar y desde que me lo caparon en casa nomás se dedica a hablar, es el chueco Emilio.

"Don Manuel Guzmán dice poco pero merece que se le escuche. Don Manuel dice que si los cabrones bolillos tuvieran cargos ya hubieran jodido a Jehú porque el bolillo no perdona madre y menos cuando se trata de mónises. Eso sí, ni para qué decirte que aquí ni se chistea mierda de Jehú cuando don Manual entra a tomar su café . . .

"¿Y qué me dices de Andrés Champión? Primero te raja un taco de billar y luego te vacía un ojo si hablas mal de Jehú. Y no es el único: Jehú tiene amigos de todas edades. Ya sabes.

"Otros hablan que si se trata de viejas y allí es cuando la cosa se pone seria. Tú sabes que los viejitos no se van a meter en eso. Pero, por parte de la palomilla . . . la palomilla le achaca a Jehú de haberse echado a una de las muchachas del banco. Pero eso es puro pedo y nadie sabe nada. Cuando se trata de viejas, a Jehú ni tú le sacas media palabra. Es machito en eso de no soltar la lengua.

"En fin, mucha plática, mucho chisme, pero poca substancia.

"¿Y tú, Galindo, qué oyes por ahí?"

Lucas Barrón es buen cantinero y casi tan buen oyente como el esc. (Interrumpe menos también.) El Chorreao está en buenas condiciones: no debe dineros ni favores; el local es suyo y aquél que no se porte bien ya se puede estar yendo.

El Chorreao no lo dice pero tampoco tolera que se le critique a Jehú.

Confesión: el esc. se pone a pensar que si quizá él, el esc., envidia a su joven amigo todas las amistades que tiene.

El esc. también piensa que sería de valor hablar de nuevo con Polín Tapia.

40

Polín Tapia

Vide #23.

"No sé nada; y no creas que es porque no quiera hablar. De veras. Uno oye, se pone a cavilar, sí; pero de saber *saber,* no. Nada.

"Ah, y no creas que he andado buscando o escarbando por allí, tampoco. Yo tengo muchos quehaceres, por ejemplo: trabajaré part-time en el despacho local de Morse Terry mientras él atiende a lo suyo en Washington. La otra parte del tiempo, no sé. Bueno, no sé definitivamente . . . quizá con el Rancho pero no . . . no se sabe en qué capacidad. Y si no en el Rancho directamente, en su banco de madera; tú bien sabes que yo sé algo de pintura.

"Pasando a otra cosa. Ira va muy bien y ha hecho varias propuestas que ayudarán a Klail City; él es un joven que tiene talento y que sabe agradecer. Ira me dice que el puesto viejo de Jehú se lo han dado a un pariente de Morse Terry y eso se debe a que las obligaciones del condado le impiden a Ira que progrese en el banco. Pero hay que ver lo siguiente: Noddy se da cuenta y reconoce los talentos de Ira".

Dejarlo hablar, no contradecirle, no interrumpir, y P.T. que dice no saber nada, se abre como una compuerta. Al esc. casi le da pena de tan bien que conoce a su amigo.

"En el Rancho, de lo poco que sé, todo bien. Ya han vuelto todos de sus viajes a La Pesca, Tamaulipas. Sammie Jo, por fin, no fue esta vez; creo que se fue a ver a unos parientes o que ellos mismos vinieron a verla; ya sabes, teniendo como tienen sus propios aviones, esa gente va y viene que es un encanto.

"El que estuvo enfermito pero ya sanó del todo fue E.B. Cooke, el hermano mayor de la señora. El abogado Bayliss bien y parece que ya salió de peligro de esa enfermedad que le dio poco antes de las elecciones.

"Y un servidor también va bien; como te digo, empiezo de pronto en el despacho del diputado. Esas son cosas de Noddy, pero también es evidencia de que sabe ser agradecido con uno por poco que uno haya contribuido".

El esc. menea la cabeza, alza las cejas de vez en cuando, se cruza y se descruza los brazos pero no dice ni *bú*.

"No habrá divorcio: Sammie Jo dice que Sidney sigue débil de salud y que necesita de su ayuda —y *eso* para que se ahoguen más de cuatro en una gota de agua. Esa muchacha, digan que *no*, es Perkins y es persona.

"Y nadie puede negar que Noddy y el Rancho no se portaron de lo mejor con Jehú. Pero ya estaba escrito: el que no sabe agradecer, no sabe agradecer . . . Bueno, mejor no empezar por ahí porque eso es cuento de nunca acabar".

Las orejas del esc. se erigieron un tanto como las del conejo en nopalera ajena que oye ruido desconocido.

"Según Ira, en el banco todo bien y como si aquél nunca hubiera pisado allí. ¡Ja!

"¿Y qué de tu vida, Galindo? ¿Qué me cuentas? Te ves malón todavía".

El esc. le agradece (hay que saber agradecer) a su amigo esa solicitud; se la agradece porque aunque P.T. tenga sus flaquezas y rarezas, treinta y pico de años de amistad no se olvidan de un día para otro. Es más, Polín Tapia tiene pocos amigos que le aguanten tanta cháchara. El esc. por natural disposición, le gusta escuchar; en este caso más. En este caso es imprescindible.

41

Vicente de la Cerda

Dueño del camión *Klail City no se raja,* es otro de los que conoce a Jehú desde que éste era niño; aunque no sabe mucho del caso, quiere intervenir.

"Bueno, ¿ve este troque aquí? Jehú me prestó el dinero para comprarlo . . . No . . . eso no está bien. Me facilitó el dinero; él no firmó la nota —ese fue Israel Buenrostro— porque Jehú, como oficial del First no podía firmar, ¿ve? Lo que le digo, Jehú, como loan officer, trilló el camino. Es hombrecito el muchacho; tiene sus vicios, pero quién no, ¿verdad?

"Mire, la verdad, yo no sé mucho de ese viejo pleito de los Leguizamón-Buenrostro, pero yo oí, no hace mucho, oí . . . oí que, a ver, ah sí, que Jehú le dio sus estrujones a la Rebequita, la esposa del Irineo Escobar, al que llaman *Aira.* P's sí; que la rellenó, como decimos en Klail . . . P's sí, bien puede ser que por eso se fuera Jehú del banco. El muchacho está joven y no es capón.

"Ahora, a la que sí no conozco es a la farmacéutica; a la niña San Esteban; la del carrito verde . . . Los del *Blue Bar* dicen que si Jehú iba en serio, que sería con ella. Buen palo, señor Galindo, no, no . . . Quiero decir que a buen árbol se arrimó Jehú. Y está bien, a cabo los dos son universitarios. Pero, como le digo, yo hablo de lo que oigo. De saber, *saber,* no, y ni pa' qué mentirle . . .

"En el *Aquí me quedo* se dice que Jehú le daba pa' los dulces a la Sonny Job (sic) de Norberto Perkins; que tenían su entendimiento, ¿eh? Sus relaciones . . .

"P's sí; que tenían sus relaciones. Que desde la *high school,* fíjese. Bueno, a lo menos ése es el run-rún enquese el Chorreao.

239

Unos dicen que Norberto sabía y otros dicen que no. Y, otros todavía, que al Norberto ni le importaba. Eso sí que 'ta pelón, Galindo, eso es descompasarse.

"Y he oído también que en un tiempo Rafa y la Sonny Job se veían muy seguido. Fíjese. Sí; en lo mismo. El primero que lo dijo fue el Turnio Morales, pero ése no sabe nada de nada. Pa' mí que es pura envidia.

"El Rafa sabe lo que hace; no por nada fue hijo del Quieto. Y Rafa también es muy, muy . . ."

El esc. no cree que debe ayudar a hablar ni de poner palabras en boca de nadie. Se supone que el informante quería decir *discreto*.

"A ver . . . Ya sé: El Rafa no es bocón, Galindo. Eso; no es soflamero.

"Bueno, aquí la mocho. A ver si más adelante le cuento más o, a lo menos, algo que sepa de seguro".

El esc. quisiera aclarar que él no siempre da crédito a lo que digan los fijos del *Aquí me quedo* o del *Blue Bar*. Pero también reconoce que tampoco hay que andar echando tierra a lo que se diga por ahí; mejor es oír y escuchar todo (y con cuidado) para así seguir tratando de asirse de la verdad que se venga distilando por la coladera.

Vicente de la Cerda, por lo visto, aunque mayor que Jehú, es su amigo.

42

Emilio Tamez

Casi de la camada de Rafa y Jehú. Peleonero de cantina hasta los veintitantos años cuando, por fin, se casó y luego su mujer lo aplacó. (Quizá no venga al caso, pero la mujer de E.T. es de lo más chaparra que el esc. haya visto en su vida: chaparra, chaparra, y tapona.)

Tamez sigue tomando aunque no tanto y los del *Blue* dicen que el día que se vuelva a agarrar a golpes en la cantina con alguien eso será anuncio general de que su mujer, la Estercita Monroy, ha muerto.

En vez de pelear, Emilio se ha retirado al campo más sosegado de las habladurías. Emilio lleva varios años de manejar una de las pickups del Rancho y se le verá de sol a sol llevando y trayendo a los pequeños herederos Blanchard que, por ser tantos, se comerán a los Cooke un buen día de estos.

"Dice mi hermano Joaquín que el Rancho ya tiene siete vagones de alambre para las cercas que piensan renovar pa' mayo; los postes, como siempre, de ébano. Joaquín firma por todo allí en la estación donde caen todos los pedidos del Rancho.

"Da gusto trabajar con gente de ese tipo . . . cuánto dinero no tendrán los Blanchard que hasta ven a los parientes Cooke así, de reojo y por encima del hombro.

"Y fíjese, a uno lo tratan con mucha consideración; hasta da pena decirlo, aquí con amigos y en cantina, pero a veces los bolillos son más personas que uno. No, no, no —no soy agringado, ustedes me conocen . . . es que uno sabe apreciar y proteger lo que tiene. Y no . . . y no como unos que consiguen más educación y luego no saben proteger la chamba . . . Sí, lo digo por Jehú que . . . si no está aquí pa' defenderse, lo mismo da; porque si pasara por esa puerta, se lo diría a la cara.

"El bolillo nos jode pero a veces uno también le da la pólvora . . ."

Emilio Tamez habla por hablar; al esc. le parece ridículo que Tamez sepa qué opinan los Blanchard de sus primos los Cooke y vice versa. Es más, tan corto de vista está que se olvida de los Klail con quienes todo empieza. Como dicen los matemáticos: hay que saber distinguir entre lo importante y lo esencial . . . y otras cosas más.

"Y ¿qué me dicen de los garage sales de esa gente, eh? Los tienen en el Rancho y esas son pa' *nosotros,* los trabajadores. Es ropa de primera y poco usada. ¡Y barata que se compra! Ah, ¿y el dinero? ¿Saben lo que hacen con él? Se lo dan a su iglesia. Ellos no necesitan el dinero; lo hacen de caridad.

"Eso es saber ser persona y no pedazo, ¿qué me dice?

"A ver, ¿cuánto tiempo anduvo Jehú con esos aleluyas locos? Y vendiendo biblias, tú . . . ¡Ja! Pa' acabar como acabó. ¡Quedando mal!

"Nosotros los Tamez somos muy trabajadores . . . Y no somos dejados. ¿Y Jehú? A ver, ¿cuándo se le ha enfrentado a alguien en una cantina . . . o dónde sea? El colegio lo arruinó; se educó y luego no dio la medida en la calle ni en el banco . . ."

Puede ser que Tamez anduviera en trago. La conversación-monólogo saltaba de aquí a allá y sin rumbo; a la deriva, pues.

Siempre han sido trabajadores los Tamez y eso no se niega; a veces hasta se les ha alabado por ello, pero bien visto, pocos hay entre la raza que no lo sean. El trabajo no viene siendo virtud única y menos cuando es propiedad muy nuestra esa de trabajar en lo que sea.

El esc. piensa también que Emilio habla y dice lo que dice de Jehú debido a la ley no escrita: lo dicho en cantina, y en trago, allí se queda. La ley tiene que funcionar así, de otra manera la vida sería intolerable.

43

Arturo Leyva

Contador y tenedor de libros públicos; casado estos veinte años con Yolanda (la hija de doña Candelaria Murguía de Salazar alias 'La Turca' y del dif. don Epigmenio) es de la edad y de la camada del esc.

Conoce a Jehú desde que éste era niño.

"Qué no vengan aquí con historias de Jehú . . . Y si vienen, que vengan preparados a que Arturo Leyva se las raye parejo, en seco, y por mayoreo".

El esc. interrumpe para informar que el informante habla de sí en tercera persona. Siempre.

"Arturo Leyva no permite que se desmanden ni con él ni con sus amigos; que Emilio Tamez o el que sea hable así fuera de la cantina, en el parque de pelota, por ejemplo, entonces Arturo Leyva viene y le pone pare a su pedo al inmediato y por entrega. Y Arturo Leyva no se detiene con Tamez; se trata del que sea".

El esc. señala que A.L. no es ni de lo más grande ni fornido que haya en Klail; pasa que es decidido y no habla por hablar. Tiene su sentido de amistad y lealtad; aún no se le olvida que Jehú, años ha, le salvó el pellejo en un asunto de amores que si sale al sol hubiera sido funesto y fatal, como dicen. Se habla en serio; si su suegra, La Turca, se hubiera dado cuenta que Arturo traicionaba a la Yolandita, el Valle tendría un contador menos.

"Ese muchacho es y ha sido servicial como pocos. Al año de estar en el banco empezaron las mexicanas a trabajar allí y fue por interés personal no por 'lo otro'.

"Así es. Que le guste el cuento y que sepa contarlo, ¿eso qué? ¿A quién no? Es muchacho del Valle; sabe respetar y no es dejado. Bien dijo Echevarría, que Dios lo tenga. 'Déjenlo solo! ¿Qué le pueden enseñar que él no haya visto y aprendido? La orfandad es escuela muy déspota y con una sola lección: no se *raje*, cabrón. ¡Déjenlo solo!' Arturo Leyva les recuerda y les repite lo que dijo el viejito Esteban en esta misma cantina: ¡Déjenlo solo!"

El esc. se complace en decir que Arturo le invitó a una cerveza; el esc. dio las gracias pero no pudo aceptar; tan malito así está.

44

Esther Lucille Bewley

Cuatro años menor que Jehú (ella mismo lo dice) trabaja en el banco desde que se recibió de Klail High School. Soltera, menudita, y de buen ver, el pelo es rubio, corto y chinito; los ojos remedan canicas azules. Demasiado flaquita para los gustos del esc., se viste sencillamente y eso sí es del gusto del esc. De voz sosegada, Esther aprendió español en los ranchos y en los campos, zurcos y praderas que rodean Klail City y sus alrededores.

"Uncle Bowly said you had come around and talked to him a while back. You didn't know he was my Mom's older brother, did you? Well, he is, and that makes *me* a Ponder on my mother's side . . .

"Let's see . . . Jehú was a Senior in high school when I was a Freshman, and I really had a crush going, let me tell you . . . but that was years ago . . . He never knew it, though . . . at least not till I told him here at the bank some three years ago. And when I did, he just smiled . . .

"There is something I need to tell you, Mr. Galindo. It's something I *know*".

Esto último se dijo con una finalidad, con una seguridad, y con empaque sin ápice de malicia. Al decir que sabía ese *algo,* a pesar de su juventud, de repente pareció una viejita sentenciada por el destino a revelar ciertos secretos que la gente ni sospecha.

"I do, Mr. Galindo; I really do . . . You see . . . I've *watched* Jehú. Closely. And I can add; I can put *two* and *two* together as well as anyone . . . But I . . . I'd *never* do anything or *say* anything to hurt him.

"Not once, not *once,* Mr. Galindo, did he send me out for coffee.

"I'd *bring* it to him, though, or he'd make it hisself —*himself*— he'd make it himself in that pot there. He'd just do it, is all. But that *other* one. ¿Sabe que? Yo hablo mejor español que él, and *he* went to *big* Texas A&M . . . well, *he* wouldn't lift a finger, he wouldn't. And you and I know the word in Spanish for *him,* right?"

A este punto Esther se puso coloradita y la imagen de la vejez que le espera y que le sorprenderá pasó como la brisa sobre las palmas: leve, ligera, tibia y calma.

"But I know something, Mr. Galindo, and I know about the fight, too. And you know *what?* Mr. Perkins was righter than he *knew* and Jehú *still* beat him. Jehú beat him at his *own mean game.* Oh, I could've kissed him, Mr. Galindo . . . Jehú, I mean.

"After the shouting, he walked out of that office, winked at me, and then he gave me that smile of his; he then turned to Ira and pointed at him, you know, like with a toy pistol? Well, he did, and he smiled again. But it wasn't the smile he gave *me.* Know what he did then? He called me over and said, real serious-like, but smiling at the same time: 'Esther, the world's full of sons-of-bitches, but killing's against the law, so you've got to skin 'em once in a while just to let them know you're here'. And then, 'Want to flip to see who makes the coffee?'

"See what I mean?"

El esc. que no es tan cínico como él cree, notó que a Esther Lucille le bailaban esas canicas azules que usa en vez de ojos. Esther no lloró y si a eso hubiera llegado la cosa, el esc. hubiera disimulado: cuesta poco, vale mucho.

"It's not important that I tell you *how* I know, but I do, and I know about *both* of them, Mr. Galindo, *both* of them".

Aquí Esther apuntó con el mentón, primero al despacho de Noddy y luego al escritorio de Ira Escobar. También se le notó la tristeza, pero, flaquita y todo, Esther Lucille Bewley sonrió esa sonrisa que la ha de llevar a su vejez cualquier día de estos. El esc. quiere que antes que la vejez venga y derroque la juventud de esta muchacha, el esc. quiere que Esther sea feliz, incluso, muy feliz.

No es mucho pedir.

45

Don Javier Leguizamón

Este señor ha llegado ya a los setenta y pico de duros años. En su vida variable que lo ha llevado a los principios de esta década de los sesenta, ha sido comerciante y contrabandista en ambos lados del río (en bruto). Siempre ha sido fiel seguidor a sus instintos. Nació y espera morir de la misma manera: con los ojos bien abiertos.

Muchísimo más se podría decir de él y del familión Leguizamón pero el esc. reconoce que aún así diría bien poco. Al decir esto, no se quiere dejar la impresión de que el esc. se tapa con la ropa de la ironía.

"Sin que me quede nada, y esto no es vanagloria, que a mi edad ahora y ni de joven, me ha gustado ese papel . . . como decía: sin que me quede nada, YO (sic), en gran parte, le conseguí el puesto a Jehú en el banco. Me siento responsable.

"Había dos puestos originalmente y YO hablé con Noddy sobre Jehú y allí entró. Un par de años más tarde, hubo otro puesto y ése le tocó al hijo de mi sobrina Vidala.

"En aquel tiempo, Jehú estaba muy necesitado y de allí que lo recomendara a Noddy. YO conozco a Jehú desde que era niño; en un tiempo hasta trabajó en una de las tiendas que tenemos aquí en Klail".

El esc. ya perdió la cuenta de toda esa gente que conoció a Jehú cuando éste era niño.

"No puedo disimular que Jehú me decepcionó algo ya que no nos ayudó durante las elecciones; no obstante, señor Galindo, si se me presenta la oportunidad de nuevo, de nuevo lo vuelvo a recomendar.

O se es firme o no. Así soy YO; así somos todos los Leguizamón. "Usted bien sabe . . ."

OJO: El esc. no sabe nada.

". . . que de los hombres, y todos nacimos el siglo pasado, YO soy el único que queda. La familia, gracias al Señor, es grande y YO ya no tengo que andar preocupándome con los negocios: Que lo hagan ellos, los jóvenes.

"Uno se dedica, como siempre, a su familia y a sus negocios. Si se cuida lo primero, lo segundo viene de por sí: conciencia tranquila, tratando de no injuriar al prójimo y si hay oportunidad de hacer un favor, que se haga. YO no pregunto a quién sino cómo, cuándo y dónde. Lo dicho, señor Galindo, se dice en humildad. Diría que me enorgullezco de mi humildad si decir eso no estuviera fuera de mi carácter.

"Sé que varia gente no me aprecia, pero eso no me molesta. En un tiempo, sí, pero ahora no. A mi edad, uno ve que no hay por qué molestarse —indebidamente— por lo que se piensa o se diga de uno erróneamente. El hombre no es la perfección andante, pero no por eso hay que irse a pique o por los caminos de la perdición.

"El trabajo, la familia, el orden y el progreso, la seriedad, la sobriedad, y ayudar a los caídos; lo dicho, si no es el lema personal de los Leguizamón, a lo menos es algo que tratamos de seguir. Asiduamente.

"El favor a Jehú no fue el primero y, como dije, seguro estoy que no será el último. Aunque pariente, ignoro si lejano o cercano de esa familia que tan injustamente piensa y quizá obre mal para con nosotros los Leguizamón, digo, aunque Jehú sea pariente de esa familia, Javier Leguizamón sabe hacer favores y no es de esos que después vienen a cobrarlos".

El esc. cree innecesario el hacer sus acostumbrados comentarios. El esc. decide no poner ni quitar *jota* a lo dicho por el señor Leguizamón. El esc. prefiere que lo dicho por J.L. quede como su monumento personal, inviolable, intocable.

El esc. tampoco ha de sobajarse a la ironía en este caso.

46

Jovita De Anda Tamez

Esposa del mayor de los Tamez, algo güila de joven, le ha dado varios hijos y pocos sinsabores a Joaquín Tamez. El esc., y no sabe cómo decirlo, oyó cuentos, rumores, equis, hace mucho, poco después de Corea, que Jovita acomodó —¿Y será esa la palabra?— que acomodó, se decía, a Jehú o a Rafa. Se hace mención de esto porque los rumores no fueron de cantina; se oían en bocas femeninas. El esc. no ofrece, por no tener, pruebas.

"Tengo años de no ver a Jehú Malacara, y a Rafa mucho más todavía. A Rafa lo divisaba cuando él pasaba por aquí a su trabajo en que el Chorreao; en ese tiempo, él trabajaba en los veranos y Joaquín y yo lo veíamos pasar desde el corredor.

"A Jehú, como le dije, Galindo, hace años . . . Y ni que Klail fuera tan grande pero en la casa no hay qué falte por hacer; ya sabe.

"Por aquí Emilio cae seguido y siempre los domingos cuando él y Ester vienen de visita; se habla de todo y apenas hace poco que oí algo, y tardillo, porque lo de Jehú es cosa del año pasado, ¿verdad?

"Lo que se oye mucho es que la farmacéutica San Esteban va a dejar el negocio para irse a vivir con Jehú; que en Houston, usted. Esto lo oí por Emilio y no sé dónde más, pero de oírlo, lo oí más de una vez. También se dice que la farmacéutica va a usar parte del dinero de la farmacia para pagar lo que Jehú quedó debiendo en el banco . . . Emilio me cuenta lo mismo y muy en serio.

"Y ¿será verdad todo eso? ¿Que ella lo vaya a ayudar? Otros dicen que no; que Jehú consiguió trabajo en Austin y que les manda parte de su sueldo al banco para saldar lo de ahí . . . Un arreglo especial entre ellos . . . Yo le digo esto a Emilio pero él me dice que no;

y dice también que la farmacéutica es una boba porque está tirando su dinero.

"Yo no sé qué pensar; yo conozco a Jehú y no lo puedo creer. Aunque eso sí, la gente cambia, no hay duda. Ah, espere, allí en la tienda de don Efraín Barrera oí que los Leguizamón habían ayudado a Jehú. Joaquín dice que estoy loca, pero así lo oí yo.

"Bien sé que una no sabe mucho, pero eso es lo que se oye".

El esc. nota que Jovita todavía está de buen ver; ésta es una mera observación y sin guisa de nada; desgraciadamente.

El lector está libre de aceptar o de rechazar lo que diga Emilio Tamez aunque el esc. espera que el lector considere ridícula la idea de que los Leguizamón ayuden a Jehú o a cualquiera que no sea de la línea Leguizamón.

Tocante a lo que se dice de la señorita O.S.E. y de su hermano y de la farmacia y de Jehú, el esc., por ahora, no ve que haya provecho con otra conversación con Olivia o Martín San Esteban.

Parte III

LOS EVENTOS CONSUETUDINARIOS
QUE OCURREN EN LA RUA*

El reportaje se termina con Jovita de Anda porque el esc., al leer todo lo demás que tiene en mano, opina y da garantía que nada de ello ampliaría lo que se sabe del caso.

Lo suprimido, por consiguiente, lo considera innecesario ya que tampoco es asunto de llenar renglón tras renglón: ése no es el caso ni es ése el camino.

---

*Lo que pasa en la calle. Antonio Machado, 1875–1939.

Las cuentas resumidas

A pesar de que cierta gente, más o menos responsable, u otra gente que debe saber, y que sabe, y también a pesar de las muchas amistades que tiene Jehú Malacara y de aquéllos que dicen que son sus amigos y conocidos, la mayoría de la raza —la gran mayoría— dice que Jehú es culpable.

En efecto, no precisan de *qué* pero eso es lo de menos. El esc. también ha oído el tono y la manera, el *cómo* lo dicen, y se pone a pensar que si todavía hubiera piedras por esas calles de Klail, que Jehú al volver tendría que andar con mucho cuidado y en constante vigilancia por su persona.

El esc. también oye que en Klail se dice que a Jehú lo habían botado del ejército y que lo echaron de su puesto en la secundaria las dos veces. Además, que en el banco, verdaderamente, no hacía nada y que se le tenía allí de muestra pero que, por su comportamiento dudoso, ahora la raza no tendría oportunidad de volver a trabajar en el banco.

Otras voces dicen que Jehú no se ha casado (a pesar de tener sus treinta años) por su temor a las mujeres y todavía otros dicen que no, que su celibato se debe a otras preferencias.

254

Los techos de las iglesias (de la Apostólica y los ramos protestantes) cuentan que siempre hubo falta de discreción, de fe, de seriedad y, por supuesto, de dinero en las arcas.

Las madres de familia dicen que *ellas* ya lo sabían y que sólo se esperaron paciente y resignadamente con los brazos cruzados sabiendo que a Jehú ya le vendría su día. *Merecido se lo tiene* es lo que se oye con más frecuencia. Los padres de familia asientan con la cabeza y les dan toda la razón a sus respectivas consortes.

Jehú, en Austin, ignora lo que se dice de él en Klail, pero el esc. está convencido de que no faltará alguien que tome la venia y luego le cuente todo sin omitir absolutamente nada. Sépase que hay gente que insiste que a esto se le llama amistad.

El esc., en resumidas cuentas, también piensa que cuando Jehú Malacara vuelva a Klail City —al fin y al cabo, de aquí es— que todos los perros en el barrio mexicano se van a poner en línea para mearlo.

Los hay con suerte.